Snow Bees

ALSO BY JOHN MUCKLE

FICTION
It Is Now As It Was Then (with Ian Davidson)
The Cresta Run
Bikers (with Bill Griffiths)
Cyclomotors
London Brakes
My Pale Tulip
Falling Through
Late Driver

CRITICISM
Little White Bull: British Fiction in the 50s and 60s

POETRY
Firewriting and Other Poems
Mirrorball

GENERAL EDITOR
The New British Poetry 1968–88
    (with Allnutt, D'Aguiar, Edwards, Mottram)

Snow Bees

John Muckle

Shearsman Books

First published in the United Kingdom in 2023 by
Shearsman Books Ltd
PO Box 4239
Swindon
SN3 9FN

Shearsman Books Ltd Registered Office
30–31 St. James Place, Mangotsfield, Bristol BS16 9JB
(this address not for correspondence)

ISBN 978-1-84861-902-9

The world is charged with the grandeur of God.
　It will flame out, like shining from shook foil;
　It gathers to a greatness, like the ooze of oil
Crushed. Why do men then now not reck his rod?

Gerard Manley Hopkins, *God's Grandeur*

One

A few hours after her accident, Agathe Oury found herself trudging across a plain of thick, crisp, sparkling snow that might, at any moment, turn out to be merely a drift over a ravine thirty metres deep: a hidden cleft. One step might plunge her to a suffocating end, she thought somewhat redundantly, but she battled onwards. Ahead of her stood a regiment of pine trees planted on a slope, above them the curling mountainous road, and beyond it, rising white slopes, peaks scarred here and there with brown wounds of torn earth, broken, half-submerged trees. It was an early spring morning, bright and clear, in the middle of avalanche season.

She knew precisely where she was and where she was going. Her breath hung on the air in short visible blasts as she battled off-track, skirting a suspicious-looking bowl-like hollow, making for the pine trees. She was clad in a thick ski-jacket which cradled her head, heavy boots and a pair of fur-lined mittens. An expensive Canon camera, capped, hung on a strap over her shoulder. When she reached the fist trees she saw the snow was thinner underfoot here, while above her heavily chandeliered pines suspended fistfuls of ice daggers above her head, at least providing some cover from the wind. Agathe saw the almost obliterated path upwards, which seemed to have been trodden out by deer or some other sure-footed creature, rather than by human feet. She was able to find footing and handholds, panting as she propelled herself upwards towards the road.

Finally she saw the small Renault ahead. It was upended, crumpled, shattered, wedged into the landscape, buried nose-first between two rows of slender pines which seemed not to have been damaged by its impact. Agathe stopped to take a photograph, bracing herself against another tree on the steep approach. The sheer neatness of what resembled a pale giant gravestone planted upright amongst the perpendicularly rising trunks of the trees was striking, as though they had carefully caught her on the way down, prepared a space for her amongst them. Agathe edged her way closer along a ledge created by the close-planted trunks of the young trees, and looked in through a miraculously preserved side window. The windscreen had been punched out on impact. The woman behind the wheel, close to the ground, was Agathe herself, not particularly appropriately dressed but decidedly, if recently, dead.

Agathe squatted down beside the window and took a few shots, mainly of her own back, although the head, its neck broken, was twisted to one side, as if wincing at a bad joke, her still face reposed horribly in that attitude. She snapped away. She saw that the glove compartment had slammed open on impact that its contents, a small bottle of orange juice, a sandwich, a sheaf of her writings, and a fat letter from England in a torn open envelope, were scattered around in what was left of the passenger-side of the car, as if in evidence of her cause of death.

This debris she also photographed, and another shot from above as she hauled herself up to the level of the road from which she'd plummeted to her quick death. She remembered nothing, had seen no sign of struggle or movement after the crash. Behind her eyes she felt the build-up of a blinding headache, the beginnings of disturbance, of the dancing visual break-up of migraine.

She pulled herself onto the narrow road, staggered and sat down immediately, her chest heaving with the effort of the climb. She felt she was going to pass out, forced her head down between her knees and closed her eyes, lights dancing behind them, temples pounding. She recovered a little, and stood up, keeping her head down. Glancing across the road and back, she saw where her Renault had gone through the rail fence, although she had no memory of it. She'd thought that maybe it had been an avalanche, a small fall from above the road, that had pushed her over the edge, but there was no sign of this.

Walking across the road she scuffed with her boot and located what must be skid marks, all but covered by a fresh dusting of snow. Obviously she had lost control; it had happened very quickly. *Oui, évidemment.* She remembered precisely but there was only an annoying gap, just after a sense of being late for her shift at the *maternelle*, an empty space somewhere behind her eyes where the blinding headache was located. She seemed to remember some sort of anger because the stupid Communists in Grenoble had been trying to abolish *fête des mères* – call it something else or something

8

– just because some children didn't have mothers. This made her so fucking angry.

But what did it matter now? she thought in utter dismay. She couldn't believe she'd lost her life over being angry about something so idiotic, so completely insignificant; but since she couldn't remember it properly she dismissed the whole notion. A small camionnette rounded the bend, winding down the mountain. Agathe stuck her thumb straight out, waving vigorously with her other hand. The driver stopped and she climbed in beside her. Another woman who made her living here in the foothills of the Alps, wrapped up well as Agathe was now but hadn't been earlier on.

"Vous avez un problème?"

"Oui oui," Agathe said. "J'ai perdu ma Mobylette là-bas."

"Ah bon," the driver replied calmly. Whether or not she believed her unexpected passenger, she didn't ask her any further questions.

Agathe said as little as possible, but the van driver didn't seem too put out. She headed back to the city centre and dropped her passenger near the end of Rue Lafayette. Agathe shared a cramped apartment above a jeweller's shop there with her daughter, whom they called Mono, and her husband, Jacques. She fished a duplicate key from her pocket and let herself in quietly. Mono – Monique – was at school of course, but she thought Jacques should be at home for lunch by now, working on his sculpture. He was, and quite enthusiastically, in raw clay, in the little studio he'd made at one end of their only halfway decent room. She looked in on him from the hallway. Handsome, and such a truly beautiful man. Tears flooded her eyes. He glanced in her direction as if to say something but obviously saw and heard nothing. He turned back to a lump of red clay in which he'd shaped a crude maquette of her lower body. Jacques would be going back to the yard in half-an-hour, to spend a long afternoon doing what he liked doing despite the fact that it wasn't really sculpture. It was monumental masonry.

There was nothing for her to do but let herself out again. Jacques was a man of abilities. His skills were honed, long-practiced. Cutting slabs, for walls or cornices or graves. But what was she doing here? she wondered. Was she just going to fade out soon and that would be that, *Ptouf!* She hoped so. At that precise moment she knew she was a ghost, perhaps the most stupid ghost that had ever existed, but afterwards everything had started to get a bit vaguer, and later on she began to understand that she no longer owned anything, nothing except this part of her which kept moving around and thinking

Two

Rob hooked his blue paper mask up around his big ears and got on the train. It was a midweek journey during lockdown, nearly Christmas Day. First class seemed completely empty but he still walked down the platform to the second class coaches, hopped on at the first one. Due to depart in ten minutes, he had plenty of time to stake out his spot, which he did, in his favourite position, a window, one of a pair facing in the direction of travel. He'd never liked the exposure of fixed tables and one of four seats: luxurious bays attractive to families with noisy brats. He swung his bag, cast it up onto the rack above his seat and settled. He wondered if there would still be refreshments.

A masked cleaner passed rapidly through his carriage, an anti-bacterial canister slung on her back and a delivery wand in her plastic-gloved right hand. Quickly but thoroughly, she sprayed everything in sight – except Rob – and disappeared towards the front of the train without a glance. The whistle blew loudly and the train pulled off from Waterloo. Rob glimpsed a yellow signalling bat, a navy-clad arm, and the train lurched smoothly into motion. There were no other passengers in his carriage. No reassuring clatter of a trolley being lifted on from the platform. Nevertheless, he sat back, relieved to be leaving the city behind.

First lockdown had begun for Rob when he arrived on the doorstep of a care facility in Walthamstow to find himself barred from entry. The key worker in charge signed his form on the doorstep and the tutor retraced his steps. On his way back to the station he'd noticed McDonalds was still open, although festooned with police incident tape, and so he popped in for a final double cheeseburger and fries. He'd hurried out with it in the bag, and that had been the last he'd seen of McDonalds for … how long?

At least a year, and the months had piled one upon another like discarded shirts.

Not for the first time he marvelled at how little there was to look at on a train. At the far end a poster advertised cheap seaside returns; nothing else stirred any emotion or invited you to rest your gaze: the moulded back of the seat in front, and the grey folding tray let into it; bristly blue and orange nylon seat covering, derived from an ancient design which had been handed down for centuries. At least the seat was fairly comfortable. You could raise the armrest and sprawl if you didn't mind a grey metal seat-partition digging into you – and the folding plastic tray was fairly useful: it made you want to buy something to rest on it. That was that. It was probably just being in motion, or the concept of journeying or something, but he'd always liked the familiar sensation of train travel, unless it was a commute on the DLR to tutor another excluded Nigerian teenager in Woolwich library. Bless 'em. Bless 'em.

He had carried on teaching kids online, and these early evening sessions with teenagers had come to comprise his human contact. Science fiction. Genuinely spooky, a banal, emptying feeling of removal and horror. Only the bubble-wrap of media to jolly all of them along in normality as the pretentiously portentous midnight bong of Big Ben grew more insistent, more urgent.

People were furloughed from work, blah blah, if lucky. Assorted idiots charged at barricades put in place for their protection. The government, whom they seemed to like, were openly lining their own pockets; it was obvious, while the people carried on expiring from the virus. Why not? Rob found himself thinking. There were always more of them. But it would all be managed and forgotten. Nothing, he realized dully, could possibly shock our leaders, our public. They had all bases covered. There was no lie they would not get away with telling.

The Nightingale hospitals had been erected rapidly to hold in readiness for dying victims to be shipped through. Nurses and care workers were falling like flies, ill-equipped, as the death toll of elderly people clicked up week by week, as they crackled up like moths in the plague's leaping flame. People stood on their doorsteps to bang pots and pans in a bizarre tribute to the carers, and all essential workers, all workers in fact, were now practically to be known by institutional handle as 'key-workers'. This seemed peculiar to him. Rob stood at his back window to listen to the rattling kitchen utensils and the cheering kids, clapped silently in the light, hoping he would be seen, because aside from this the streets were empty when he took his exercise, walking a circuit around baked out pavements empty of passengers like the silent blue skies.

He'd woken to a nasty headache from the most disgusting dream he'd ever half-remembered. He stood up, mistakenly shook his head and tried to focus on the dim, gloopy images still moving across the polluted surface of his brain. Stagnant water, dripping with torpor in a low hollow … a large muddy dip in marshy ground stinking putridly of decay. Vegetation of a half-familiar sort fringed the blurred edges of this huge pond of waste-water. It looked like an enormous eye, a wide-open rheumy eye staring blindly up at heaven, and above it hung the largest red sun he had ever seen: like a bowl of tomato soup.

Things had been moving just under the surface of the lake, horrible things – horned inhuman creatures skimming along under greenish sludge, a habitat which was otherwise as dead as dead could be. On the fringes – ill-defined, hovering – twitching legions of elongated flies. They were feeding on something and they were the most revolting creatures he'd ever… Rob hated those fucking dreams. He gave them to himself deliberately as an order to wake up, a sort of alarm clock of disgust he managed to programme somehow or other. But why did he have to dredge up such disgusting filth? Fuck! His head throbbed and he stumbled through into the bathroom. At first he gingerly held up cold running water near to his face and his forehead, then splashed it all over him before staggering blindly into the kitchen. He choked down a couple of paracetamol. The kitchen was dancing, breaking up, and he realized with a sudden jerk of panic that it really had been a wake-up call.

He looked at the time on his silent radio. It was 9 o'clock on the morning of Christmas Eve. He was supposed to be travelling today. Leaving soon. He was going to catch the last morning train down to Devon. Everything was already packed: a couple of shirts, a couple of parcels, and cards for his father, his brother. In fact, he was ready to go.

He washed and shaved, evacuated the night's evils, gradually pulled his wits together. He didn't feel like going out of the front door, let alone on a three-hour train journey. Perhaps he should put the radio on to check the travel advice – but he knew it already: Don't. He didn't wish to hear any crisp, punctilious tones. He drank a cup of dark hot coffee, which made him think of long ago. Again he'd felt dark and heavy, sluggish, and had to jerk himself out of it to get downstairs, through the front door and down to the hidden steps of the train station at the bottom of the right prong of Tottenham Lane, forked hill of deserted nothings.

At the first stop he glanced out of the window at Clapham Junction. A few people were milling under an electronic departures board but none got on. From further up the train a solitary young black woman seemed to have disembarked and walked down its length, a small purple bag slung over her shoulder, her black mask still in place. They pulled away again and Rob rested his head against the window, feeling the vibrations go through him. Tiredness swept through him also and he thought he might doze off for a while. But an odd thought nagged at him.

Perhaps it was the way the train moved, snaking and clattering over the rails, or the sheer lightness and smoothness with which it seemed to rattle along, but somehow – he was almost convinced this was the case – Rob felt he was travelling on an empty train.

After a short interval of watching outskirts, he was again stuck by a feeling that the train seemed mysteriously light, almost flimsy as it flung itself down the rails. But was it empty? He got up and headed down the carriage to the first door. This led directly onto a second door, so that you had to open both of them to pass through, which he did, pausing for a moment as he stepped over the coupling where the metal plates moved slightly, grating over one another as the bogies followed the tracks.

For a moment he paused with one foot on each side of the coupling, and planted himself there, feeling the train bucking and squirming. He closed the doors behind him and passed down a short corridor, past the WC and into a carriage identical to the one he had just left. This too was devoid of passengers. Glancing up he saw that the information display happened to be showing his final destination, and that the train would be separating at some point, and that he had settled in the wrong part, the part that would be left behind.

He decided to go back and fetch his bag, repeated his negotiation of the double doors, and, bag over shoulder, paused again between the two carriages where, he supposed, decoupling would take place, and felt the energy there, the sense of hurtling along. Soon he was back in the other empty carriage, walking along it slowly, leaning forward in the direction of travel, as the train seemed to try to escape from under his feet. On the return journey he would be flying along, he thought, rather like an astronaut in horizontal weightlessness.

In the third carriage, which carried the legend 'quiet zone' on its sliding door, he found somebody. She was dead. She was dead but reading a book, her legs drawn up under an old fashioned pleated skirt. Was it the book of her life? Her hair dark and tumbled across her face, she was glancing out of the window occasionally, the landscape danced across her reflection, and as Rob passed by she looked up at him. He decided not to let her know he recognized her. Instead he asked her if there was a refreshment trolley or carriage on the train. But she looked blank, didn't seem to understand. Didn't speak English, he thought. She didn't recognize him either, which was hardly surprising. He smiled at her and passed on, as she adjusted her mask over her nose and her gaze dropped again to the page of her novel.

The fourth carriage was again empty. Rob propelled himself down it, using his hands to grasp the green plastic holds projecting from the tops of the seats. He glanced into a vacant four-seater bay and saw that a folded newspaper had been left behind. He couldn't see which paper it was, didn't stop to pick it up, but couldn't help noticing the front-page photograph: a deserted city square with rubbish blowing across it. Trafalgar Square? There had been a demonstration yesterday, he remembered, against restrictive measures, but he'd missed it on the news, had left quite early, around lunchtime.

In the fifth carriage a corpulent man in his thirties filled up a four-seater bay all by himself. He had dark, curly hair, a light, scrubby beard, and quite a feast spread before him on the green-edged table. An open packet of crackers, three or four open small tubs containing hummus, some other sorts of Greek fillings Rob couldn't immediately identify, and a piece of soft French cheese on an open square of grease-proof paper. The man also had a bottle of red wine, and a plastic cup contained a measure of this, its surface rippling in the vibrations of the train. Between long, messy-looking fingers he held a broken piece of cracker, and was hesitating as to what he should dip it in next.

He didn't see Rob coming, but as he passed by him the man looked up and smiled indulgently. Rob nodded and passed on. The dead man continued to consume his feast. He picked up his cup to take a sip of wine. Nothing about Rob's demeanour revealed that he recognized the man, who in turn disclosed no sign of having known this passerby. Rob was relieved to get to the next set of doors, to push through into another short corridor, where he entered the WC and locked the door behind him. After urinating and flushing, he sat on the closed lid of the toilet and pulled a pouch of tobacco from his pocket. He quickly rolled a cigarette, lit it, and filled up the small compartment with smoke. There seemed to be little chance of his being interrupted. He listened carefully but could hear no approach, and felt himself sliding from side to side on the toilet seat as they rumbled lightly along.

He finished smoking his cigarette, put it out in the small sink and tossed it under the toilet lid. He flapped his arms around to dispel the smoke, picked up his travel bag, and unlocked the door. Out in the corridor a guard was waiting for him.

"Ticket, sir?"

Rob produced his tickets from his top pocket and, squinting at them, passed the one for the outward journey to the guard. The man took it, said nothing. He didn't seem to register the obvious tobacco smell wafting from the WC. He scribbled a loop on the orange card with a loosely-held black pen and returned it to the nervous passenger.

"You're quiet today," Rob ventured.

"Yes," the guard said. "Unnaturally so, even in these strange times." He smiled crookedly, pleased to be able to pretend to be in an old horror film. "I believe, sir, you are the only passenger on this train."

"Not the only one, surely" Rob laughed, "I've just seen two others."

The chap regarded him blankly.

"Am I in the right part of the train for –" he mentioned his own destination, "– only I wondered if..."

"Yes," replied the guard. "You're okay here. Quite near the front."

"Is there a refreshment car?"

"A trolley's supposed to be coming on at Basingstoke. Don't know if it will though," he added jocularly. "I'll offer no guarantees."

Rob turned on his heel, back the way he had come, and the guard proceeded. But before he could trigger the door to the previous carriage, he remembered the dead man he had just seen feasting in it. Once upon a time they had been friends, but now, as in the old bluegrass song, they might as well have been rank strangers. He couldn't however resist a temptation to poke his head around the door. But he found that the presence had departed, and of his recent feast not a crumb remained. Perhaps, Rob thought, he's moved further back, or maybe, while he had been in the WC, his old friend had decided to move to the front of the train. What about the young woman he had spoken to? They had been lovers once, and she didn't seem to have aged a day since those long ago times, before any of them had been in a position to know anything at all.

A reassuring image from another one of last night's dreams came back to him. In the dream his fingers on both hands had been knotted together into a sort of cat's cradle he couldn't get out of. But then, somebody had helped him to untangle them. It had been easy, he remembered. Just a bit of patience was all that was required. There had been no real reason why it had happened in the first place.

He decided to walk through to the front of the train, just out of idle curiosity. He turned and followed the guard into the next carriage, but there was no sign of him. He had passed on further – and this carriage too was empty, as might have been expected. How many carriages were there, he wondered, six or nine?

But that mystery was soon solved when he passed into the next carriage, evidently the final one. He saw clearly down to the end, where a different door, a locked door, led to the engine, to the driver's cab. Just beside this door the guard was seated. He was doing some paperwork, checking off things that needed to be checked off on a few sheets of printed paper, and didn't look up from his task, which he seemed to be completing with rapid efficiency. About halfway down this final carriage two more dead people sat opposite one another in a four-seater bay. This time they recognized him instantly. The small woman, who sat with her back to him, turned and waved, and the spindly red-headed young man pointed and called out:

"Rob," he said in a soft Scottish accent. "I thought this might be your doing."

Rob hurried towards them. He saw that they had been playing cards, but the woman lay down her hand face down on the table. "Well well well," she greeted him semi-derisively in a familiar Northern Irish brogue. "I can't believe it's you." But she didn't really seem surprised, not at all.

When he got there they didn't immediately offer him a seat but looked up at him awkwardly, as if unsure how to proceed. It was as if he were some sort of interloper to whom they were compelled to be polite. Rob stood there with his bag uncomfortably over his shoulder, bracing himself against the opposite empty seats, and looked down at them, wondering how to break the silence that was opening up between them.

He remembered their deaths clearly enough, around ten years apart; both violent and unnecessary, but only one was definitely self-inflicted. That had been Stuart, who'd thrown himself out of a train similar to this one, although of older slam-door stock and on a different route in a different part of the country, and for no good reason, or none that Rob had ever grasped.

Marie – how tiny she was – looked up at him, her head moving from one shoulder to the other, as if she was trying to see him from more than one angle, to get him into focus. She wore the same squarish steel-framed glasses, her hair clipped back with old-fashioned girlish clips.

"Great to see you!" he said, forcing the words out. He wanted to hug her but something kept him from doing so. Perhaps it was a certain

16

coolness that had descended between them all due to the ticklish fact of these two being dead. There were also the new etiquettes of social distancing to consider. Both of them, he noted, wore the familiar blue surgical face masks, only Marie's was pulled down below her chin, in order to allow for unrestricted movement of her jaw, he supposed. Stuart looked resigned, as though he'd been doing a lot of listening. He held an open can of Tennent's in front of him. He lifted it up, pulled down his face mask and sipped from it, pursing familiar cracked lips to receive this Hibernian sacrament.

Although unexpected, it made a kind of sense for these two to be travelling together. They had after all been pretty good friends. Marie had missed Stuart Mcleod after he committed suicide, and always had said that she had really preferred him to Rob. He stood there, swaying, looking down at them, and as if to break the spell of a sudden indifference – should he just say oh well and walk away? – Mcleod pulled a second can of Tennent's from a plastic carrier bag beside him and passed it across to Rob. "You'd better sit down," he said. "Go on, Marie. Budge up, why don't ye, and let your lovely boyfriend sit down next to you."

Marie did as he asked, and he slid in beside her, into her still warm seat. He opened the Tennent's and took a slug of it down. Marie picked up her cards and they resumed their game, as if nothing out of the ordinary had happened, ignoring him as he tried to frame questions that would make sense of this situation. None came to him immediately. They played on silently and intently.

"Guess what?" he said, remembering suddenly. "There are a couple of other old friends on this train. I couldn't believe it. But they didn't even recognize me."

Mcleod didn't even deign to look at him, just frowned at his cards, but Marie, typically, couldn't contain herself for more than a few seconds.

"Who?" she asked sharply, eagerly.

"It's Agathe," Rob said. "I don't think you ever met her."

"I remember you talking about her sure enough," Marie said.

Her obvious indifference brought back uncomfortable memories of how he'd used to mention Agathe to various other girlfriends, probably giving an impression of some unfinished obsession, some high place he had put her in that was impossible to compete with – if they could even be bothered. Rob had taken a long time to realize that his friends, these two anyway, had had a less than rosy view of his heart's holy affections. "Stuart," he said. "You liked Agathe, didn't you?"

"Yeh," he said, not lifting his eyes from his cards. "Agathe was great." He remembered their escapades, the three of them together. Travelling up to Edinburgh by train, and a few days later him and Agathe hitchhiking back to the south of England having run out of money. A long and probably dangerous journey but it had welded them together in the bright forge of memory. Stuart had decided to take care of himself. To be fair, there hadn't been a lot of other options at the time. Rob thought of the casually made choices, the rash acts. Things he had embarked upon easily just because he knew it would all be alright, that he could handle whatever came up. One thing he'd learned to do back then was to throw himself on the mercy of other people, even complete strangers, and somehow that had worked for him early on in his adult life and soon became part of his repertoire of trusted tricks for coping with difficulty. It hardly made him feel good about himself. Stupidly, he began to wonder what these two people wanted.

"So, did you speak to her?" Stuart enquired.

"I did," Rob replied. "She didn't even know who I was, it was obvious. I don't think she even understood English."

"Who was the other one?" Marie asked. "You said you saw two friends."

"It was Paul Hubbard."

"Paul Hubbard!" said Stuart. "Paul – that's really great!"

"So what has Paul been a-doing with himself?" Marie's voice sounded its sardonic sing-song, her sharp intake of breath unmistakably implying that she still exhaled, still lived.

"He didn't say," Rob confessed. "He didn't seem to know me either. He seemed friendly though. He was glugging down wine and feeding his face. You remember how he used to do things like that?"

"Paul was great," said Stuart. "I always wished he'd stayed in touch, but he preferred you."

Rob attempted to demur, shaking his head.

"It's the truth," said Stuart.

"Let's go and find them," Marie said. "Come on, I'd love to see Paul Hubbard." She started pushing Rob's shoulder, forcing him out of his seat. "Come on, where are they sitting?"

"They're not together," Rob explained. "They don't know one another. Never did. Then, when I went back, Paul seemed to have disappeared. I thought he'd come this way."

Rob squeezed himself out of the seat and stood up. He happened to catch the eye of the ticket collector whom he realized had been listening to their conversation. "Not this way, he didn't," the guy said. "I'd have seen him passing."

Mcleod buttoned his short denim jacket across his narrow chest. It was actually fairly chilly on this train; it seemed the air conditioning was

18

blowing in icy air from somewhere. He gathered up the cards and slipped them into his top pocket, picked up his carrier bag, which appeared to be his only luggage, and in a familiar gesture which Rob remembered, he poked his loose gold-framed glasses back up the bridge of his nose. "We'll soon find them," he said. "Wherever could they have gone?" He gave Rob his stupid look, an expression which had always said, follow me if you like.

But it was tiny Marie who led the way back along the carriage, practically flying through the air as the train's forward motion turned her small steps into giant strides, carrying her rapidly backwards into the past. Mcleod followed her and Rob brought up the rear, trailing in their footsteps, as it seemed to him he had always been doing, quite long ago when they'd all of them been alive and kicking.

Three

Paul Hubbard had been running along the hard shoulder of the dual carriageway, his stride long and even, powerful. His arms pumped, moving in tense unison, performing Kung-fu dance moves at his sides. His breathing was deep, controlled, and his enormous brain firmly in the driver's seat of this great articulated contraption of his body. He was bidding it to perform, to carry on as it could easily, under the firm control of his will. For him, it was an instrument of mind, and it was a sort of over-mind he tapped into to dissociate himself from the pain of actually running, so long, so far, all the way down the dual carriageway between Stockport and Manchester.

Blood thundered in his head. In his chest he carried a pounding hammer. Heavy articulated lorries thwacked past him in both directions. He doubted if they could see him; it was dark and the road was not particularly well-lit, but headlights raked over him, and once or twice they had given him an almighty blast of the Doppler horn. Paul had felt like waving, but simply held up his arm above his head in greeting. He was floating, he felt, not way up at treetop height, but just above his head, vertically, so that he could look down at his own crown, his flopping hair, his moving arms, his legs pumping in a long, slow, almost lazy rhythm. It was a feeling of disembodiment.

He was trying hard to remain centred in the moment, in the present actions of his body and movements of his mind, but found himself involuntarily moving ahead, in anticipation of his arrival at the family home. What would they think of him when he burst in casually to tell them he had just run all the way from Stockport? His father would be incredulous, say he was mad as a hatter. His mother, Polly, would doubtless have some witticism to hand, and his sisters would pretend to

20

be unimpressed, although he would point out that none of them would be attempting a similar feat anytime soon.

It was at that instant he looked up and beheld something strange. There were bars pushing up from all the bright corners of the sky, cross-crossing above his head, flashing in the spill from the dipped headlights of the trucks and cars, as if bracing the dome of the firmament, which seemed nevertheless to be lit up from behind. And here he was flailing along beneath, a puppet in the mist of rain that oozed from a million holes in its taut fabric, bathing him in heavenly coolant.

Paul eased himself back a little, trying to absorb whatever he was seeing. The point was to test your physical limits, to see what your mind could really do, not to over-wind, bust your mainspring and be chucked in the bin.

He tried to be in touch with whatever resources his body held, to feed them out through his lower limbs at the correct rate, like fuel, neither conservatively nor rash in expenditure. Meanwhile, his mind, part of which took care of these autonomic systems, was free to roam, or to be emptied at will, an ever-replenishing bucket of nonsense whose water tended to turn murky, needed freshening up a bit. There was no point, he always thought, in being parsimonious with water.

And so he looked down and ploughed on. There were interesting dreams he'd been having recently. His dad called them wise old man dreams, seemed to think that they meant something good, which Paul was willing to go along with. He too felt they meant something good. His younger sister thought they were simply more evidence of his delusions of grandeur. She thought it didn't matter what a wise old man thought in your dream, because he was ultimately your puppet, always telling you what you wanted to hear.

His mother thought such dreams meant you would never be that wise old man yourself. Otherwise, why would you make up such a splendidly non-existent creature as a wise old man? It was something you aspired to but would never achieve in your life. It meant you knew you weren't wise at all, not really. And your mind was gently trying to tell you so. You were trying to let yourself down easily by passing everything off as a joke, which is what the wise old men usually did. His dad had said that he should go on reading Jung. It was good for him.

Thanks, Molly. Thanks, Jim. He leapt a puddle, slid a little on landing but recovered, feeling a strain in his left calf muscle, which he thought he might have hurt. He winced with pain and powered on, not too far.

Perspiration flowed from his body freely, a warm river between his shoulder-blades, burning on his forehead and sizzling down into his eyes. He wiped his face on his sleeve and saw it was dark with sweat. But he kept going. He had to really, because he knew that if he stopped and tried to walk he would be immediately lame, unable to take another step.

The wise old men in dreams laughed at authority, made it all too obvious that all this earthly stuff was just a silly game. Nevertheless they were authority, they knew nothing else, and they played on the world's approval ratings to the hilt. His parents were like that, he realized. And so was he, Paul Hubbard. He was in actual biological fact their only begotten son. He ploughed on, took the slip road, ran straight across the centre of a roundabout, under a railway bridge, and tottered through the little streets, where they lived in ostentatious, scruffy modesty but stopped for a breather at the end of their road.

He leaned forwards with his hands on his knees. Chris Chataway, Roger Bannister. The quiet public modesty of these English heroes: pride under restraint. His father sounded a bit like them, not the lower-middle class bus driver's son he was in reality. A social imposter, he had assumed the wise old man role as quickly as possible, so he explained cheerfully to his children. Whereas for the bastard Freudians it had all been just another ego-dream: you were reassuring yourself, like their mother said. Dad had pulled his famous glum face. Molly, the famous one, stood there with a spatula in her hand, laughing.

Paul's brain told him he would soon recover his wind, saunter up to the front door and ring the bell. His body thought otherwise. Unable to straighten up, he staggered forward at a half-crouch, feet weaving crazily like Roger Bannister at the end of his record-breaking four-minute mile. He reached up for the bell, reassuringly there in the hall light. His sister Carol pranced joyfully down the hall to let him in, and when she answered the door, he fell straight through it, collapsing at her feet. For almost a minute, as her parents and her sisters crowded into the hall behind her, until Paul began to stir, Carol believed that her brother was actually dead.

Four

They caught up with Marie midway down the third carriage. She was standing with hands on hips over Paul Hubbard. Paul looked as if he was just waking up, huddled in the window corner of a two-seater, his head comfortably nestled in a pillow he'd made of his folded car coat. "Paul! Paul! Wake up!" She was laughing maniacally, her thin voice poking at him like a sharp stick.

Paul's eyes were open by now, but a film appeared to have been drawn over them as he blinked and gazed sightlessly around him. His hair was matted, crumpled by sleep, his body large, bear-like, and the unravelling, greenish jumper he wore was adorned with crumbs from the feast Rob had seen him consuming earlier. Suddenly he looked up. Marie was clearly in his sights, a withheld, jowly grin took hold on the bottom half of his face. "Anne," he said quietly. "It's Anne, isn't it?"

Marie's small, mobile face immediately screwed up in disgust. "Marie McIlvoy," she said precisely. "M-a-r-i-e," she spelled it out for him in English. She'd forgotten Paul was a bit of an idiot. "So, how've you been all these years?" She was counting on her fingers, seven or eight, until a stagy glance skywards suggested a total that was well over the sum of her combined digits.

Paul had no ready answer as to how he'd been, but by this time had spotted Rob and Stuart in the aisle behind her. He held up a stilling hand. "Is this really happening?" he asked of the same airborne deity, but then he reminded himself such events occurred all the time. He had only to remember two old friends he'd almost walked past at Waterloo a few months ago: unrecognizable for a moment or so, abruptly settling into once-familiar shapes. "Rob! Stu!" he called. "Long time no see. This is fantastic!"

Neither of them responded immediately. They were too amazed to see their old friend, as large as life, there in front of them. Rob was particularly relieved to be recognized. He, after all, had been much closer to Paul in the old days. Perhaps, he thought, the three of them together created a stronger force-field – or something like that, the way spooks do.

"Can I ask you all a question?" he called in a loud voice.

Three faces turned at once to look at him.

"You know you're all dead, don't you?"

"Yes!" they said in unison.

"But not me," he said. "I'm alive. At least, I was when I left home."

"No, you were not," Marie exclaimed.

"Think back," said Paul.

"Yeh," said Stuart. "Remember anything unusual by any chance?"

Rob didn't remember anything unusual, just leaving the house and walking down to the station. Anyway, there was no percentage in falling out over this sort of detail. Somehow it had been decided that they should all move over to one of the empty four-seater tables, so that there would be room for all of them. Soon they were settled around an empty table and Paul Hubbard began pulling things out of his shoulder bag. Crackers; several little tubs of things to dip them in; olives in a jar; an unopened litre bottle of Italian red wine. Stuart retrieved two more cans of Tennent's from his carrier bag, but that seemed to be all it contained.

"I always bring my own refreshments," Paul gestured towards the dainty feast he had set before his friends. "Help yourselves," he said encouragingly. It transpired that he also had a roll of unused plastic cups in his bag.

Soon they were all tucking in. Paul opened his litre of Italian red and splashed a generous measure into each of their cups. However, there was little conversation. Even Marie had been struck dumb by the momentousness of their meeting up, if it was momentous. Why had it happened? Why at this moment? These were the questions everyone was afraid to ask, and so they went on guzzling and nibbling, occasionally glancing at one another with raised eyebrows, as though they were all back –

Back where? They seemed to have very little memory of anything, Rob thought, whereas he –

Memories! It all seemed to pour through him, in cataracts, every harsh remark, look and glance, fold of clothing, toss of a tangled head. Once, a couple of years ago, he had even seen two people he thought were Stuart and Marie on YouTube. He'd been watching some audience footage of an old rock concert, Bob Dylan at Blackbushe Airport, and there had been Stuart, a long-haired ginger beanpole in swift jerky motion, lurching along a line of ground-seated people That was Mcleod: a gangly, scruffy bag of bones with bad skin, terrible teeth. If he was invited to a fancy-dress party he'd always want to go as Jerry Cornelius; and, heart-stoppingly, Rob caught a brief side-view of Marie's head, her tiny silver earring. She was squinting into the viewfinder of an Instamatic camera to take a photograph of somebody who sat next to her. Himself.

Naturally enough the Super 8 footage immediately jerked away to alight elsewhere amongst endless ranks of suburban young people in their not very extravagant or stylish clothing. They were only a type, perhaps, part of a loose class of people who followed this particular thing, at best half-heartedly. Paul, he remembered, definitely wasn't there. It had been a Hubbardless experience. And as for anything unusual about him setting out that morning: there hadn't been. This too was clear in his mind. They were dead. They knew they were dead. He was alive. Apparently they didn't know the difference.

Marie put down her cup and jumped out of her seat, her movements sudden and elastic as they had always been. Without looking at any of them she walked jerkily down towards the rear of the train. She'd gone to look for Agathe, which should surely have been his own job. But as soon as she'd departed, Paul and Stuart Mcleod struck up a lively conversation. Mcleod had already downed a couple of cans of Tennent's, now he was getting stuck into Paul's wine. "A cheeky little vintage," he sounded his adolescent note of the mock connoisseur. "Fruity but not a bad finish – not the usual crap one encounters on British Rail."

Paul laughed in his distant, chuckling manner. "A lot's happened to me since I last saw you lot," he said, adding diplomatically, "But I expect that's true of all of us, isn't it?"

"Last I heard, you were in Berlin," Mcleod said. "Visiting Hegel's grave, or something, wasn't it?" There'd been a newspaper photo of a shaggy Paul pointing at the name of the venerable philosopher.

"I had a paper round over there. It was so cold in my fucking flat, I burned all the newspapers one night in the grate. So that brought my paperboy career to an abrupt end. Then it was Paris. We lived in a VW camper van, played in a punk band, The Exits, got a record deal from Eddie Barclay. But –" he laughed in a way that wasn't quite self-deprecating "– it all fell through at the last minute."

"The best laid plans, eh?" Mcleod murmured.

He himself hadn't been anywhere or done anything half as interesting, Rob well knew, but there was a belated comfort in knowing that Paul Hubbard's exploits hadn't completely covered him in glory. All this had been decades and decades ago of course, but Mcleod seemed to think some sort of gruelling recap was required. "So, you're back home again," he added, "in dear old Blighty."

"I'm here," Paul said. "I don't know where else I am."

"Sounds reasonable," Stuart admitted.

Paul's face flushed, became wreathed in smiles, genuinely delighted to hear Stuart's sarcastic Scottish tones again. Hubbard had always sought out people from the past, Rob recalled, as if they might have something to tell him about it that he'd missed at the time. He could see Paul was getting ready to ask them a lot of questions. Or perhaps just to tell them more about his many adventures. More precisely: to tell Stuart. Stuart had died years before most of this had occurred.

Rob felt uncomfortable with the situation. It was awkward, stilted, and he was stone cold sober. He helped himself to another refill of the Italian plonk. It seemed to him that the dead got drunk very much faster than the living.

Marie felt as if she was flying down the length of the train, like a small insect riding on a wild draught. She lifted herself on the green handholds on the tops of the seats and propelled herself forward with great leaping bounds, like a space-walker. She really liked the feeling of being out of control, and if pressed she would have admitted to being completely addicted to this. It wasn't until she'd cannoned into one of the sliding doors, which calmly opened to let her fall through, that she finally managed to take control of herself.

She found Agathe on the right-hand side of the train, tucked up in a corner, exactly where Rob had left her. Her book was in her lap and she was looking out of the window, deep in thought.

"Hallo," Marie said. "Are you Agathe by any chance?"

Agathe turned to regard her blankly.

Marie pointed at herself. "Marie," she said, and then, at Agathe. "A-gat."

"Ahh," the young woman looked astonished. "*Agathe*," she said, pronouncing her name correctly. But she was obviously at something of a loss as to how this odd little woman knew who she was.

"Friends," Marie said. "You have friends on this train. Rob. Stuart. You know them, don't you?"

"Rob," she said slowly. "Stuart." She still sounded baffled, but appeared to recognize the names. "Yes, I know ... I *knew* them." Then she said, "Je suis morte. Vous aussi?" Her large brown eyes threatened to fill with tears. She was unabashed but stared straight back at this small unknown woman.

"Yes," replied Marie. "*Moi aussi.*"

She noticed that the open book on Agathe's lap was a French edition of a novel by Kazuo Ishiguro: *Les Vestiges du jour.* It was this book, she remembered, that her murderer had carried into the dock with him at his trial for a crime they'd decided was after all only manslaughter, or woman-slaughter, murder of an Irishwoman too – a far less serious offence.

"Come," she spoke gently, holding out both her hands. "Come with me," she sparkled a bit in encouragement. "They both want to meet you again." She shrugged. "Weird, isn't it?"

"Where is my daughter? Where is my husband?" Agathe said in halting English. "Please, I want to see them."

"Perhaps they are still alive," Marie suggested. "They aren't here."

"Oui, c'est ça," said Agathe, and the thought seemed to cheer her up. Irlandaise, she remembered hearing of her, perhaps. Now she rose from her seat, dropped her book into a gaping shoulder bag and followed Marie back along the carriage, her dark green cashmere coat slung across her long right arm.

On the way they were met by the guard, who was hurrying along to the rear of the train. He was looking from side to side just in case there were any passengers he'd missed. But he didn't see the two women; he passed right through them both with little more than a shiver, blissfully alone on the almost empty train hurtling across the smear of countryside, on which a few large snowflakes were beginning to fall in considerable numbers. Away across the scrolling, whitened fields, Rob saw something strange skittering away, an animal of some kind, disappearing before he could focus, leaving a slender scar in the new snow.

Rob looked up as they came through the door. This time it hadn't slid open for them; they slid right through it. Agathe brought up the rear. He couldn't help but notice how different they were, these two old girl-friends of his. Marie was only about four and a half feet tall, striding along proudly; Agathe towered above her by about eighteen inches – a thin, slightly stooped figure, hair wild; but although still a beauty, she looked both nervous and careworn. He stood as they approached, to leave the girls the two vacant seats, which they slid into readily. He would sit in the opposite aisle. He'd grown a little agitated in the company of his two male friends.

"Look who I found!" Marie called. "Lurking in a window seat. Dodging the ticket collector."

Agathe didn't understand her joke but she smiled wanly. Her eyes flickered briefly towards Rob in the barest of acknowledgements. She seemed to recognize Mcleod, said hello and smiled. Paul Hubbard offered a hand in gallant greeting, and she bobbed her head slightly, like a young girl at a dance.

Rob was being pointedly ignored by all of them. Rather than sit down, he decided to perform an experiment, walking down the carriage towards the sliding door, which began to slide open as he approached, so that he had to rush at it in order to bump against it, which he did, but it slid implacably open to let him through. He tried the same in reverse with the same result, only confirming what he knew already. Both he and the sliding doors, the whole train in fact, were solid matter. Whereas the four dead people currently trying to get to know one another back there weren't substantial, not really.

Another idea occurred. Perhaps it was that the dead, or their ghosts, although they probably knew they were dead, couldn't actually tell who else was alive or dead? Perhaps they also didn't know that such living people were alive in a different way.

This time they looked up at him when he approached, all of them looked up in acknowledgement of his presence. They'd missed him, he thought. And somehow, they seemed to be saying by means of their looks and glances, it was he who had brought them together on this train. But for what reason? Their guess on this point was as good as his own. There was no credible answer he could give them.

Their eyes dropped back to their cards. They had changed games, he noticed, in the short time he had been away. This time the cards were larger. They were Tarot cards in fact; doubtless a Waite–Rider deck pulled out of Stuart's other top pocket. Rob noticed that a hand of four cards had been placed face down on the edge of the table. These were his cards, ready to be picked up and to reveal whatever they had to offer by way of prediction. But he didn't pick them up, just sat down in the nearest seat opposite and watched them look at their own. They'd all slackened their masks, which were now looped incongruously around their chins, like baby bibs, for ease of communication, he supposed, perhaps because they realized, if only unconsciously, that they couldn't catch the new deadly infection which had been raging for almost a year across most of the planet. After all, they couldn't die twice, could they?

As far as he was concerned there was more than enough to worry about amongst the living right at the moment. The long-anticipated virus had ebbed and flowed, been beaten back. Hospitals had been built but not yet used. People had protested against masking and staying indoors. It was all a hoax, a conspiracy of lies. Others had simply ignored restrictions. Death stalked the land, and the roisterers thought they could kill him by getting drunk. The virus had mutated and rallied. America had blown up, Sweden proved delusional. France simmered, and the leader of the UK parliament kept blustering through and largely got his way.

Rob was tempted for a moment to reach across and pick up the cards Mcleod had carefully dealt for him. But whatever they had to impart, he knew from experience it would probably turn out to be something he didn't want to know.

Five

Agathe walked across the bridge sedately, pushing her blue mobylette. She was tired, because although it was not heavy, she had had to lug it up the slippery steps. It was approaching midnight, and the bridge would save her a little time, but she preferred it anyway. And below her the river flowed on in darkness from Belgium out towards Champagne country, where it would sparkle later. Here it was a sluggish blackcurrant river below her, its darkness untouched by the few street lamps further along the Quai Rimbaud, shrouded by lindens on the far side of the road.

Behind her, faintly, she heard the clamour of the clock in the Place Ducale, which it now being midnight unreeled the entirety of its pretty eighteenth century melody, followed by a dozen chimes, echoing and fading in the cool spring night. Agathe thought this was the most reassuring sound on earth. She liked well to hear it. She paused to catch every one of its fragments as it was minutely reassembled and sounded delicately, fully, in the right order.

On the far side she descended with her mobylette, prepared to mount it and pedal it into life, but something made her wheel it down silently towards the flower clock by the camping. The clock was really blooming, bursting with red and yellow roses, she could see it in the moonlight, but the heavy scent was what really hit her, knocked her back almost, both pansy-covered wooden hands pointing straight up in brief agreement before inevitably falling out again. Over in the camping there was a solitary tent, a family-sized one, a softly bent glowing rectangle of light, which went out abruptly.

She pedalled her machine into life, puttered away up the long hill which would lead her circuitously around and back onto the wide road that led out of town, past Rouget de Lisle, her old school, the spider network of oft-trodden roads and pathways, the tall blocks of flats, and on the opposite side of the road flimsy-looking buildings, flaking stucco, a few modest shops, and the Maison des Jeunes, where if she had been asked she wouldn't have known where it was, although she had been there plenty of times.

All these scenes of her childhood, shrouded in night, slid by invisibly into the past as the road opened up, empty and dark, between open fields, and the chill wind whipped at her buttoned black cord coat and her hair was torn back, her eyes squinting and crying as she sped along behind the feeble spark of her headlight. A large truck came past in the opposite direction. She was briefly blinded by its lights, blasted by its slipstream as it hammered past. Another big truck came up behind her, and this time it was really scary because he didn't seem to see her, and he blasted past with a great cry of his horn.

Agathe was bathed in headlights and rocked off the road for a moment; she literally didn't know where she was, but managed somehow to recover.

Her father's large self-designed house was on an estate occupied by other successful local businessmen, a development newly carved out of forest still roamed by Ardennes boar. His children were protected by a tall wire fence, the house an airy modern prison which none of them could wait to escape. He had made his money out of selling carpets to Algerians. In fact, he sold anything to Algerians and he liked to boast about it with a certain measure of defensiveness and a certain jeering quality, whether towards the Algerians or towards those who might criticize him for dealing with them … but they were people, people who needed carpets, and he got on with them fine, and he spread his arms wide in the family photographs arranged on the walls of this large modern house he had built, L'ardennais typique, a part he was born to play, sewn into his costume at birth, the stocky proprietor of a lucrative kingdom of forced bonhomie, paved by rugs and carpets.

She turned her engine off and coasted the last hundred metres or so to the darkened rectangular hulk of this house. She unlocked the garage and slid the door up, pushed her cooling mobylette into its place against the wall beside her father's metallic blue 505, pulled down the door and locked it carefully from inside, as she'd been nagged into doing. She was still shivering as she pushed through into the laundry room and mounted the slatted wooden stairs to the first floor. A soft glow spilled down from the hallway, telling her that, unfortunately, somebody was still awake.

Her father had waited up for her in the kitchen. In front of him on the table was a timetable he'd drawn, which he'd photocopied in the office, of how late his daughters were allowed to stay out,

"C'est moi," Agathe said timidly, and tried to slide past to her room.

"Ici, mademoiselle," he said precisely, insistently, "Viens ici, s'il te plaît."

She could see he was holding himself in check, that he'd been waiting for some time to speak his piece. She stood before him, muttered a few apologetic words, her head down. A well run house, he said, needed rules. He'd drawn up these rules clearly so everyone would understand them. There could be no excuse. No misunderstanding. He was concerned. He was a father. And he wanted her to give a copy of these rules he'd quite reasonably drawn up to her boyfriend. So that he could have no excuse for keeping her later. Because – he pointed a stumpy finger at her, his lower lip trembled – he would in future be held responsible – personally – for his daughter's timekeeping.

"Mais, c'est à moi," she cried in exasperation. "It isn't up to him what I do. It's up to me. You understand? Me." She had never spoken to her father like this before.

"Take this with you, Ga-Ga," he said not unreasonably. "I need to know where my daughters are at night. If this boy is decent he will stick to this. Tell him he won't like it if I have to come looking for you." Her father offered one of his wide possessive shrugs, and a bit of a sharkish grin. She preferred when people laughed at something because it was funny, which this wasn't. Not really, except, in a different way, to herself.

My name is Agathe," she said coldly. "You have named me this."

She had no choice but to take a couple of copies of his Horaire de la Maison and retreat meekly to her bedroom. It was a small room, the smallest in the house. Her older sisters got the bigger rooms, they were both young ladies now, and her little brother needed space to spread out his toys. She didn't mind the small room, but it didn't seem very private, people were always wandering through it, more like a corridor with a narrow divan, and a wall above it where she had stuck up paintings she liked, including one by Rob, a colourful ink drawing of his school friend he had sent her years ago.

She undressed, put her nightgown on and scuttled under the duvet in the dark, making herself as small as possible until she was warm, then stretching out to relax and poking her leg out to cool off. She slept easily, not particularly worried by her father's blowhard threats. He was an idiot, a bit mad, that was all. She hated him.

In the morning, of course, it had been school again, up at seven and out of the door by seven thirty to get to the Lycée Chanzy by eight o'clock. It was a beautiful old building, in a sort of classical style, with a sculpture of General Chanzy on the lawn, a lofty chapel and a wide arched gate, this grown-up best lycée in town, unlike Rouget de Lisle, which was about the same age as she was, seventeen, in the *terminale* year of her bac. She wasn't late, just not exactly on time, but she couldn't resist her usual circuit of the square du Petit Bois, past two little shops she had bought gum in and the Café du Stade, not yet open, around the permanently crumbling concrete velodrome with its profiled modernist cyclists hunched down over their handlebars and a man on an ancient style of moto, like hers, pacing them. She chained up her battered machine and swung in through the gates.

Agathe was a good student: quiet, thoughtful, alert, but not, this morning, as quick at note-taking as usual. The philosophy teacher discoursed on about Descartes and Diderot, giving them a thorough grounding in the types of passages they would have to interpret properly, precisely in their examinations. She lost the thread for a moment, looked up and accidentally caught the eye of a patrolling peon. This peon simply glared at her in cold contempt. He didn't want to be asked, as some of these girls had a habit of doing, "What's that he said, mister? Qu'a-t'il dit?"

She looked down steadily at her paper, catching up, and began covering the tiny squares on the pages of her notebook in a neat orderly hand. Denis Diderot, she decided, would never mean anything to her. From History to Geography to French, the most boring part of all, hardly a break between them, except for a few minutes to eat her orange and her chocolate biscuit. Béatrice came over and rattled on for a few minutes about something she didn't manage to take in, but after a close reading of one of Montaigne's passages about women – everyone laughed at his disgust with the female smell – she just wanted to get out of there at once.

Béatrice understood well, although Agathe was too shy, too reticent to say anything about where she was going.

When she arrived at the attic room in the Rozoy house, which had a reputation amongst kids for being full of junkies, she was flustered, with a lot to tell that had nothing to do with school work. Rob had just woken up. She unpacked the feast she had brought for them from her mother's kitchen. She gave him a copy of her father's Horaire de la Maison, and explained what had happened when she got home last night. She repeated her father's threats to Rob. She explained why she'd been especially angry about this, not because he would do anything, but because he didn't accept that whatever she did was her responsibility, not his, or that of some other man.

He understood exactly how she felt, but somehow couldn't help wanting to go along with her father. It suggested trust, this placing of some sort of male responsibility on him. After all, he was two years older than Agathe. He stood up and opened the attic's skylight, just in time to hear the chimes of the town clock in the Place Ducale as it began to reassemble its inevitably unfolding afternoon melody.

Both felt as if they were being spied on, caught in a tight controlling web, handed rules and conditions over something which had just happened between them, and with which they knew there was nothing wrong. On the other hand there was something comforting about this cat's cradle of constraints and regulations. The clock had a pretty tune. It gave a little; accommodated their sexual relationship, after all. Papa had said yes to that. He knew he couldn't stop it. There was something reassuring about this. Rob had been dependent on the good graces, kindness and acceptance of others. They ate some nice fresh ham on a baguette Agathe had bought, and some chocolate cake of her mother's, wrapped in baking foil. They climbed back into the sleeping bag.

Rob glanced into the long window at her reflection. He was relieved she had one, a reflection, that is, although it didn't fit in with anything he'd previously heard about ghosts. Agathe looked a bit younger in hers, just like everyone else. If she had been a living person riding along beside him, she might well have glanced at it herself, but she didn't. As a girl she had always been scruffy. Rob had loved her lack of interest in self-grooming, in anything like clothes or make-up. Actually, he realized, she looked smart, as if she were on her way to a function, an interview. It was an older woman making this journey, a woman travelling on her own.

For him Agathe was poetry – that's what sprang to mind when he thought of her: it all came together.

Six Spirits of Place

1.

Downstairs the policemen tell each other stories to try and make themselves feel healthy and whole. I'm not fooled by that, I know there are no salmon in that sweet stream and that dark glasses only stop the suns from seeing you and passing their cruel judgement.

Downstairs the policemen still shout and roar, they have seen prostitution of the soul and they have played this game before.

All the new mothers of the little policemen tell stories too, but theirs are different. They tell stories about amazing women and their pregnancies. They have bad eyes.

2.

It is wet in the Place Ducale today and the chocolate and underwear sellers all throw curses at each other across the great fountain. Most of the stalls are empty, waiting to be photographed by those with intelligent eyes and no film left.

Sky, you are sodden, you don't blink enough, something heavy will fall into the eyeball of the earth! We must not damage the wet black heads must we! Each one is golden in the sight of the holy fountain mermaid.

The earth is running away in the Place Ducale today and all the arches are angry. Someone has to put out his cigarette to watch the gush and they are already scraping suicides from the walls.

But even when the stalls crash, no-one moves and the fountain continues to overflow.

3.

French breasts are not blue, dry and normal, but are slicked back with nicotine. They are cut off when their owners die, varnished and put in shop windows to advertise soap.

I have seen people stubbing out cigarettes in the avenue Charles Boutet.

I have seen people biting their nails in the Bonbonnière.

4.

The Meuse flows along the Quai Rimbaud, unfrightened by the brothels and the children playing at being poets.

The Meuse is as brown as evening and has watched the fishermen stub their toes and cry in secret.

The Meuse is longer than the Quai Rimbaud and they say that it has a short memory.

5.

Time moves slowly as the talkers hang upon the bars of the down train in the square.

The children have all hidden behind the aprons of the past and only the grown-ups are left, limping round in small circles and swaying in the warm breeze.

Time moves slowly in the square and some of us pretend to read magazines.

6.

It is very dark in the spare bedroom and impossible to recognise your friends.

When you see the one you're looking for she tells you that her parents are watching and as you glance round they look down and continue eating.

Too late, you have already truck the hungry pose and arranged d to meet outside in the cold air of the Metz road. Fortunately nothing happens.

It is very dark in the spare bedroom and impossible to remember your friends.

Much later as you sit counting the morning in and drawing on your fingernail you realize that you've wasted time.

That was about as good as it got. Charleville, in a small yellow *cahier de dessin*, when he was seventeen years old – but now he didn't remember it right. There was a lot more packed away in the wardrobe, but he had put it behind him. He thought himself a poet no longer. He'd been failing to write poetry since he was about fifteen years old, when he'd largely got away with it due to generous teachers, those wonderful women, one of whom wrote helpfully in his notebook: 'Keep working, keep thinking – but learn tolerance.'

Trouble was, you couldn't get rid of the poets. He hadn't. He still read them, read about them too, always, and his own frustrated poetic journey had dogged him for years: the why of why he wasn't good, the techniques and struggles of the great poets who often had not much to show for their lives except for what they had written. As a tutor he'd had to pore over a lot of syllabus poetry by good old poets and well-connected contemporaries, pointing out connections between their dead metaphors for teenagers who would never like this stuff anymore than did he. Its main effect on him had been to foster a habit of juggling with word-orders until they seemed awkward and old-fashioned to most people.

Poetry, he had found, was a hobby one pursued in solitude. Gerard Manley Hopkins was his latest fad. This more or less failed but devoted

Jesuit priest had written stuff that would knock your eye out if you allowed it to do its dirty work on you.

Manresa House, Roehampton was, and perhaps still is, a squarish neo-classical mansion which once stood in isolate rural grandeur and relative seclusion up behind a long lazy descending road that for well over a century now had been choked with traffic. At the top of the hill, he remembered, had been an old hospital where prosthetic limbs had been first developed. Forty years ago Rob had undertaken a year's postgraduate teacher training certificate there as a further education lecturer in English and Communications. Garnett College, it had been called, but before then a Jesuit college where Gerard Manley Hopkins, fresh out of Oxford, had begun training for his own vocational qualification, the Roman Catholic priesthood via a noviciate in the Society of Jesus. At a later period he had returned to teach classics there, one of few subjects he had really enjoyed, and genuinely excelled in, which had otherwise been of little use in his ministry or theological studies.

Small teaching rooms up circling flights of stairs, where young apprentice Jesuits had studied and knelt in prayer, an old refectory, a high chapel with some sort of decorative rotunda. Rob seemed to remember being shown relics of the famous poet-priest, perhaps up amongst the rafters of the chapel, a tiny work-space where he had made the discoveries that led to 'The Windhover' in sprung rhythm, to all of his mature work. Rob was unsure. It was the kind of memory you couldn't trust. Memories which flooded in to occupy fresh ground recently excavated by reading and imagination: a hollow place filling up quickly with snow. Everything brought up to the same level. He seemed to have read that the Society of Jesus had sold the old place off or leased it out in the early sixties, when high-rise housing in compulsorily purchased grounds had threatened the privacy of the noviciate and therefore its integrity as a place of secluded study and worship.

Gerard's first spell at Manresa had been for two years in which he struggled towards beginning his final vows. In Rob's day behaviourists and fucking educational method had been the main time-waster, the bane of the whole place. Anything to do with poetry, creativity, student-centred learning approaches, already old-fashioned, were on the way out as the Margaret Thatcher era swept on and on with the vigour of a new managerial broom. All those blue-suited behaviourist types liked nothing better than to chop down humanists and democrats. What was this inwardness you spoke of? How could it be proven? It can't, it can't, they would crow triumphantly.

He was particularly intrigued by Hopkins' notion of inscape and its peculiar sister concept of instress. The ambitious young priest had written a lot about this, but used both words in a vague way, redefining them with each use. Inscape sounded like it meant 'inner landscape', which perhaps it did, but also something like 'essence'. What was the essence of being – a human being, a kestrel, a stand of felled poplars, a kingfisher, a dragonfly, a box of old tools – or anything else that attracted him but might not ordinarily be thought beautiful? It was still a created being, or more widely part of God's Creation, a creature like us, a creature made by God. For him each thing was specific and unique. Its inscape was the essence of its being but also our ability to perceive it empathetically, to recognise and know God in it. Instress, Rob thought, meant both the act of perceiving or understanding those beings, drawing them into ourselves – which could be stressful, an act of will for certain – a grasp, a mental holding of a thing together in the mind, and also Hopkins' own making of differently stressed poetry which might be able to do them justice.

His sprung-rhythm, his surprising and surprised compression, lavish verbal tricks of alliteration, hyphenation, line-breaks, contorted syntax – all seemed to record a battle of understanding, a wrestling match with what he saw as a created world. A labour of love which paralleled the Almighty's labours, a model-making activity, perhaps, of the kind Rob had been fond of as a boy. But, Rob knew, there was an understanding and a huge ability implied by this, faculties he knew would be forever beyond him. At the same time, he knew that for most people they would be just strangled, all-but-incomprehensible verbiage.

No wonder of it: shéer plód makes plough down sillion
Shine, and blue-bleak embers, ah my dear,
  Fall, gall themselves, and gash gold-vermilion.

The Society of Jesus hadn't liked them much. The Jesuits had thought it all a bit unorthodox, a waste of his time by somebody who – although counted a genius at Oxford – wasn't even capable of passing his final theology exams, and had been consigned therefore to lowly service in unpopular places. Liverpool, Wales, Ireland. His works weren't published until many years after his death.

This tormented, unhappily failing aspect of Gerard Manley Hopkins – as with many other poets – was deeply attractive to Rob. Also attractive to him was this self-denial, this stringency with himself, and his stubbornness, the way that – on his knees, at retreats – he had begged God for permission to continue writing, and believed he had been granted this dispensation, provided he asked permission and didn't do it too often.

In his most famous photograph he reminded Rob physically of another schooldays friend, Rick Nimble, a relentless logician of the art room. Gerard posed in a dog collar as if butter wouldn't melt in his mouth, smooth brow, book in his hands, the calm expression of a man enjoying his uniform. Hopkins had sometimes been known as "Hobby" or was it "Hoppy"? Rob imagined him as a small, darting, enthusiastic creature, always stopping on his way to look intently at this or that.

Hopkins had been a man of diminutive stature, 5' 2" and easily dragged by his heels by his Dublin students around a polished table to demonstrate the manner of Hector's death. His one regret, he told them, was never to have seen a naked woman. These were said to be his eccentricities. He was not, as a rule, very fondly (or accurately) remembered.

Recently, desperately, Rob had typed Ask God into Google and come upon a well-presented website where you just typed in your question. But the only visible question was a double: 'How old do i am when die? How many kids do i get?' The answers were 'never' and '69'. Consultations appeared to be private, but there were plenty of genuine endorsements, thanks for sound detailed advice. Rob had been unable to formulate a question. He wondered how many people were prepared to engage with this useful God. Not that many. The comments were years old; which meant it had an abandoned, disappointed look: it had appealed neither to atheists nor believers.

According to the black box merchants your job was to provide and document results, to serve the demands of the state apparatus, and as subsequent research proved, treating people like black boxes did mainly cause them to shut down most of their brain and emit black box type responses. Just as it had been in Hopkins' day, as long as you put forward the Duns Scotus argument against Thomist orthodoxy, that's as long as you would be held back, and like all but the most obstinate trainees, you learned how to fill in the homework grids the way they wanted. Trained to be a corrected form-filler, box-ticker. Foolish to resist. If you did you were indeed stupid. The questions weren't hard, and the only way (an easy one) to a secured living under the provisions of the 1944 Education Act. Rob had a delirious feeling of having truly arrived in the middle classes.

It had been easy in the end to get through teacher training. But they had kept poor Gerard's nose to the grindstone, bloodied it many a time. Rob had seen people who seemed determined to abort their ascent into the middle classes, who just would not let go of some crude workerist belief in the authenticity of soul music, or D.H. Lawrence, or some other crackpot idea deemed silly, but even social laggards like these had been thrust through the none too strait gate of accreditation. In the end you felt you were being foolish, making a bogus stand as an excuse for failure. By this time Stuart had already failed to become himself, and Rob had begun to abandon him.

Six

The Tower, The Hanged Man, The Devil, Death. All appeared in the hands of those around the table, not exactly *Good News Bible* material, reversed or otherwise. Rob picked up his own hand – which still rested on the edge of the moving table – and saw it contained the King of Swords, upright. Marie, he noticed, without wishing to, had the Queen of Swords reversed in front of her. Death, also. He put his cards down immediately and turned away from the others. None of them was speaking, just glumly looking down at incontrovertible evidence of disasters that had already occurred, and were by now some time in the past.

"Cheer up," Mcleod said tonelessly, "it might never have happened." He gathered up the cards, including Rob's, and replaced them in careful order in the Rider-Waite deck, which he stuffed straight back into his top pocket. "Life and soul of the party, as ever," he added, half-apologetically. "I only tell the absolute truth."

Rob wanted to say something, one of his old jibes. But he remembered one of Stuart's older sisters had once asked her brother at the dinner table: "So, how's the intergalactic revolution then Stuart?" And Stuart had hung his head, unable to reply. Skewered by his own sarcastic flesh and blood for living in a fantasy world.

"I've always hated those things." Paul was the first to come to his senses. "I don't know how people can enjoy that sort of stuff, I never did."

"Means you're superstitious, probably," Rob said.

"True," Paul replied. "Easily spooked, that's me."

"I used to like them, that's all." Stuart muttered.

Agathe had taken on a wall-eyed look. She was visibly sagging, a half-hearted smile quivering on her wide mouth. Unable to comprehend what was going on. Rob had never really understood what was going on in her head either, and her ghost was no more communicative than she'd been as a girl. So long ago. Rob hoped he hadn't been responsible for summoning her from whatever limbo she usually dwelt in. If so, he wished he hadn't.

Sensing his eyes upon her, she turned towards him. Her smile twitched, a thought formed. "Do you remember *l'Écosse*?" she asked.

"Yes," he said. "We'll always have *L'Écosse*."

"*Oui*," she replied. "I have always remembered this," adding, "I looked on a map once, to see where we have come." She smiled again, suddenly more relaxed. "A long journey."

They'd come a long way since then. He remembered hearing of her death. A phone call from France, from Mathéo, one of those conversations that began, "I have bad news," and proceeded to convey it as your mind hammered, went still. But why had she died in that pointless way? There was no rhyme or reason in it. Same with the rest of them. They had been the first four of his friends to die. There were others later, but these sudden deadly punctuation marks, spaced over a decade or so, had each hit him pretty hard.

Paul rooted around in the bottom of his capacious bag. The crackers were finished, and the dips, wrapped in a plastic carrier, stowed carefully inside. "Ah ha," he said, then "No I shouldn't," then "Yes I should," and "Hmm." He paused for a moment, was frozen. Then with a flourish he produced, on his splayed hand, a large Italian Panettone cake, wrapped in thick white paper and tied up with a red ribbon: an expensive one he'd bought at the station, perhaps for some other purpose. And so he'd captured their attention. Marie applauded loudest, she was transfixed, an excited bobbing girl again. Stuart put away his surliness; Agathe offered a swift beaming smile that lit up her face, but then her eyes crinkled in a peculiar way and from across the aisle Rob could tell that Paul Hubbard, the dead clown, was instantaneously and completely smitten by her.

What an absolute fucking tool, Rob thought. Always up there in himself. His desires seemed to him like divine promptings or something, for the world spirit to realize itself through him, and he insistently censored and denied anything that got in the way of his vaulting self-esteem. One of the great ones, Rob thought. A truly devoted and good friend; somebody who'd cared for him, believed in him; one of the most well-meaning people on earth. Paul presided over his unwrapped cake like a grandmother, doing the honours with a plastic knife that produced more crumb than slice. In his scheme of things everyone got a generous portion, and they all took theirs gratefully.

"Is good," said Agathe, cracking another of her wide smiles – this one disgustingly crumby.

"You know how to treat your friends, I'll give you that," Mcleod spoke awkwardly.

"Actually," said Paul, "I got it for someone else." He left that mystery hanging in the air while Stuart and Rob went "hmm hmm" in unison. Paul Hubbard had always known how to work a crowd, or at least he'd thought so. He tried to brush crumbs from his baggy jumper, but the effect was negligible.

Rob glanced through the window and saw that, as if to confirm their happiness, thick snow was pelting hard across the light grey open countryside of fields and distant stands of spindly trees. Huge flakes of it suicided against the long windows, making long smears like the entrails of a white army of attacking bees. More and more of the fuckers continued to sacrifice themselves, until sills began to form on the windows, and a white crust of snow framed their reunion feast.

Snow bees: that's what they looked like. One or two of those monkeys thwacking you round the side of your head would sting considerably. Christmas on Earth! And suddenly, in a clear announcement of something, the train was slowing down fast and the LED display began scrolling its message of a fast-approaching delay. The snow-swept platform at Basing-stoke was desolate; and the town rose behind it shrouded in a sort of dull mystery. A uniformed man, his cap pulled down, stood beside a door under the departures board, ready to step out and wave the train on in a moment or two. But they could see no further, and a distant slamming of not one but two doors informed them that some passengers had boarded the train after all. The platform guard whistled the train off and raised his white paddle and they jerked into motion once more, easing out past snowy roofs, rimed fences and chandeliered garden firs. This was heavy snowfall and the train edged out carefully into it before again picking up speed.

"The train of doom!" Mcleod cried out in puerile irony. "Ah wouldnae go there, sir! No tonight!" He seemed to be feeling called upon to act Scottish. It had all been Tom Nairn back then, for those who thought about those things, like Stuart Mcleod. *The Break Up of Britain.* And here it was, in actuality, and he was acting like a clown.

Nobody seemed to think this was funny. God's put a stop to all that, Rob thought. For God there was no advantage in the dissevering of kingdoms, not at this time.

Paul busied himself with another slice of cake. "Help yourselves," he said to them through his first mouthful.

They were leaping forward over Hampshire, over villages strung along the River Test, places which literally manufactured money, centuries of banknotes, were able to establish churches and workhouses for the relief of the rural poor, corn mills, wool churches, the Black Death, all these had passed through here in a long procession. One boomed, honoured by a royal residence, a flurry from its paper mill filled the skies above lush countryside dense with combed wheat, its proud workhouse later the subject of a Victorian scandal of systemic cruelty, routine abuse of every sort.

There was rich connective tissue to the present, deep down layers of Anglo-Saxon laws, golf courses and munitions dumps; but these sites of wealth and rural poverty, gradually emptied, tranquillized into supine beauty, were looked at and away from by most travellers, their secrets never unravelled. Nowadays inter-fractal parishes boasted of the latest fibre optics as they had once been proud, prosperous railway towns, and before that new freight-bearing waterways had been cut through to Salisbury, Southampton, Bristol … he wondered how they would cope with being snowed in tonight.

He'd passed so many times through these loops of recurring Adlestrops. They were silent, sleepy, but no birdsong of any particular counties seemed to be ascending to heaven, just smug decimated places that had been forever fading down to weathered brick, pebbled gardens, walled away behind glass, spelling out a local name. Country halts that could have been anywhere in the south of England were tonight in deep freeze, sparkling out there beyond the spilled light from the paused train. Edward Thomas had known, there had been plenty going on behind those apparently endless moments of repose; the fastest bricklayer in the village had been caught in a single photograph by Gertrude Jekyll, his hands a speed-blur, constructivist poetry in motion.

On Sundays the squat villagers had dressed up in their white corduroy suits, offering their rough music to any wife beater in the Devil's Punchbowl. Edward Thomas must have realised that the emptying of all this was well underway, as did Jekyll with her gentle, painstaking account of a vanishing life in *Old West Surrey*, they seemed to know somehow that the great cull of the trenches was rushing towards them, an armoured bullet-train from the none too distant future.

Agathe said she wanted to get out. Marie sprang up to let her pass. "I want to speak with Rob," she said. "I haven't seen him for long … I must do this now."

Rob budged up and Agathe sat next to him. "It's good to see you again," he said. "I upset when you didn't recognize me."

"I was sleeping," she made a twirling gesture beside her head. "Dreaming or somewhere. Your friend's cake brought me here; I have eaten this cake before."

They were still young, all of them. He was old. He could see it plainly enough in his reflection in the dark train window. But while he was here with them he was still young himself; they were all still in it together. He was making them dance to his tune, unpleasantly enough. He didn't want it that way, but how else could it be?

He was standing at the intersection of several lives. Perhaps he had drawn the lines together, in a sort of distorted perspective, gathered them around him like one of those mirrors that enabled you to see around corners. Rob himself could see nothing much, just the rim of his memory's surface, organized around him, a bowl in which he'd brought his friends to life, forced them up to dance again to the same old tunes. It was an addiction, automatic. He couldn't help it. Locked into his phony religion of memory. At least he wasn't the sort to look away.

"It's amazing this," Rob said. "All of you are so young, that's what I can't get over."

"But Rob," Agathe said. "You are young too. Look –"she pointed at the window.

Stuart turned and looked at his reflection. A younger man looked surely and squarely back at him. A man in his early thirties, perhaps, but no more than that.

"It is *génial, merveilleux*," Agathe said eagerly. "What is happening to us is very good. It must be."

Rob hoped this didn't mean he was dead.

Agathe's head rested on his right shoulder. "Do you remember walking out of Scotland?"

"We didn't walk all of the way out."

"It felt like this."

"Until the first lift, a newspaper van – *avec les journaux*."

"Ah bon? Je croyais que c'était un van de boucher."

"A butcher's van? No it was an early delivery to a florist."

With their heads almost touching it was easy to talk. The whole shared dream came back: walking arm in arm, leg in leg, singing Old Macdonald and Frère Jacques and Gentille Alouette for miles and miles on the long trudge out of the benighted Caledonian empire. And then that first lift, with the butcher, the newspaper delivery driver, the florist, only for a few miles, then a longer lift in a panel truck that took them across the border into England. Rob had made her laugh by kissing the ground when they were dropped off on the edge of a roundabout in the middle of Sunderland. It was still pitch black and the next lift was such a long time coming. Although, they agreed, it had really been a time of excitement, happiness. Rob remembered trying to make it so, drawing on reserves of buoyancy he'd never known he possessed.

There was freezing and fainting, being cold and keeping warm together, and a long lift high up in the cab of a sixteen-wheeler, drowsing, smoking, listening to the radio, chatting to the driver about nothing to keep him awake in the warm fug. Another, others. They'd ridden on the big trucks with the generous lorry drivers down into the heart of England. Hopped a coach from Lancaster to Birmingham, ran out of money there and took to thumbing again, finally picked up on a grass verge in the lower midlands by a police car, which deposited them by a police phone box and made Rob phone his father to come and collect them, which he did, but none of it was too serious, all had ended happily. Rob's father could appreciate the adventure they'd had, but his mother had hit the roof in hysterics. This had only to be expected; it all flowed off them like water off the backs of the lucky ducks they knew they were. They'd had an experience that, in some way, they felt should have bound them together for life.

"*Oui, c'est vrai,*" said Agathe.

It's true, Rob thought, it really is true that's how it happened. He had been trying to make life exciting for her, by throwing themselves on the mercy of a fate which he had understood to be merciful, to some anyway. In the belief that people were okay, and that the working-class world would quite happily take care of you. It had worked pretty well, proved true at that time and in those places he hadn't known anything about. It was an early attempt at making something good happen, which hadn't misfired. It had worked. It had bound them together.

In his work with teenagers he'd quite often came across kids who seemed to want to die of shame or embarrassment over something they'd done. What had they done? Hit someone, poured flour in someone's handbag. Poured a bottle of water on the desk during a maths lesson, laughing gleefully. Now they wanted to atone, to be forgiven. In the end they all wanted to be good, to pass their exams. He had felt the same way at their age, in truth still did. He wondered where his own reserves of confidence had come from: his breathtakingly cringe-making belief in his own capacities. Straight out of a Christmas cracker, he shouldn't wonder. But it was still there, prodding him along.

Seven

On specified days in the late nineteenth century, Gerard Manley Hopkins' head popped up and looked out over the back wall of the grounds of Manresa House – across the oak and aspen-lined edge of Richmond Park, whose inscape was that of a velvet-antlered stag which he partially instressed into the jigsaw branches of trees whereupon leaves were layered in shingled tiers interlocking at the quoins of their spiny spokes.

July 11th (1866) – Oats: honey blue-green sheaths and stalks, prettily shadow-stroked spikes of pale green grain. Oaks: the organisation of this tree is difficult. Speaking generally no doubt the determining planes are concentric, a system of contiguous and continuous tangents, whereas those of the cedar wd. roughly be called horizontals and those of the beech but modified by droop and by a screw-set towards jutting points.

July 19th ... Alone in the woods and in Mr Nelthorpe's park, whence one gets such a beautiful view southwards over the country. I have now found the law of the oak leaves. It is of platter-shaped stars altogether; the leaves lie close like pages, packed, and as if drawn tightly to. But these old packs, wh. lie at the end of their twigs, throw out now long shoots alternately and shiny-leaved, looking like bright keys. All the sprays but markedly these ones shape out and as it were embrace greater circles and the dip and toss of these make the wider and less organic articulations of the tree.

March 12th (1870) – A fine sunset: the higher sky dead clear blue bridged by a broad slant causeway rising from right to left of wisped or grass cloud, the wisps lying across; the sundown yellow, moist with light but ending at the top in a foam of delicate white pearling and spotted with big tufts of cloud in colour russet between brown and purple but edged with brassy light.

But what I note it all for is this: before I had always taken the sunset and the sun as quite out of gauge with each other, as indeed physically they are, for the eye after looking at the sun is blunted to everything else and if you look at the rest of the sunset you must cover the sun, but today I inscaped them together and made *the sun the true eye and ace of the whole,* as it is. It was all active and tossing out light and started as strongly forward as a long stone or a boss in the knop of the chalice-stem: it is indeed by stalling it so that it falls in scope with the sky.

The next morning a heavy fall of snow. It tufted and toed the firs and yews and went on to load them until they were taxed beyond their spring. The limes, elms and turkey oaks it crisped beautifully as with young leaf. Looking at the elms from beneath you saw every wave in everything (become by this the wire-like stem to a finger of snow and of the hangers and flying sprays it restored, to the eye, the inscape they had lost. They were beautifully brought out against the sky, on one side dead blue, on the other washed with gold.

Hopkins' natural descriptions were a result of the way they seemed to extend from the movements of his pencil on the sketch book he carried with him. This laden branch, moving and mopping in its visible complex geometry, an acute quoin, a spray of leaves, sprouts, shoots, fine womb-like tubers which curled mathematically around the hidden encirclement of a bole, a bloom, a seed, and the lashes of a slowly blinking watcher, the eye of God from which all filaments descended, criss-crossed, binding together visible and invisible worlds: a continually opening bud, a hatching insect, an ovary from which all created beings fell forth in the precise order of their utterance by the living mind, his pencil changed direction with the swift, unimaginable dexterity of that agile, invisible hand in a swift apprehension of the interconnectedness of beings.

Instead of holding himself apart, as Hopkins had learned to do, and placing whatever small resources he had at God's service, Rob had been largely content to freewheel, to see what came his way. All the same, starting his 'A' Levels at St Anselm's College, Isingford had been an exciting time, a moment of seemingly abrupt transition. He'd walked along the pavement to the looming sixties grammar school, past dappled private establishments, infant prep and music schools, beyond a swampy green hollow ringed by well-established oak trees. Old red suburban villas stretched off along dappled ways, now suddenly within his reach, deservedly, or so he'd imagined. He burned with curiosity to know what was happening behind every door, to be admitted into these calm beautiful rooms without fuss or argument.

Hopping over green-filled cracks on the mossy pavement, he experienced a sense of becoming detached from his lower body, somewhere way up in his perched head, or even floating high above himself. Suddenly he achieved complete disconnection, and was looking down on all this for the first time from waving treetop height. The sense of being able to do this, perhaps to leave his own body behind, reassured him of his capacities but was also somewhat disturbing. He carefully reeled himself in before he went through the school gates, feeling light and rocky in his brand new desert boots.

It was tempting, looking back, to see the whole experience as one of induction into a larger, superior kind of life, towards which, willing or no, he was being gently if insistently propelled. Some people, new teachers, fellow pupils, had pointed out this privilege, and its highly conditional nature. But if he was being put on trial for his life, he felt quite easily up to the challenge.

One of the first friends he made there had been tall, insistent Malcolm Rivers, another new boy, expelled from his nearby public school for refusing to be thrashed for stinking out the common room with Disque Bleus. He had a car. A 1962 Austin Cambridge, A60, an impressive, solid wagon, ancient-seeming although only ten years old, and he often gave Rob a lift back to Cobham once they'd made friends at the first Christmas disco. Sometimes he wore a long, black cape, complemented by heavy blue eye-shadow, and when he appeared at the back door Rob's father would call out: "Dracula's here!"

They used to stay up half the night drinking instant coffee, locked in endless disputes about the true meaning of libertarianism and what have you. And then there was Zoe Spott, a promiscuous Catholic girl who instantly offered to read your Tarot cards, to whom Malcolm had remained devoted for so long; and Abi, Rob's first girlfriend, whose German mother had kept her Hitler youth dagger in a felt-lined case; and Tom Rivers, a bluesman from nearby Claygate. He'd had the whole attic of his parents' considerable Tudor semi to himself, full of guitars and humming amps. Tom had approached him one day and they started jamming, soon afterwards playing gigs together at The Swan on Claygate Green.

Easy and charming, this life of the middle-classes, with its assumptions and strong repeating patterns. The idea that you could do something, for example, there were possibilities. It had all seemed so harmlessly pleasant but there were also quoins where people split off abruptly, divided in two, changed direction. Looking back you could see when these characteristics first revealed themselves. Malcolm had always been the sort of person, always would be, who would make sure Christmas was achieved. His life seemed to have run on rails. Rob glanced up at the end of the carriage, at a poster for a cancelled production called *The Play That Goes Wrong*. That was life according to Malcolm. He'd realized long ago that the only way to stop it turning into a mess was to impose the plot at every moment, impose and reimpose, keep it straight, on the rails. Tom Rivers was still playing blues, still repairing old guitars; he too had had it all sorted out from the beginning.

St Anselm's was also in transition, from grammar school to sixth form college, but some of the older intake who'd passed the 11-plus exam appeared to be somewhat recessive. One of these was a scrawny Scot with greasy red hair and an incomprehensible accent, and a fight had broken out one day between him and another boy in the form room. They were rolling around on the floor punching one another, desks kicked over. This skinny kid's glasses were knocked off as he swore and punched a larger boy, who had insulted him grievously.

Rob picked up the red-haired boy's glasses, and tried to pull the two of them apart, succeeded in separating the fighting boys, calmed them down by telling them they were childish. Stuart, he said, was too intelligent to be fighting like this. This set him off again, pointing and swearing at the other boy, whose face Rob could recall in precise detail. He was smooth-skinned, light-haired and had seemed harmless enough. Stuart was shaking from head to foot with adrenaline. He calmed down, and the other boy turned away, after being called an English cunt one more time. Rob handed him his glasses, which he put on. Rob wondered to this day why he had intervened, just why he had befriended this skinny, apparently violent kid.

Possibly because he was a Scot. Rob had never met a real Scottish person before. He also fancied himself as a peacemaker, and discovered that being an outsider – from a secondary modern – gave him a certain leeway. Rob said that he hadn't expected to find that kind of behaviour at a grammar school but it was the way the rage had come flaming out of Stuart which was so impressive.

Mcleod's family lived near the school, and once they'd become friends, Rob often went round there at lunchtimes, to play darts on a board that hung in the living room of their semi-detached home, drink coffee, and talk. Stuart was vociferously left-wing, and also, if Rob remembered accurately, also had interests in astrology, Tarot cards, science fiction, and religion in general. They were a large family, seemingly happy and jolly, very welcoming, and Stuart had a couple of older sisters who were student nurses, a younger sister, and a pair of young identical twin brothers. He was also on valium ... for his nerves, for his temper.

Thinking back, it had always been obvious Stuart would never be able to cope with real life. Mcleod had steered a car, a big estate he was attempting to learn how to drive, right across the middle of the Scilly Isles roundabout, due to being in a valium-induced trance. Perhaps that was why he'd been interested in Tarot, astrology, the occult, even Christianity – and then philosophy – they were each of them ways for a not-powerful person to achieve power, or that's what they promised anyway, quite falsely. And his politics, although common enough in Scotland, in the south of England had been an obvious affront to what everyone else believed. Perhaps in looking for a certain way for the weak to be stronger, you found this faith.

Last night's dream sprang up again upon his inner eye. It had been horrible alright. Rob's dream landscape hadn't been washed in gold, outlined no such joy, no promise of renewal, just a fetid swamp of dying things which seemed like it might stretch on for eternity. No inscape to discover, no instress to take up, to pull into yourself, nothing in which to intuit a deep overall pattern. In Rob's dream the final destination of God's manifold creation had been shown to him all too clearly. But when Agathe and he had walked out of Edinburgh, the roads, and the darkened fields surrounding them, their synchronised steps and the trucks which stopped for them had all been interlinked, articulated, levers pushing against one another in what seemed a more or less friendly world.

Mcleod had always been drawn to violent solutions to political problems. You and whose army? Who knew? He had come to rest, as it happened, at a point where justice was clearly always on the side of the weak, but completely unobtainable. As usual, Rob thought bitterly, there was a flaw in Stuart's reasoning, a useful *because* for every single *why* none of it could ever happen. Nietzsche had helped him discard religion, but as far as revolutionary socialism was concerned, he had never noticed the flaw which broke the lovely fork, although he had loved the Brecht poem.

Eight

At Salisbury they stopped again, and this time the platforms were well lit. People were waiting for connections through to Southampton and Bristol, but a few got on their train, including four younger people who entered heir carriage, a pair of young men – laughing teenagers, travelling light – and two women, separately, each laden down with a weekend bag and two shopping bags full of wrapped Christmas gifts. They passed by in file along the aisle, but glanced neither to left nor right, apparently not seeing the five travellers.

On the other hand they didn't try to sit down on anyone, just spread themselves out further down the carriage. The two boys, casually unmasked, took up a four-seater bay halfway down the carriage; the women, first stowing their luggage on the empty overhead racks, occupied separate twin seats, one behind the other, on the opposite side.

The train banged on through the darkness, which had fallen rapidly; the windows were reflective lozenges, long occluded mirrors against which legions of snow bees continued to sacrifice themselves, crazily confident of eventual victory. He thought of the Roman invasion. They'd been all over the West Country, though this was denied for years by local history buffs, until relatively recently a few enterprising detectorists had taken some sonar readings and found plenty of evidence. They'd built on the long barrows and the iron and Bronze Age forts, scattering dud coins, dead straight roads, butchers' shops, broken kitchen equipment, cloak brooches and caches of skeletons. The inhabitants had settled eventually into layers of sediment

Paul packed up the angel food. Marie nodded off against her folded coat, her features angelic indeed in repose. Stuart had pulled out a paperback and was reading it bent over against its spine. Stuart could never stop reading. The day he stopped reading was the day he died. Reading had ended then for the present. But here he was consuming another paperback. Rob wondered what it was – could be anything up to the early eighties, some long reformed or suicide Marxist theoretician perhaps, the fifth volume of Trotsky's Fourth International documents, a Russian science-fiction novel, a biography of Oliver Cromwell.

"What you reading Stuart?" he called, leaning forward. Stuart unexpectedly opened up the cover and held it up. It was a current bestseller, at least something Rob had seen in piles at the station bookshop: a popular volume about contemporary working practices, it looked like. *Surviving the Gig: How Long Till the Lights Go Out?* Something like that, he only caught a glimpse before Stuart bent its back and drooped his head to the small, densely-printed page. Stuart was obviously bringing himself up to date, or maybe just rekindling an old habit. Exactly what he should have done in the first, or last, place, Rob had always thought, just carried on and on with his interests come what may, do another degree, an MA in something or other, repair the damage, prove himself once and for all. He only had to settle down to it. He could do that. If not, a simple TEFL qualification would have been far from beyond him.

Whatever he should have done to prevent Mcleod's death, his glib suggestions had missed the point, as he had well realized at the time, pushing empty or mocking notions at him as if by rote, just as he was doing right now. He'd had every single and absolutely no idea about Stuart. In other words he hadn't understood him at all. It was almost as if he had been trying to teach him a lesson about his shallowness and lack of comprehension of the world and its workings. Teaching him that you can't make things come out how you want them to be just by thinking it's so. You have to actually be right about something.

As if overhearing these thoughts Stuart stood up, buttoned his thin denim jacket, and pushed past Paul who retracted his legs to let him pass. He was moving stiffly, as if in great pain. He stood in the aisle and glared down angrily at Rob. His carrier bag was hanging over one thin wrist, his hands thrust in the pockets of his jeans.

"This is where I get out," he said, and marched back to the sliding door.

Marie reacted first, getting up to follow him, Paul craned around to watch with already startled eyes, hooded in suspicion. Stuart began awkwardly to push past sleeping Agathe; but before they could get far he had passed through and they heard the violent explosion of the outside door slamming back against the side of the fast-moving train, and glancing back quickly into his window Rob saw his root-pale human form diving out purposefully, finally, again, to be swallowed up instantly by the storm's swarming white-out. They heard the outside carriage door crashing back and forth angrily, its lock smashed, wide-open.

Marie in the lead, they ran in shock to the sliding door and piled through it. But the outer doors on both sides of the train were perfectly intact, the sliding kind, quite impossible in any case to open from inside a moving train. There was no sign of Stuart, not in any direction.

Rob had actually seen him go. Stuart had stared at him full of hatred, and then plummeted past his window. Now he was no longer here but somehow the door had been healed. And unlike the first time nobody had pulled the communication cord. The others relaxed a little, as if relieved to have been had. Rob couldn't stop shaking, crying involuntarily, his mobile face crumpled in sudden grief.

"Well, I suppose that means he found us boring after all," Paul said. "Poor Stuart."

"You're right there. You're not wrong," Marie said.

Agathe just stood there looking stricken, baffled. "He has played a trick?" she asked.

"I saw him dive past my window," Rob cried out in pain. "Just like it must have been, like it was."

"Of course you saw him," Paul said wryly as they jostled back to their seats. "The whole performance was for your benefit."

"If you see something that doesn't look right," a tinny female tannoy voice perked up, out of the blue, "Text British transport police immediately on 61016. We'll sort it. See it. Say it. Sorted." It clicked off abruptly, finally.

Stuart Mcleod had been dead almost twice as long as he himself had lived, and he, Rob, had lived in his place. He had slipped into his seat. Stuart. Stu. Stewball. These were his various names. For unknown reasons he had always had to keep Macleod alive, always had to be referring back to him in everything. Well, not everything. But he was always stupidly resurrecting the idiot anyway, and now he was playing games of revenge, exacting payment for the irregular life he had been permitted to live. The old paranoia crashed through him, his spirits virtually extinguished.

There was a phase when Stuart had acted as a buffer between Rob and his girlfriends. Come to think of it, that had started with Agathe. Someone to fill up her silences, to try and bounce her (usually without success) into a conversation. It was difficult to get her to utter a word of English. She'd liked him too but was shy, too shy to speak.

Marie on the other hand had never stopped talking from morning to night, yakking or sulking, full of despair over her university life, hatred of her snotty teachers, and her and Stuart got on easily and well. He knew how to get along with Marie and they would reappear talking from a shopping trip or a walk in an air of good humour and calm. He would talk to her about his family: his brothers, the twins, and his three sisters, and Marie would turn down her own memory-steam and listen with interest. They were both Celts and issued from large contentious families.

Further down the carriage the two boys still had beers and empty cans in front of them but each had retreated into a private world of headsets and miniature screens; the women, according to the tops of their heads, were also bent in attitudes of prayer to screen or book or magazine, equally oblivious to anything that had happened.

The four friends sat together around the same table, keeping close. Rob slid into the window seat Stuart had just vacated. It didn't seem so bad after all. Perfectly natural. He saw that Stuart had left his book behind, stuffed down the side of his seat. He retrieved it and laid it on the table, straightening the bent covers. To Rob it looked like the most unappetizing object on earth. He couldn't conceive of any circumstance in which he would want to read it himself. But he had always, as Stuart would remind him, been an ill-informed and unjustified literary snob of obscure pretensions.

"Do you remember Stuart?" Paul asked Agathe, who stirred suddenly.

"Yes," she said, "I remember him in Edinburgh, of course, with Rob, when we were there. He was very nice, I like him well. But I cannot understand him."

"I met him through you, Rob," Marie said. "Right after we got it together. We just hit it off straight away,"

"We were a team there for a while," Rob said. "Wasn't it brilliant, hanging out in that house in Braintree, just flopping around listening to reggae, reading books, smoking dope? Cooking up something to eat. What was wrong with that? It was the perfect domestic situation," he recalled fondly.

"You were a wee bit boring," said Marie. "Stuart was absolutely brilliant, you couldn't touch him. He had you beat in everything except looks. You were an annoying person, Rob, to be really honest with you!"

She let out a peal of laughter, leaning over the table and to poke him with a finger, laughed some more, an irritating little sister seriously *asking for a slap*.

Agathe had understood most of this. She laughed in sympathetic recognition: she too had found Rob to be a type of an annoying idiot.

"He was always a difficult person," Paul said. "I found him obtuse, to be honest. I never knew whether to take him seriously. But I didn't, not really." He was rather pompously tapping a long finger against his tight lips, as if considering a verdict in some heavenly law court in which he presided. "There was something interesting he said once," he began, "But I can't quite – no, it's gone. He was a great bloke – I know you thought so – but I just don't buy it. Look. Why couldn't he just have accepted things, had a flat, had friends, lived a life like anyone else? You don't throw yourself off a train just because your plans didn't work out."

"Not everybody can be like you, Paul," Marie said. "You had your family's plan."

"I've been privileged to be born into such a brilliant family," he said. "Between us we know everything."

"Thanks for sharing that," Rob said drily, but he knew instantly, if Paul had been alive he would have said nothing.

"There weren't many people I could share it with. People are jealous of you. That's what dad told me. They're jealous and they bite deep, if you let them. But don't let them. I found that to be good advice."

"What terrible advice," Marie said. "It's what did you in, Paul. Your parents' advice. If you just ignore everyone's opinion, and then you go be frightened of Tarot cards, it means you can't accept any kind of outside contradiction – you can't admit you might be wrong – you're living in a fantasy world where you can do anything you like, and that's why you're frightened of those stupid cards." Her eyes glittered behind her girlish spectacles as she plunged her long Irish gimlet into the heart of this idiotic middle class Englishman. "And you can't, you idiot, you just can't. Because, well, basically, you're completely unintelligent compared to the average Irish paddy." She spat this out, laughing joyfully in contempt. "Even my brother, even wee Dermot is cleverer than you, Paul Hubbard." She laughed again derisively.

Paul held up his hands, as if that would hush her. Some chance. He'd had this trouble with Irish people before. This was something else his father had explained to him carefully, warned him about: how the Irish, that sort of Irish anyway, they hated us, and that he might as well accept it and move on. Don't even try to get any sense out of them. He had found it to be true, but he didn't bother explaining this to Marie.

Rob looked on in admiration at the way his old friend withstood the onslaught. He rolled with the punches, didn't contradict her. He knew better. Marie herself, it had to be said, didn't know better. She pursued her advantage – she was fantastically arrogant in a way – so gleefully, so relentlessly, so perversely, it was impossible not to imagine, since that's what happened, Marie pushing someone so far with taunts and insults, that they battered her to death with an ashtray while her baby slept in the next room. Paul had predeceased her by a few years; he'd never known about her death. But Rob knew. He had once been pushed far enough to hurt Marie just sufficiently to shut her up. He had been drunk though, not mad or homicidal. He had frightened her a little and humiliated himself. That was the beginning of the end of their relationship, before she went to Iceland, and came back, and lived, and had her child: the girl baby he had looked at, a tiny crumpled scrap of nothing asleep in a carrycot.

"I know what I could fancy right now," Marie said. "And that's a wee glass of Bushmills." She looked around at them, as if expecting somebody to pull a bottle out of a bag, but disappointingly none of them had any whisky about their person, not even Paul Hubbard.

Molly Hubbard had been a household name for decades, his father on the face of it a bearded house-husband named Jim. Jim Hubbard had done most of the childcare, but apparently little else apart from muttering on about Hegel and Günter Grass and assembling ships in bottles. He sold advertising space in Early Music and had collected a copy of *The Times* for every day of his life on earth. This was according to Paul, who was proud to take after his Dad, rather than his celebrity mother. Leave that to the sisterhood; he knew they'd never be able to fill her shoes.

His mother hosted a long-running high-culture chat show. Everyone in the land, who watched BBC2, had heard of Molly Hubbard. She had been more or less an institution. She'd crossed swords with Pinter and a young Salman Rushdie, got Martin Amis to come out on air. Amis wept. Something about her air of straightforward, friendly inquiry, her cocked blonde head suited the role. She had listened attentively to Doris Lessing's cat stories, treated Berger with due religious awe. She had compared pubic haircuts with Germaine Greer on live television – heart-shaped and zigzag respectively – but that had been a long time ago. Ratings soared.

A woman like her, as might be guessed, was more to be feared than loved. Her affairs were legion, legendary, whereas Jim had been the meek stay-at-home type, sexually and otherwise frustrated.

Anyway, such had been Rob's impression, nailed in place now, true or otherwise. In that respect Paul had been determined not to follow in his footsteps, but being the allegedly brilliant son of Molly Hubbard – notorious presenter of *Mother Hubbard's Cupboard* – had done him no harm at all. He was handsome, articulate, and personable. This top-drawer media profile-by-proxy had opened a good many doors, not so much in television itself – like his entire family, he scorned it – but in the peripheral worlds of book publishing and advertising. And, to a degree, in the left-wing politics they all espoused. That too had been a long time ago.

Earlier in the year Macbeth's witches had glooped up out of the mud once more to intone their anti-human curses, this time with special relevance. GCSE mocks always necessitated a certain amount of discussion of the evils of witchcraft, as well as its possibly amusing and justified aspects. Owls chasing eagles. Horses devouring one another in their stables under a roiling sky. Nature was in an uproar alright. She was getting upset and preparing to exact her revenge. This was the part he relished explaining over and over again to his online prisoners. How the witches were really the good guys.

Rob wondered idly if Paul's sisters were similarly driven to use the ambitions of men against them. Perhaps they would blow up the world! But no, he supposed not. They were in reality more or less caring, do-right people whose malevolence was kept largely under wraps, manifested only in a certain relentless smugness. When shall we three meet again? How about another orgy of self-congratulation? But all that was wrong with them really was they thought they were alright,

The Hubbards seemed to evidence the second of the two dominant attitudes towards class he had met with in Surrey. The cultural one, which more civilised middle-class people held, admitting we were all in the same boat, shipmates on a leaky tub, equivalent beings perhaps but created or simply bred to order for the places we occupied. The more common opinion was harsher and held more nakedly that you, Rob Goddard, and your sort, would never be anything other than lesser beings. This was apparently what most women thought, especially Paul Hubbard's sisters. I

Molly Hubbard herself wasn't anything like them. Off-screen she was kind and interested in people, unassuming to a fault. She had a residual St Louis accent, rather refined, slightly Irish-sounding, and these odd, engaging tones had been part of the spell she had cast over her small but fiercely devoted TV audience. After a few years it had been rechristened Hubbard's Hub, became more dignified, sharper, but eventually petered out an anachronistic institution of late Friday nights.

The doors slid open with a huff and Mcleod stiffly walked past the empty luggage racks back into the carriage. He carried, precariously, a travellers' fare bag hung over his thin wrist, and a grey moulded cardboard tray into which four lidded paper cups were neatly slotted. "Look what I found!" he announced cheerfully. "They put the trolley on at Basingstoke."

Three of them looked at him, speechless. Paul appeared to take this reappearance in his stride. "Much of a queue?" he asked.

"You'd be surprised," Mcleod said. "I didn't know what to get," he continued, putting down the tray. "So I got two teas and two coffees. You'll have to fight amongst yourselves." He reached into the travellers' fare bag, pulling out a handful of milk and sugar sachets, and dumped them on the table.

Nobody moved, they just looked at him in silent dismay. Mcleod stood there, until Agathe reached forward and disengaged a lidded cup with the string of a teabag trailing down its side from its place in the tray. "Thank you," she said, prising off the lid and beginning to prepare the drink.

Rob looked away, at his own reflection, then back at his battered friend. He had immediately taken Stuart's seat, he realized.

Mcleod turned away, resigned to sitting alone. Rob noticed that the back of his head was caved in, his thin red hair was matted and gouts of blood and brain matter were splattered down the back of his jacket, which, like his hair, was saturated with the entrails of snow bees. He was shivering, his teeth chattering. Rob noticed that one of his legs was badly broken, a loose flapping twig, but it didn't seem to bother him. His own provisions were stowed in the travellers' fare bag. He sat down opposite, folded down his tray and pulled out his own survival rations, which included black coffee and a sandwich: a cheese ploughman's. He tucked into these things, ignoring his friends.

"Have you got my book?" he called through a mouthful of sandwich. Rob picked it up, leaned forward and threw it hard at him. Mcleod reached and caught it in mid-air with a lightning reflex. He soon found his place and continued reading about disorganized capitalism. Rob opted for coffee, and prised out a cup. He picked at a couple of milks and a couple of sugars, tore them open with his teeth, and shot the whole lot into his cup, not without spilling milk over his fingers and scattering brown sugar granules over the table. Marie too was a coffee person. Paul took the remaining cup, the last tea, which he usually preferred anyway, not needing any further jolt to jump start his metabolism.

Rob again, trying to cheer himself up, leaned his head against the shining black window against which the snow-bees still crashed and disintegrated. He drank in the chaotic assault of these perishing beings, safe from them, but drawn out into the madness of the battle for control of the world, in which he tried to lose himself completely.

At that moment the driver applied the brakes sharply, lights flickered. One of the women further down the carriage stood bolt upright in her seat, pulled down her mask and began to scream. The lights flickered again and went out completely. The woman was still screaming. He heard the other woman shout harshly: "For fuck's sake SHUT UP!" The train was still moving at speed. Sliding out of control, it seemed about to buck off the rails. The standing woman abruptly stopped screaming.

Rob had a sudden flash of understanding that those two women were also dead. The one who had screamed had resembled an automaton.

Nine

When the lights came on again, the train was still moving fast, and craning his neck to look behind him in alarm, Rob noticed that the two boys were undergoing some sort of transformation. Their loose clothing bulged and tore and their dull brownish carapaces cracked open. They crawled out and extended damp, trembling wings to dry in the warm recycled air. Immediately they began to pump themselves up, and were soon hovering in the air near the roof of the carriage. They moved themselves slowly along the ceiling by means of the rails of the luggage racks, which they grasped lightly with pairs of grappling mandibles protruding from the remnants of their hoodies.

Each had become a long-bodied creature, kept aloft by a double-pair of battering gossamer wings; their faces were narrow, recognizably those of the kids he'd seen earlier but their eyes had moved further apart, enlarged, conjoined: compound insect eyes. Feeding tubes – or something – hung down from their mouths. They were undeniably beautiful creatures, twitching as they seemed to struggle along the carriage's ceiling towards the bemused ghosts. But they didn't come any closer, just hovered there, lit up from within, nervously equidistant between the women and the five travellers.

"*Elles sont belle, les libellules.*" Agathe cried out. And while the carriage lights flickered intermittently, those of the giant dragonflies remained constant, glowing: drawn out tongues of flame. "*Ce sont des anges célestes, regardes!*"

"We're alright here," Mcleod shouted up at them, "you can fuck off home now."

Twin beams shot from the enormous segmented eyes of the striated blue dragonfly, bathing his head and body entirely in violet light. When it blinked off again a few seconds later, he had been completely healed.

Stuart felt vaguely disgruntled. He offered them no thanks.

Little by little their train slowed to a halt, and a dead silence of achieved immobility fell. They all listened intently. No announcement was made. The display board was blank, the overhead strip lighting failed. Emergency bulbs flicked on, powered by a chugging generator. They gave out a dim illumination at various points along the ceiling, against which the delicate finery of their guardians shone from within like drawn flames. The dark train lay quietly somewhere between Salisbury and Tisbury. Snow covered it over so that it soon resembled a long chocolate Yule log nestling on the ground, encased in a crisp cylinder of sugary icing.

Marie was transfixed by the hovering creatures. She hadn't taken her eyes off them for a moment since the emergency lights flicked on. Mcleod, on the other hand, determinedly ignored them, grimly straining to read the text of his bent-over book, following the new trajectory of the future present. Rob, on the other hand, built mental snowmen, or some such activity, his head still leaning against the dead glass of his shared window, devoid of response. Meanwhile, the glittering creatures hovered above them, in abeyance.

Paul gazed into a middle distance, just above everyone's head. This was an irritating 'thinking of higher things' posture, but it was also how he genuinely happened to feel at this moment. He too had left people behind long ago, mainly his family. He missed his folks, Jim and Molly, something rotten. Even his God-awful harpy sisters. He pulled out his gold Samsung Galaxy S10 from his pocket, and tried to get a signal. He knew it would probably be impossible on a night like this, but he enjoyed trying.

Hubbard's phone still seemed to him like a Star Trek communicator. He'd acquired his first mobile a few years into his post-death existence, but they still seemed amazing. He was reassured by a quizzical look from James T. Kirk. He seemed to recall Mr Spock using his device to access some marvellous ancient Klingon poetry, in the only known language more beautiful than Erse. He couldn't contact his family on it, only listen in on them sometimes when he could get a signal.

He wished he'd been alive to make use of the internet properly. Living people didn't seem to appreciate it properly, especially if they were young enough to take its capabilities for granted. *Why would anyone need to do that?* he imagined them saying incredulously, as they took another of those self-photos on a long stickie. The truth had been revealed to him posthumously: it wasn't the world that was boring, just most of its population. But his incarnate personality, which remained, just wouldn't let him change his mind about anything. He'd always been optimistic. He couldn't let go. Not of anything as big as that; but he still tried to make the best of things.

Taking yourself off somewhere was anyway what you were supposed to do on a train; it was what journeys were for, Rob thought. Suspension. Even when something was really happening it wasn't, at least not this time. No bombs, no derailment. The women further down the carriage had fallen silent. The dragonflies hovered, effortlessly radiating goodness, light; the soft thrumming of their beating wings was the only sound.

They appeared restless, however, as if waiting for something important to happen.

Agathe nudged at his shoulder. "Rob, Rob," she said. "Réveilles-toi, regardes les anges. Je n'en ai jamais vu de pareil!"

Rob sat upright beside her and looked.

"Only *les tout petits* can see the angels," she said in a barely audible whisper.

Where did they pull this crap from honestly? "Trailing clouds of glory," he intoned indifferently.

"*Oui, c'est ça,*" said Agathe. "Perhaps this is why the libellules fly into the trains. It is why there are always so many of them. They fly in when the doors are open."

"But they don't fly into the trains," Rob pointed out. "There aren't any, not usually."

"Oh."

"Not usually," he explained. "They hang around rivers. They're mainly river insects." He didn't know if this was true exactly, but it was better than her foolish ideas.

"Ahhh," said Agathe.

"But why did you think they fly in? Why onto trains?"

"Because the doors are open?" She faltered, searched his eyes briefly, and looked away, hung her head and began quietly to cry again.

It reminded him of their partings, their silly lingering farewells. These had been life rehearsals. Sitting there, waiting for something to end, not with any relish, just ticking off the hours, the minutes, the seconds, perhaps studying those stark graphic Ricard coasters, or posters on the walls, old brown beer advertisements – in one of them a beer-drinking woman was breast-feeding a baby who pissed into a bucket. But there were only their faces, really, to come back to again and again, lit up in frank love. A light too bright to stare at continuously, it had to be circled and circled around and about in an endlessly stretched moment of rediscovery.

Until they had to say goodbye, eyes hanging onto each other's faces, trying to hold every detail forever, every gesture sacred, until we have to say goodbye. All those rails, ribbons, iron ways, fire paths, had tied them together, but it was a long way, they both knew, across on the ferry to the upside-down land of unlikelihood. E PERICOLOSO SPORGERSI. But what if you did lean out of a moving train to catch one last glimpse, and what if you could travel along those rails like incandescent light? Where o where would you get to then? Until they had to say goodbye, bright eyes hanging on each other's gestures, trying to hold in every detail forever, every gesture sacred, until we have to say goodbye.

The ghosts didn't altogether understand where they were. Anything could go in any direction for them. They always watched him surreptitiously when he looked away, as if for clues about etiquette in this peculiar situation. He put his arm around her shoulder and eased her to him. Agathe yielded in a way that was almost automatic. She seemed to take comfort from his enclosing arm, as she had when a girl.

As if to break this spell the guard reappeared from the rear of the train – Rob thought he'd been left behind somewhere before Salisbury – but here he was again, and this time he could see everyone easily enough and asked to see their tickets. The two women complied readily enough. He glanced at the now empty bay still littered with beer cans, where the two boys had been sitting. They seemed also to have dumped the papery husks of their bodies. He halted, looking up at the giant dragonflies buzzing around on the ceiling.

"Tickets, please!" he called up sarcastically.

Each of the newly-hatched creatures extracted a ticket with laborious care, awkwardly passing it down to the guard in an extended mandible.

"Yes, that's lovely. Thank you very much," he called out loudly, as though they might be hard of hearing. He scribbled casually on their tickets with his black ballpoint, passed them back, and the enormous insects swiftly regained their former height, brushing against the roof of the train.

"I've seen yours," he said, holding up his hand as Paul and the others fumbled for their tickets.

"Are we stuck here all night then?" Stuart asked from behind his book.

"Well, I'm glad someone asked," he replied jovially. "Anyone would think you didn't have any homes to get to. In answer to your question, sir – yes, we have indeed been stuck. You may have noticed it's snowing rather heavily, but I've been just informed we will shortly be continuing on our journey."

He smiled and moved on, but as soon as he pressed the button for the sliding door the dragonflies made their move, darting through the opening into the corridor, where they seemed to prevail upon the guard to use his special emergency key, because the next sight the travellers saw was two celestial beings making a rapid spiralling ascent up through the snowstorm, flaring iridescent torches as bright as magnesium flares, still visible for a few seconds as fading dots high up beyond the low-laden snow clouds, and after a brief interval the train creaked into motion again. There was a jangling announcement over the tannoy, but no one could make it out properly except that it seemed to be employing an oblique, jocular tone, and soon the train was racing on towards its next stop, which was probably not far away.

Tisbury sounded a bit like Cissbury, where they had a ring around a hill and a flint mine, but Tisbury still had its standing stones, albeit shifted out of sight. A great hoard of bronze artefacts had been dug up there not long ago, and earlier the stone to build Salisbury cathedral, and a handsome tithe barn in which to pile up a tenth of all your goods for a farmer's ticket to God's forgiveness. No doubt it was still an important place to some people, but none of them descended from the train. The station itself had passed from picturesque to unrecognizably swamped in heavenly dandruff. Surely history – or their bit of it – couldn't be disposed of so quickly? The train whirred briefly, recharging itself, whipping itself up like a top, and pulled out of the station towards the hazards of Dorset, towards Gillingham.

Mcleod wasn't sorry to see the dragonflies go, no, not at all. Were angels part of the gig economy nowadays? Certainly looked like it. They probably had another pizza delivery of some sort to perform, probably something like their redundant and unwanted repairs to his fucking dead body. Piecework, strictly by the timesheet, the perfect atomized social labour force under the regime of disorganized capitalism. Stuart was dead before the rise of chaos theory into respectability, but he got the SF version, he had grokked entropy. After all, he had been a sociology and philosophy student.

The writer of his paperback was a good popular critic, but something disturbed Mcleod about the exposition: it was the ill-concealed glee with which the author leapt and vaulted about the globe, showing connections where only disconnects occurred, setting forth obvious reasons why the working-class as it had once been envisaged would never again be at all powerful, except perhaps as consumers. The best way to survive the gig economy was to accept your place in it, obviously, smile nicely and do your job. Adapt and service. What on earth made you think you were worth anything more? He seemed to be crowing over the powerlessness of workers, or maybe Stuart was misreading him. He knew in his gut this was totally wrong, and that he was right, although no more than a fragment, to completely disregard this guy's puerile and self-serving analysis.

Rob felt much the same about the departed creatures. He and Stuart were really two sceptical peas that grew side-by-side in the same semi-comfortable pod; but he'd had enough of these people long ago. Blood suckers! Killjoys! Now he wished they would all let go of him. And yet, he thought sentimentally, they had loved him, of course they had, back then. At least, they'd found a space for him, weirdo Rob, that permanently zoned out good-looking fool. They had definitely, all of them, come back again and again for more of the same old same.

Marie, no longer distracted by the hatchlings, seemed to have drawn new confidence from their brief ministry. She'd seen nothing like it since her uncle Pat produced a perfectly formed leprechaun shoe he had found on the hill above the farm, trapped in a bramble twig, so he said. She had marvelled at it, believed in it utterly, although when Uncle Pat tried to give it to her her mother had said she wouldn't have it in the house. Then there was the fucking banshee she'd heard on the night Anne Devine died. No fucking joke at all.

Now she glared across at Rob. Somehow he had got away with everything, had it ridiculously easy just for being a fucking English idiot. Marie wanted to shout at him, tell him to stop drivelling, because although his lips weren't moving she could see this was exactly what he was doing. She could practically hear his ceaseless inner patter of murmuring self-justifications and stupid ideas which didn't lead anywhere. Stuart and her used to enjoy nothing better than getting together to tear him to shreds. She laughed to remember how much fun it had been, ripping off the flesh of a prize idiot.

Ten

Marie and Stuart had tried to insist on it. They thought that he was dead as well. What if they were right? Rob struggled to reconstruct his walk from the front door to the railway station. But he couldn't remember anything unusual about it. The picture perfect front window of next-door's house and the beautiful life on display behind it: a charming domestic theatre for two young children, who also had a trampoline and a swing in their back garden, now up for sale. No sooner were they settled than restless, wanting to move on, create a similar but better environment elsewhere, while in his adjacent subdivided flat, Rob's rhythms were those of somebody maintaining a slow steady habit: inhaling dust mites, the poor man's cocaine, *dégueulasse,* and logging on for the occasional contact high of Zoom tuition.

Next-door's life was a little different. They'd excavated the back garden, installed swings, paddling pool, trampoline, knocked the front room through. They celebrated holidays, pasting cut-outs made by their children onto the front window. There had been work going on ever since they arrived; continual hammering upstairs; but now, all improvements completed, a for sale sign was strapped to their front wall; it seemed they were moving on. Perhaps that was next-door's job: refurbisher of domestic dreams. Always on call, he did them up and passed them on to people who couldn't manage their own happiness.

He didn't remember noticing anything particularly, nor a peep out of his sullen in-house neighbours but that was hardly unusual. But wait a minute. There had been a most foul stench coming from somewhere … the drains, he supposed. There had also been a police helicopter in the sky above his quadrant. High up. But low enough to hear their rotor blades, like a lawnmower with worn out bearings, hacking at the sky. It had seemed to be following him, especially when he looked up. But ... someone else had been looking into the air at the same moment. Somebody else looking up and saying, in effect, bring it on. Come on. Come down here and arrest me mister po-lice-man if you think you're so fucking hard. But he couldn't picture that other person, a woman he thought, and had carried on to the railway station.

And then ... but the details were coming thick and fast. The trees had been hacked back, not pollarded exactly because they weren't proper trees – just a clump of fast-growing bushes, including a squat, yellowy palm, on the island in the pavement behind which two benches had once lurked. Nobody could sit on them because they'd been uprooted years ago, post-holes filled in with concrete but still visible. Although one or two people had been there in the summer, he remembered, crouched on the low wall in the shade from the bushes, drinking, smoking (Would that ever happen again? Of course, but it was hard to imagine), next to the car tyres, shopping trolleys, the ... what else? He couldn't remember what had been dumped there. Only that you had to slide past on your way to the station, on one side or another, past the empty bench alcoves or along the road. That the shrubs and bushes had been cut back recently, he'd noticed, leaving a lot of naked rubbish which passers-by thrust away in there in moments of casual irresponsibility.

He wondered why the benches were ever planted in the first place, concreted in, facing away from the hill and the road, but the answer must be there was once something obvious to look at on the other side of the tall industrial wire fence. This fence ran in front of what had once been a showroom for Lotus cars, preserved in pristine dusty emptiness, and a wider yard behind that sold building supplies, there were a few low warehouses, assembly sheds, perhaps, and a service road which led back to where you could see nothing. The largest visible unit was a flourishing Self-Storage facility. People squirrelled away the trappings of former expansive personalities in them for a brighter day. A patch of used land, but not what had been there before, towards which the absent benches, blocked carefully into recesses let into the brick-enclosed retainer of out of control shrubs, facing out as though those who sat in them, old people perhaps, resting on their way up the hill, had been supposed to be able to look out at something.

The Shi-Shi Lounge was gutted but not yet refurbished, abandoned for now. That place hadn't worked since it was Funky Brownz but the Turks were willing to have another go at something. Another night-spot. And then the empty bus stop, wide empty steps leading up to the platforms and the open ticket office. The local train slid in, a nice new one, and he stepped into a nearly empty carriage, cool behind smoked glass, and slid away, stopping and starting with bleeps and slides as a tiny number of mid-morning passengers had boarded and dismounted from the smooth, mainly automatic service, which he had sometimes tried to imagine was sinister but which was actually reassuring.

The new engine and rolling stock, the brand new seats and elegant railings and animate arrowed displays … made it seem like an oasis of luxury in the drab, buried lives of its users, who, he had also noticed, eyed one another more critically on the new trains than they had on the old, as if their fellow passengers simply weren't worth all this extravagant expense. Nobody was ever going to speak, but if they did it would have to be in common agreement that this was indeed a good service. Actually, the people on the deserted commuter train had been perfectly okay.

Gillingham was yet another ancient settlement, had in time had become a rather substantial municipality. Originally a Saxon town, its name was a Dorset dialect corruption of that of the titular character in the *Epic of Gilgamesh*, an early medieval copy of which had found its way to an abbey thereabouts. Locals had particularly relished the scene where Enkidu fucks the temple prostitute for fourteen days and nights. He felt a bit more human after that. Cider all round. This was a long time before the Black Death wiped out half of the population. A talented itinerant labourer from those parts had cut the club-wielding Cerne Hill Giant.

Paul scrolled down further on his golden device: a hunting lodge frequented by kings; a founder of the Massachusetts Bay Company; an early petrol engine plant; a flood of evacuees in World War Two, leading to a considerable baby boom. The platform was deep-piled alpine, and no one was arriving or fleeing that highly historical place. The train grumbled on with belated caution, sneaking over the obliterated border into what was still Somerset.

Paul was stirred by his quick scroll of it. The uses of new technology were almost limitless, he realized; he couldn't believe all this had happened. As they pulled away he tried to hold its significance steady in his mind, tried to remember why exactly it was supposed to be so important to remember things, and what. But he was remembering nevertheless, pulled back by specific gravity to revisiting Christmas with his parents and his three sisters.

Not one of them but many, stretching along through his childhood, in the various places they had lived according to the dictates of his parents' careers.

There was a composite, a pattern out of which they had all been built. Repeated features – food, drink, charades, competitions, quizzes, and no-holds-barred arguments. It was also the only time of year when their atheism was mentioned – but in their way they thought of themselves as a typical communist family. Happy Hanukkah, they said, raising a glass at the end of the first course. Jim and Molly couldn't really be bothered with anything to do with religion of any kind.

And they each of them had had a character they played within the family group, a role they must follow but a permissive one nevertheless in which one's true character – as defined by Mum – could be fully expressed. Paul had always been the daft dreamer who was allowed to style himself as a philosopher, which for Paul (although not his father) meant somebody who could run a long distance in a straight line, by force of intellect or will, if only to be mercilessly antagonized by his most critical sister.

Somehow he had been awarded a sword of honour to cross and parry with, in the jousts they carried on with the wide world of everything their parents knew, and, for his family, were the ultimate measure of. Molly Hubbard, a can-do person, was used to making things happen. Their father was an indulgent man whom they indulged in turn. He was just an ordinary journalist, he said. But was that really so? Rob wondered, attempting a fused instress. Their father had been a mysteriously powerful person: his children were obliged to live in the stories he made up about them – but their mother, the great Molly, had got away with living as she pleased.

Marie and Agathe appeared to care nothing for their surroundings. Each slid along in her own capsule, or so it seemed to Rob, but there was no getting away from their presence. They were forwardly absent in a way, and nothing much remained behind their pale facades. Not for him, anyway. Mcleod was his self-contained self. He had never been able to muster any interest in the boring English countryside, but he continued to burrow ahead in his up-to-the-minute book about the gig economy.

Marie tried to remember how she'd been in those days, her first days of getting away from home, times and friendships that had defined her whole life, all her photo albums of connection and consequence. But first she'd hooked up with Sheila and Emer from her first year's classes, brilliant girls both of them – particularly mad Emer – Sheila, come to think of it, had been more of the quiet, sensible type, not like her, more like Dervla, who loved her and really would do anything for her.

She drank to extinction, of course, every night, and within three weeks she'd met Rob at a tower party, who was just fascinated obviously. And then Stuart, they lived in one another's pockets. Stuart was the clever one, Rob the shallow parasite, so she thought. And from the flat, Dan, from Roanoke, Virginia, and through him a whole lot of other gay young men. Irish guys in particular found her congenial. They all went crazy together, rubbishing everything, and one night they had planted her in a large galvanized wheelie bin for refusing to shut up.

Rob had never known what he was on about, just continuously smoked dope and stared into space, listening to music, staring at sheets of paper he'd rolled into his Olympia portable and trying to pull words of genius out of his head in reply to essay deadlines. Rebuffed, collapsing syntax, empty words out of language-sets he only vaguely recognise. He thought he understood things but he was just not intelligent enough; it was more than obvious to her.

Their relationship consisted mainly of fucking, fucking around the clock, and in every position available within his narrow room with its thin borstal mattress and angular wooden fittings, castle slits for windows up there on the fourth floor rarely peered through in daylight. They fucked until they both contracted scabies, which were creatures generated spontaneously by excessive rubbing, but still they couldn't keep their hands away from one another. That was about it with Rob and Marie. Neither of them had ever experienced anything like it before. They lived in their own pornography. They saw it led to death, in the end, or rather that there was nothing at the end of it except more deathly rubbing of unhealed raw patches.

Rob had gone to the student health centre. At this stage he hadn't grown put of seeing doctors as all-knowing all purpose dispensers of life-wisdom. He told this doctor he was incompatible with his girlfriend due to an age gap between them of two or three years. The doctor had found this slightly amusing. "I think we're intellectually incompatible," he winced to remember saying, "not on the same wavelength. I've been getting really depressed about this, nervous, unable to concentrate. I was wondering if there was anything you could give me to help." He looked at the doctor with a look of utmost sincerity. "It's the stress of essay writing."

But it hadn't worked. The campus doctor was unwilling to prescribe valium, and he'd had to rely on Stuart's supply. A Cornish head-type gnome creature from Castleford, cider and psilocybin capital of the far west, always had plenty of everything. It had been immediately obvious that such people were dangerous. They didn't care what happened to themselves or to you. They'd already given up the ghost. Given it up, and their prescription was always bleak. They liked to see you gobbling down your death. They defied the straight world. Terry enjoyed watching Rob pass out. Who fucking cared? They used to do amyl nitrate and ether together for a while, until one late night Rob's heart had lurched, fluttered, and he collapsed on the floor, and after that he'd eased off.

He had been waiting for Templecombe. It was a small, precarious station, which had been opened, closed, and later reopened. A prize-winner at floral displays, much celebrated English whimsy had perhaps played a role in its original construction. Part of it was disused, and there was an impressive statue in the garden of a man tearing pages out of a thick timetable and scattering them around himself. Rob had enjoyed passing it for years, but now, incredibly, only the tips of his vandalizing fingers were visible above the deepening drift as he tossed torn paper into the air. He could've have had little cause for complaint tonight. It was a pity he couldn't tear himself from his stone base and lurch over to join them. But it didn't happen. Unfortunately, it never did.

The people these ghosts once were had all had the same propensities for self-immolation, except perhaps Agathe, although even here he suspected something. She'd also been a fan of Leonard Cohen. Stuart Mcleod had always liked The Doors, especially *L.A. Woman*. Anything fairly extreme, preferably involving black magic or Celtomania, but basically he had been more serious than that: a serious intensive reader. Paul had batted away his carefully worked-out ethical arguments for the sovereignty of pleasure with amused but eloquent ease.

Rob – incapable, almost, of regulating his own drives for failure and defeat – had tried instead to take responsibility for a scrap of turbulent Irish perversity, Marie. Once, when she'd got a splinter, possibly a glass splinter from drunkenly punching a window, Rob had got up in the middle of the night to find her in the kitchen, a bottle of whisky in front of her, gouging at her thumb with a razor blade. He tried to stop her but she told him to fuck off, leave her alone. If she died it was her own responsibility, none of his fucking business. Eventually she came to bed with her wrapped hand cradled in front of her, well-sluiced with the magic healant of whisky, and next day she was fine, spitting venom, but still adamant that she would never trust an English doctor.

Rob and Marie went their own ways, to an extent, but stuck together as long as they could. He seemed to remember they shared a large room on the other side of Greenstead, which hadn't worked, they were too thrown back on one another's company, her back turned to him, her zipped up white night garment, and trotting across the estate to get to classes on campus, past the munching goat moored in a front garden, reminding her of home. But she'd dropped out – was it at the end of the first or second year? The events of those fleeting, marginal times crowded in on him, multiplying – her trip to Italy, her misadventures with Emer, her fierce affair with glamorous blonde SWP bombshell dipstick Marco Pontelli, and how it had never been the same when they got back together afterwards. Not that it had ever been that good. Marco Pontelli was later caught masturbating at an open window dressed in women's underclothes. He hoped Pontelli wasn't haunting anyone. Eminently forgettable, a brief wannabe star of campus politics, some sort of flirty blonde recruiter appointed by an omniscient SWP central committee.

Rob looked at Marie across the table. Her bright eyes were boring into him; Agathe's dreaming head was on his shoulder. He smiled at her, gave her a sparkle. Marie sparkled back. Then she lowered her head. She didn't want to be here either, but where had she hoped she would end up, with the way she had always carried on? Rob realized, however, that although his companions had doubtless all been found wanting in various courts of no appeal, it was he himself who was on trial. Trial by ghost: it was traditional; wasn't it?

He had never got over his disappointment that Sherborne wasn't Shelborne, home of the 18th century naturalist vicar Gilbert White. His *Natural History of Sher(l)borne* had been recommended to him by a bona fide poet. Rob was no naturalist and had concluded that 18th century vicars had had a lot of time on their hands. But it was frustrating how you were unable to correct yourself. Every single time he'd stopped there he had had to go through the same loop of error, which had killed any interest in the place.

He knew his way along the West of England line alright, but although he'd been vaguely tempted never once got out to investigate. Well, you wouldn't, would you? This time however there was somebody on the platform. A small, muffled man. He got on the train near their carriage, but instead of turning to left or right, he walked straight through and out the other side. He seemed to be suspended in mid-air, at the height of some absent walkway. Rob and Paul exchanged a glance and watched him glide obliviously across the far platform and into a small closely-planted wood that lapped at the edge of the station.

Paul was back, if not in the land of the living, at least scrolling on his gold Samsung as they pulled away from Templecombe. His face broke into a smile. He read aloud: "It was here, in his castle, as he enjoyed a pipe of tobacco beneath the spreading branches of a great oak, that one of Sir Walter Raleigh's servants was said to have doused him with a pitcher of beer in the mistaken belief that his master's beard was on fire."

"Do you think that was him?" Rob felt a little put out. "Shouldn't he have been in Elizabethan costume?"

"Perhaps he's travelling incognito," Paul shrugged, pleased with himself. "He loved the place," he continued. "I wouldn't have minded having a look around myself. Another time perhaps."

But they both knew there wouldn't be another time, although Rob didn't like to broach the subject.

"From here he was taken to the Tower of London, accused of treason for marrying the Queen's favourite lady-in-waiting," Paul read on. "Finally he was executed by James I – for pillaging El Dorado. Still haunts the castle, so they say."

"I think it was him," said Rob. "He's up to something on the quiet. He's involved in this somehow."

At that moment Mcleod stood up and with abrupt violence wrenched his own head from his narrow shoulders. He held it aloft in his bony hands, then balanced it in his left hand and plunged two long fingers of his right into his eyes, his thumb into the head's gaping mouth. Holding his head up like a bowling ball he swung and released it down the long aisle towards the sliding doors. It was a good shot. Mcleod's head, trailing blood, his straggly red hair wrapping rapidly around it, ran quickly and smoothly down the carriage to be stopped by the doors with a muffled thud.

Headless, he lurched down the aisle in its wake, blindly feeling his way by reaching for the tops of the seats. Rob watched, transfixed in horror, as he casually picked up the bloody bowling ball and reattached it to the stump of his neck. Paul quite simply turned away his eyes from the whole performance, refusing to see it in a kind of impatient distaste. You wouldn't catch him out with that kind of thing. Stuart sauntered back towards them, fingering his hair back into some semblance of order as he approached.

"So who d'ye think that was supposed to be?" he grinned at them.

Paul and Rob said nothing. Marie seemed highly amused. Unnoticing, Agathe had been looking towards the window, past her own reflection into shining nothingness.

"Sir Francis fucking Drake," Mcleod giggled insanely. "C'mon. Who the fuck else could it be?" Somehow he'd turned into a complete exhibitionist. He picked up his book again and resumed his agitated reading. The book really didn't make sense to him. It had been misdescribed on its back cover. The book seemed to him to be saying nothing whatsoever.

Eleven

Hopkins had tried to celebrate the mixedness of being, what he'd called pied beauty, of dappled things, objects which might not be beautiful at all to a lazy eye, whose beauty seemed to glimmer unexpectedly out of dullness, to flash out in stripes, in fungus on a fish, which turned out to be necessary and perfect after all. Everything was always mutable, always temporary, its value and function always in contention. Gerard had always known God's creation didn't make perfect sense. It wasn't perfect, was it? But it must be somehow. It definitely was, if you looked at it right.

PIED BEAUTY

> Glory be to God for dappled things –
>   For skies of couple-colour as a brinded cow;
>   For rose-moles all in stipple upon trout that swim;
> Fresh-firecoal chestnut-falls; finches' wings;
>   Landscape plotted and pieced – fold, fallow, and plough;
>   And áll trádes, their gear and tackle and trim.
>
> All things counter, original, spare, Strange;
> Whatever is fickle, freckled (who knows how?)
>   With swift, slow; sweet, sour; adazzle, dim;
> He fathers-forth whose beauty is past change:
>   Praise him

True value he could only attribute to an endlessly creating father. Then there was his odd poem about Margaret, a small girl who bursts into tears when she sees all the beautiful leaves lying dead on the ground. They have fallen from the branches of her favourite grove of trees. They remind her of her own mortality, Gerard is saying, although she doesn't know it yet. He seems to wag his finger at her. Her tears are selfish obviously. Now she's only a bud but one of these days soon enough she'll be withering herself. Woman's vanity! he seems to imply, fast-forwarding through her imagined life.

Poor girl. She was obviously mourning something, something real. Beauty on previous occasions had lit up her eyes, and she thought she owned what she saw: her whole kingdom had gone to rot, which was surely worth a tantrum or two. Perhaps her fastidious companion might be able to put it right, if he is death, or God almighty: the sun, the ace and eye of her inscape.

Hopkins says she grows up to grieve, for which this is just a first call. Rob found this hard to swallow. How should a small child understand what she couldn't possibly know? On the other hand he was trying to inscape her, sympathetically understand her by writing about child development, human development – he was trying his best to understand those processes. In another poem, Binsey Poplars, he is pulled again into the perspective of this young and horrified girl who has met death on a Sunday walk.

> O if we but knew what we do
>   When we delve or hew —
> Hack and rack the growing green!
>   Since country is so tender
> To touch, her being só slender,
> That, like this sleek and seeing ball
> But a prick will make no eye at all

Do we really know the consequences of what we are doing to nature? Sometimes, on his retreats, he achieved equilibrium. Going through St. Ignatius Loyola's *Spiritual Exercises* one by one, he took the vow of poverty as read. He trusted in God, and practiced a careless self-neglect as a result. But even here he managed to find justification for cultivating his own abilities, tuning his own faculties. His is the only self he can experience, after all. It's good to polish God's apple, he seems to say, but in order to do so you must practice detachment, as Loyola suggests, from other created beings, however brightly they might shine for you. The practice of detachment will help him perform works for the glory of the Creator. And he believed God had heard and assented to this prayer to let him save his works, possibly to be disposed of later.

He'd been happiest when he seemed to stand aside with relief from the latest work of his compulsive precision. As arrogant as he had always been, he was an enthusiastic servant and self-denier. Nevertheless, if he took what seemed to others a wrong turn he always insisted on it. He played it out to the end, through to the last appalling consequences. He was unable to doubt a decision he'd once made. Intuition wasn't worth a light but it was all he had. Meanwhile he maintained an ironic detachment when he could, almost a machine at his duties when fearsomely depressed. It was a considerable relief to arrange everything carefully, just so, under a Victorian equipoise lamp.

His poems were all about the Immanence of Christ in the world. Christ was worshipping God through his engagement with the creation, particularly humans. God saw his son 'in the features of men's faces'. Hopkins is worshipping God through his poetic apprehension of nature. In these incandescent poems he reveals God as a living presence in the world. It's not a metaphor for him; it's reality he is disclosing. Nor was he particularly hostile to Darwin's ideas. He was an evolutionist in a jokey sort of way, recommending a book to his mother which explained natural selection and squared it with orthodoxy in one of his last letters.

His anguish had nothing to do with nature, which knocked him out usually. The breakdown of his faith had more to do with experiences in the human world. The order moved him around eleven times, each time to a less congenial posting. The horrific living conditions of the poor, especially in Liverpool, shocked him. He was full of pity, yes. He also felt aversion, physical disgust – but one of his most tender poems was about visiting a poor parishioner, a dying blacksmith.

In Felix Randall, Hopkins' adult voice was speaking: the playful tone of his letters mingled with the unctuousness certainties of a suffering priest. He hears of the blacksmith's death without much surprise or interest, apparently relieved not to have to go and see him any longer. It has been painful to watch him diminish, lose his senses, and to see several illnesses contend for the honour of killing him. He has watched the man curse and fight back, and appear to rally. Hopkins believes that receiving the sacrament had helped him. But it is both reprieve and ransom, this last word implying with a certain sinister levity that Felix's soul has been kidnapped by God.

Sickness broke him. Impatient, he cursed
    at first, but mended
Being anointed and all; though a
    heavenlier heart began some
Months earlier, since I had our sweet
    reprieve and ransom
Tendered to him. Ah well, God rest him
    all road he ever offended!

But it was the way it shifted, into the dying blacksmith's inscape, walking in the road of the man's native speech, stepping alongside him. In the sestet the priest is transformed into an intimate friend, even a surrogate lover. Suddenly he is addressed as *thee* and *thou*. Gerard the priest has tried to comfort the big man with his tongue, his touch, his heart, this man who has become again as a child. Felix Randal closes with affirming memories of the blacksmith in his virility, working at the 'random grim' forge, for Felix's vocation had been inherited, unchosen, and harsh although he had excelled at it. But in the fashioning of the bright and battering sandal, Felix's almost god-like power is revealed. He made his bright sandal for the foot of Christ the worker, tireless hauler of heavy loads, striker out of these forms.

A few months before Paul Hubbard rubbed out, they had gone to the cinema in Leicester Square with their girlfriends to watch *The Big Easy*, a New Orleans-set crime thriller. Paul had seemed desperate to disappear into the action. He'd insisted they sit right at the front beneath a vertically towering screen, as if he didn't realize that you couldn't really see anything from there. But he had been stubborn, leaving them to sit where they liked, then, a petulant child, crestfallen when they left him to it. He often seemed to remember Paul doing things which involved a childish expression of willpower, an attempt to seize and control the day.

One long ago time he'd sat down on railway tracks at a level crossing during a local demo, insisting that everybody join him to bring Essex to a standstill. His fellow students had ambled away under their red banners, leaving him behind in disgust. Exactly the sort of puerile student voluntarism the trades council despised. But here he had been trying to lose himself, climbing over folded seats to get nearer to the screen, reaching for total immersion; to be surrounded by booming music and gigantic images, dialogue of the gods, shadows of ideas.

Not long after that he'd spilt with Blim and – though he didn't know – was fast approaching the hour of his death. He fell in love with a Chinese waitress whose uncle ran a restaurant and a menu printing business. The young woman didn't offer him much encouragement, more baffled than anything by his extravagant interest. However, she gave him one of her uncle's menus, and told Paul she couldn't go out with him on Saturday because she worked at night in their small print shop. The address was printed on the bottom of the menu, and late on Saturday evening, obsessed with the idea that this young woman could be his, he decided to declare his love for her by climbing there over the roofs of Chinatown, then down into the print shop. He imagined her delicate, inky fingers as she operated a small printing press, and the look of delight he hoped would suffuse her features when he clambered down through the skylight.

Shinning up a drainpipe in a quiet alley, and once high above China-town on the old, crooked roofs of the West End, he experienced a sense of exhilaration and mastery such as he had seldom felt … since he didn't know when. This is mad, he thought. The maddest thing I've done in my life. It was dark, it was highly dangerous. What if the bricks crumbled under his feet, as they were already crumbling, or a sudden rift opened up between buildings? Would he jump across like a cat? But he was committed now, and in deep shadow, with only spillage from skylights far below to light his way, he clambered in the direction of the uncle's premises. The gold dragons, lanterns strung across narrow streets he glimpsed dizzily, peering over an edge, looked flimsy, impostures, cheap advertising for something that didn't really exist … he loved the bright, immediate trashiness of it all, the heady rush of monosodium glutamate.

But now he knew it existed. The Chinese girl was real. He had met her. The elderly woman he visited every couple of weeks to brush up his Tai-Chi and solicit life wisdom was also real enough. Acupuncture was real. He had tried it and felt at least something: numbness, a tingling absence. Nothing like the rush of climbing over the roofs of Chinatown. She would be forced to believe in him, not that he believed in forcing anyone to believe or do anything, but still. He would forcefully convince her by the gentlest means at his disposal. It was worth a try. He was committed, anyway.

His journey over the roofs had been a crazy escapade, Rob thought. At one point he had to find a way from a high, broken promontory to a small sloping roof far below it, discovered an ancient rusting fire escape ladder miraculously in place to carry him down; at another he kicked a loose slate, which was dislodged and fell like a whirling assassin's blade into the alley below, and counted what seemed like a full minute before he heard a distant shattering sound. No cry of pain. He carried on, unsure of his direction, until finally he crouched motionless beside a cluster of chimneys, each topped by a red clay pagoda tile from before Chinatown ever existed, now exhausted, and scared shitless.

But he had raised his head, sniffed the air – sweet, cloying – and engaged his direction-finder. And so, inching crabwise, he spied at last the glowing pane below where his Chinese girl was industriously printing off menus for every restaurant in Soho. He tapped on the glass and she looked up, incredulous.

"What happened?" Rob asked.

"Well, she let me in eventually," Paul replied. "I climbed down into this little room. It was just as I'd imagined: a really cramped place. She was on her own in there, fitting tiny Chinese characters into something like a John Bull printing outfit with a magnifying glass. But –" he smiled a resigned smile "– she was pissed off, really angry. She thought I was a complete idiot. She kicked me out through the front door and told me never to come back."

They had been drinking Kingfisher and sopping up lamb tikka masala and a shared cauliflower bhaji with an outsize almond-encrusted nan. Paul had grown enormous, he was big and fat (although his height and large frame meant he could carry it: he looked dangerous) and obviously he didn't care all that much. Rob found it difficult to imagine him climbing over rooftops, but there, he'd done it. He was mad, that was sure. Rob felt himself dissociating from this scene, retreating inwards, observing from afar. Separating himself, which he usually did, playing his friend along. Paul didn't like being called out or contradicted.

"I'm getting fat," Paul said. "I've got to stop doing this. You too, Rob. We're getting too old for indulgence."

Rob agreed, insisting to the eager waiter that his friend needed to lose weight. To him Paul seemed out of control, no longer firing on all mental cylinders. He had retreated into a wonder-world where his desires could be easily acted out and would come true. Something any decent person knew to be nonsense. Still, if he did manage to lose weight then he could go climbing over the roofs after women every weekend. He'd be certain to strike it lucky sooner or later.

"You know," Paul said, ordering another Kingfisher, refusing the menu. "I know this is crazy. I can't get any freelance in advertising, but I have a strong feeling that something really good is about to happen to me."

Rob was left to wonder what this good thing might be, with a sense of unease bordering dread, and then it clicked suddenly. He wanted to get away from Paul Hubbard, get home to the flat.

Paul smiled a wry, beatific smile, pulling out his credit card.

Paul, only slightly sleeker than he had been at the end of his life, but still looking rumpled, like he could do with a good wash, was sitting opposite him as the ghost train rumbled on its way to hell – next stop Yeovil Junction. Paul gazed at the darkened window, perhaps at his reflection or perhaps he could see through it, Rob thought, to something beyond, as he'd always pretended, or believed. But it hadn't been the end, not at all. Here they were. There it had been though: plain evidence that going along with Paul was never a good idea. Somehow the nature of their friendship had dictated it. Rob could only behave acceptably in the role of indulgent foil, when Paul could have done with a good talking to, a good shaking instead of the indulgence, the endless opportunities he had been gorging on since birth.

Going along with somebody deluded didn't do them much good. Even if they did try to make it a condition of friendship. And it didn't do you any good either. Yes-man to a foolish fool. But it was demeaning and corrupting to allow yourself to be put in such a position. Left you with nothing except the dubious pleasure of watching somebody you'd after all quite liked run over a steep cliff and fail to bounce back up again.

Paul's had been the second death, the second time it happened. Rob had been on his guard, but the same thing had unfolded just as before. There had been other cases. You couldn't save somebody's life, so it was said with a lesser or greater degree of shrug, cynicism or even desperate sadness. But why not? Of course you could save a life. People were talked off ledges, pulled out of icy water. Happened every day, didn't it? I want to make a difference. This is what you were supposed to say in job interviews. The interviewer nodded in understanding. It was what he or she believed in too, a condition of any sort of employment.

That was the end of that. Except it wasn't, not for Rob. Whenever he'd tried express this feeling he could never pin down adequately, people looked at him as though he'd missed some basic point about existence. What was wrong with selling a few yards of mislabelled old rope to young people? What else were they supposed to be doing with their oh so valuable time? *It's all blood under the bridge* his boss had commented wisely, when Rob told him that his friend, Molly Hubbard's son, had died.

In real life nobody seemed to believe in anything of that sort. You were a fool if you didn't keep your eyes on the treacherous road ahead. De-icers on their tea break would be preparing excuses. Rivals would be allowed to keep their remarks brief and perfunctory. Friends would grimace.

The funeral had been as splendid an affair as the Hubbards could manage. None of the famous people had been able to make the service, but several of Paul's old girlfriends were in attendance, walking like the night. Rob had been asked to read, which he did, a passage from Heidegger chosen by Paul's father: We are too late for the Gods but too early for Being, and a stanza or two from Shelley's 'Adonais' which Rob thought had seemed to go with it. Shelley had been Paul's favourite revolutionary poet. He'd told Rob that he had once scribbled in his copy of the poems: "To Paul, from promethean Shelley".

Rob had cowered in the shadow of a huge coffin propped up on trestles, declaiming these things. He had an irrational fear that it was going to collapse on him and his bloated corpse would tumble out onto the nave of the local church. This didn't happen. Jim Hubbard had been in a state of hysterical excitement, as people sometimes are at funerals, and laughed at the slimy ushers in black top hats he had himself specified and ordered.

Molly tried to keep her bright empty smile in place, but what else could she do? Paul's girlfriends were particularly friendly to Rob. Paul had been so "special", that had been the word of the day, to be used again and again, whenever in years to come his name came up, a word you use when there isn't one, a fudging word. Maybe just another word for an idiot, he'd thought, disassociated, performing, looking around him.

Now he thought of a sentiment from Gerard's journals which Paul might have liked, if he'd known it:

July 19th (1872) ...Ovary of the blown foxglove ... I thought how sadly beauty of inscape was unknown and buried away from simple people and yet how near at hand it was if they had eyes to see it and it could be called out everywhere again...

Paul had also been somebody who thought there might be a simple solution to everything. Rob remembered him one morning when he'd stayed over in the uncladded tower block in Acton, doing Tai-Chi exercises outside on the grass before breakfast. Unselfconsciously turning in excruciatingly slow half-circles while Rob's neighbours trudged past on their way to work, perhaps hoping to inspire them to reject the clock-time they were living by, whatever it was, and to synchronize with the coming time, the time of being.

"There's a game we could play to help the time pass," he said, "if any of you feel like playing a game."

"Not I-Spy!" Stuart called derisively. "Something beginning with S."

"What might that be?" asked Marie.

"*Snow*," Rob spoke the word silently, jerking a thumb at the white deluge beyond the windows, dropping his head to his book.

"Bastard," Stuart replied.

"We used to play it at home at Christmas," Paul continued. "It's a bit like charades – my mother made it up. It's called 'What did your last servant die of.'"

"Charades," Stuart put his book down. "Great. OK, I've got one. It's –" He made a whirling camera sign for a film, held up a bony index finger.

"Alien," Rob said instantly.

"Fucker!" Stuart exclaimed. "How did you know that?"

"We saw it together at the Odeon in Colchester, if you recall."

"Oh yeah, yeah," Stuart said vaguely. "OK, your turn."

Rob made the film camera sign and held up two fingers in a fuck-off gesture.

"Umm, I know." Paul pondered, tapping his teeth. "Don't tell me. Is it based on a book?"

Stuart nodded. It was indeed a film – based on a book.

Marie wanted to know what kind of film. Romance? Comedy? Crime? Adventure? War?

Patiently, Paul made her ask all of her questions one at a time. A series of shakes and nods eliminated only the first two categories from Stuart's list. It was crime, it was war, and it was adventure.

"Brilliant. That narrows it down," Marie said. "I don't believe you. I don't believe there's any such film."

Stuart nodded, getting excited, happy to be commanding the floor. He held up a single finger followed by two. He made waves with the flat of his right hand.

"Waves."

"Sea."

Stuart mimed drinking slowly from a glass.

"A sea of beer," Rob suggested.

"Water," Paul guessed, then suddenly got the whole thing. "Watership Down."

"What a boring film," said Marie.

Paul felt miffed that they weren't playing his game. He said he didn't have any ideas, but elected to nominate someone else to carry on – Agathe perhaps.

"Mais non," said Agathe. "It is too difficult for me."

Marie wanted to play so she did another two-word film. It looked as if it was going to be difficult, but as soon as she held up four fingers for a four syllable word –

"Apocalypse Now!" Rob cut in, and again he had won the round.

"I loved that film," Paul enthused.

Rob remembered seeing it, with Stuart and Marie, at the same Odeon, full of rowdy squaddies, in Colchester.

"One more," Paul said "It's a –" He made a couple of quick guitar moves, then brought his clenched fists together as though wielding a giant pair of cymbals.

"The Clash," Marie and Stuart said simultaneously.

But they had no further ideas between them, so there was a lull broken by Paul saying out of the blue, "You know, in all my life I've never admired anyone more than that guy John Strummer."

"Joe Strummer," said Rob. "It was Joe."

All the ghosts actually laughed together, even Agathe seemed to know this joke.

"OK," Paul laughed too. "So let me just explain the rules of my game then. You have to pretend you're dying of a disease, right? An illness you might get through your job. An example would be Housemaid's Knee. Or a back ache might be –"

"A car mechanic," Rob said.

"Right, you've got the general idea. My mum made it up. She did it live on her TV programme." He chuckled to himself. "It was incredible, really difficult. They had hundreds of complaints as her guests began to mime cancer and blindness and heart attacks. My mother has the most appalling taste in the world." For a moment he seemed ridiculously proud to be its inheritor, but then looked at each of his companions dead seriously. "My mother, Molly, is an incredibly good person. People don't always get it. But she is."

None of them, not one, wanted to play his stupid game.

"How about what did *you* die of?" Stuart looked around at the faces of the other ghosts. Rob realized Stuart didn't know how any of them had met their deaths, perhaps none of them did, although he knew about all of them. "OK, I'll start," Stuart said. "Although I expect you guessed already. I committed suicide. I threw myself out of a train."

"Ah!" Agathe inhaled a soft, low breath. "I am sorry, Stuart. But you were happy, I have known you a happy person I have thought!"

"And you?" Stuart asked, "How did you end up here?"

"A car crash in the mountains," she said. "It was in the snow. I was so stupid and I have lost everything. My daughter, my husband." She shrugged violently, but tears flooded into her eyes. "Excuse me." She pulled a small crumpled handkerchief embroidered with tiny blue flowers from her sleeve, and dabbed them away.

"How about you, Paul?" Mcleod asked.

"Epilepsy," Paul said. "I had it as a kid, but then it came back. They were changing my medication. I had a bad fit when there was nobody there. I was stupid too. I wasn't taking care of myself properly." He pretended to rummage in his bag. "And you Marie," he said. "You were so full of life when I last saw you. What happened to you?"

"I was murdered," Marie said tonelessly. "A glass ashtray to the cranium." She bent her small head forwards to show them, and they all saw a large circular indentation at the rear of her dainty little skull.

A slight Irishwoman … passed over, easily dismissed. She wouldn't have lasted long in the company of the Hubbard family, but her politics were nonetheless perfectly reasonable if you grew up a few miles from where the Burntollet March had been attacked by marauding stick-wielding Unionist thugs in 1969. Rural Derry. She had been about eleven years old when they stopped overnight at Claudy for a meeting about the aims and strategy of People's Democracy.

Perhaps she had been there, among a crowd of well-wishers, when they set off the next day, numbers swelled a little from amongst the local people. She said she had been. Her account was graphic: the rocks, the bloodied broken heads, the vicious beatings of young women, conniving police, out of uniform specials joining in to beat the shit out of the Fenian scum.

She'd told him about these things, in the same breath as she had the banshee and the leprechaun's slipper, but was more inclined to believe her as her stories were widely corroborated by witnesses and cameras. She was a republican, but she thought the Provos were real bastards. One of them had near-raped her in a hedge on the way back from the pub where Marie had been holding forth at a table of grown men, no doubt giving them the benefit of her views on the position of women. That had been her answer, It wasn't what he had done that was necessarily a problem, but his jeering attitude to her afterwards. Women were nothing to him, two a penny those girls who submitted. Why wouldn't they? They were wee hoors and he had put her in her place.

"Gerry Fitt, Gerry *Fitt!*" Her small mouth screwed up in contempt as she spat out the hated, compromised SDLP leader's name, making her look as if she was about to have one herself.

In Rob's opinion they – the Social Democratic and Labour Party – were a fairly impressive bunch, but what did he know? Well, they were articulate, they spoke for their people, and they tried to show a constitutional way forward for the aspirations of nationalists and Catholics. Constitutional! In a gerrymandered state, in an area where a two thirds Catholic majority had returned a Protestant council for more years than the number of hairs on the chin of Paddy McGinty's goat, where the police were all Protestant, and were in cahoots with Unionist terror groups! Ian Paisley was a demented ranting puppet calling down damnation upon the civil rights protesters in a choking, enraged voice hoarse with the promise of the violence he incited, his own eyes alight with devilish glee. He identified the marchers for housing equality and non-discriminatory job opportunities with the antichrist of papistry and hurled his constituents upon them, issued with a licence to kill.

The hunger strikers had come and gone much later, one by one, after she had gone to Iceland and got married. Rob still thought of her, and of the strikers themselves, particularly if they were from Derry like Mickey Devine, Francis Hughes, Thomas McElwee, as friends of hers, neighbours, possibly second cousins. They all had that look about them: a wide open look, unlike any politician he'd seen, uncomposed except perhaps as themselves, for a cheeky sideways smile like McElwee. Rob and Stuart and plenty of others had carried around pictures of them on sticks, as newspapers argued over their satanic or angelic status, and quite horribly they began to cross themselves off the pending list and to die, one by one.

The small group of local protesters laid their wreaths and placards on the war memorial in Colchester, wrote to the papers, met the local Tory MP for a chat about Irish sentimentalism, but none of it made a jot of difference. They all died for a recognition of political status not achieved at the time, although it would be granted later, retrospectively, and these self-starving men and the civil rights marchers a decade earlier would be declared to be victors, of sorts. Marie had died too soon to see the Good Friday agreement signed and Martin McGuinness and Ian Paisley earn the nickname 'The Chuckle Brothers' for their comedy antics in Stormont.

Marie's politics were reasonable enough, and she spent the rest of her life talking about her overdone home statelet. Forever angry, not too far below her surface, while her English employers tended to think her merely cute. But she had been shaped by that place, shaped by its pain, which seemed to Rob to explain her. A school friend of hers, she said, had been accidentally shot by an IRA sniper outside a dancehall, in a gun battle with the army. But in truth he had never been able to work out exactly what her pain was about, her lassitude, her despair, her lack of interest in growing up, or where it came from, apart from those obvious things around her, and the death of her mother from cancer at the age of fifty, and her family's expectation that she should step straight into her shoes, should cook and clean for them. It was being a woman she didn't like, she never would like it. Perhaps it was all this which had somehow pushed her so far into a wired present where she relived it all, sometimes, and other times fell silent and miserable for long weeks on end. Anyway, he could find no way to staunch her tears, her share of Ireland's blood, which she seemed determined to shed, and did, in a way Rob knew he could never reveal to anybody and never would. She'd become a grandmother a few years earlier, a fact of which she could have known nothing.

There was a single photograph – all that remained – of the three of them in Braintree. They'd stayed for a week, house-sitting for a gay schoolteacher friend of his and Marie's other gay friends. The photo had been taken by Jake, another friend on a flying visit, whose father was a school photographer. Despite expensive borrowed equipment, it looked like an ordinary snapshot.

Rob stood well back against the garden fence. Wincing with self-consciousness, he pulled extravagantly on a cigarette. He'd just crawled out of his shell, hatched into unwelcome daylight from a cocoon where Peter Tosh's heartbeat had been nursing him along nicely through this latest instalment of a bad dream he had been living in pointlessly.

Marie was also smoking intensely, small, ironical, her face's gesture half-turned away in mockery, looking at him as if hypnotised by an attractive idiot.

Mcleod planted himself squarely in front of the aperture, his greasy red hair raked into a centre parting: a grimacing orange insect, presenting himself as ringmaster of this sad little circus of refugees. Refugees from what? Perhaps from their lack of importance in this world, but from that obvious truth they had been granted a temporary respite. After all, it had been bright-eyed Jake Rubin who had imposed this vision on them, forced them to reveal themselves to the wide unblinking eye of his father's camera.

Once Rob and Stuart had been taken down to be introduced as interesting friends to his family in a beautiful house in Winchester. They had been polite and deferential, but Jake had been looking to exercise his father with a good argument and had needled them until he got one. Stuart obliged by putting forward his pro-Palestinian views and Jake's father had given them a bloody good talking to and sent them off to watch *Victory at Entebbe*, a film about the Israeli helicopter rescue of hostages from Uganda, skyjacked by the PLO. They had sat through it glumly, a lesson in what other people thought.

It then it had all turned into a version of weary old jokes about an Englishman, an Irishman and a Scotsman. After having been bullied by the other two for a number of years, the Englishman survived their deaths. The Jew – who had been included in the joke – laughed at them and prospered by being part of a middle-class tendency he had always known would win. There was no conspiracy, he insisted. He didn't mind being left out of Rob's story. He preferred his own, the one where he sailed around the world on his yacht, picking up a different teenager on each island. Each island he landed at was a small green fragment of heart's desire. He was a scoundrel, just as Hopkins had known Whitman to be, although you had to admire the savage music of the American.

Twelve

By the time they pulled into Yeovil Junction legions of snow bees were volleying hard across that normally open, airy space, its attitude of agreeable retrospect was intensified, as the restored WW1 rolling stock which had once been transported to a transit camp somewhere in the Ardennes, was rebombarded. High covered footbridges and neatly painted galvanised roofs resembled flimsy walkways from an abandoned emplacement, and ever-replenishing hammering drifts of snow-bees were dumped in a crop of glittering white apples.

Paul thought it was ludicrous that the line was still open, but he supposed the crew would just take this last train down to Exeter St David's and shut up for the night. He imagined all the stations they had passed through, blinking out one by one as staff and passengers made their way home through deep drifted streets to little flats above shops, bungalows, houses with welcoming baubled trees behind the frosted or leaded glass, behind half-drawn curtains, beside solid reassuring doors.

The two women stood up and gathered their possessions without fuss, passing by self-consciously. Now they could see everyone plainly enough, and it was obvious too that they were as dead as a pair of dental implants. Looking more closely at their wrapped packages and shopping bags, the latter had a reused appearance, as did the ribbons and wrapping paper. It was difficult to believe that their elaborately decorated packages actually contained anything. Marie glanced across at them, attempting a smile, but had to turn away when they looked through her.

She could see that the first woman's neck, under her loosened scarf, was almost rotted away, a stick of bone with a few shreds of decayed flesh and muscle attached. The second woman's eyes were loose, wandering in their sockets above her well-fitting floral face mask. Her weekend bag seemed too light, as though that too had been cosmetically packed with a lot of dead air. For Stuart they were more casually employed observers, moonlighting from their graves to pay for their upkeep.

As they stepped through the door it was clear that they were walking directly into a drift several feet thick on the platform, almost to the height of the windows, but they didn't let it detain them, they ploughed straight through it in line the first had chosen, one behind another, towards the safety of the covered stairs up to the exit, a pair of half-submerged sub-marines: they didn't feel the cold, and it was as it had been with the departed angels: there was a sense of resolve and purpose in the manner of their movement, and they passed onward into the mutable world of the snow pygmies.

In his own bag, up on the rack, Rob had the usual hastily bought presents for the ritual he pressed on his remaining family every year, which they barely endured. Why did he even come? But, for him, there was always something to recommend it; even the most dilapidated Christmas was worth celebrating.

If there was one thing Mcleod had always known about Rob, it was that he needed careful monitoring. He was light-fingered and had the theoretical apparatus of a Christmas card designer. They told him to be more generous, but what was the point of generosity when people's ill motives so often danced out in front of you? They cavorted and straightforwardly showed off the body of their desires: for your appreciative inspection, seemingly. They weren't ashamed of being judged or of judging others, and nor should he be.

Judge the judgemental fuckers by all means, was his philosophy, but never forget that you yourself are subject to the same noose: the kind of which drops over your head from on high and is impersonal justice and constitutes the absolute truth of how things really are. Pre-ordained, in a way, like membership of the Presbyterian elect. Well, he'd always tried not to doubt that he was a member but chances were had been looking a wee bit slim for quite some time.

But he was still here, not in the other place. That was something, anyway. He saw now that he'd been foolish to set any store by things such as Tarot cards, and he repented of it silently. But they had helped him understand others, revealed their fatal weaknesses to him in a way he could sometimes put to use. Not usually though. Usually he was a convivial reader of the cards, trying to understand himself above all. "If … but if … and there is this great … but then again this terrible … either /or … greatness or the most terrible wipe-out, complete disaster."

At least he knew now what such a pair always meant. The stronger card was always the darker. We're drawn towards failure and death, or at least have to come to terms with it, although for some poor bastards…

That was the secret of the cards, and why fearful people had been drawn back to them for centuries. Needing to find the limit, to look into the face of the thing that was going to control and finally destroy them. Also they were a key to power over others. Those being read were always terrified. It always seemed to be coming in a bad way next week. But then, it was always inconclusive. Just a few spanners thrown in the works of the blithely cocky.

And Mcleod knew a fucking mind-parasite when he saw one. His delightful friend had turned into the most disgusting leech, on every conceivable level. It probably started at the beginning, as it usually did, but Stuart couldn't quite put a finger on it now. "Don't believe anything Stuart said to you," his father had told Rob after the funeral. "Read Freud, then you'll understand. Just read Freud."

"I have read Freud," Rob said quietly.

"Then you know it already. Accept it as the basic truth. People are competitive, Rob." His round sad face almost smiled. Rob thought it was the face Stuart would one day have grown into himself. "They'll do anything to put one over on you, and that's the way Stuart was with you. I could tell. You're just more intelligent than he was, that's all. If you have to remember anything, just remember something he told you, something you shared, not what he said about it."

Oh yeah? Mcleod had thought, hovering around somewhere near the ceiling. He would see about that later, he had already.

"No use looking up there, Rob," his father said. "The dead are nowhere to be found. I know that much, Rob. I shouldn't say what I've said if I thought he was listening. Rob, you've got to believe in the truth, like they say, it sets you free. Not some wishful thinking by academic Marxists."

This was after Rob helped bring all Stuart's books home – a huge library of philosophy, sociology, history, and anthropology – now they had been piled up in boxes out in the family conservatory.

"I've looked at some of them myself. Stuart could never have understood all that stuff, I know it, Rob. He was my son, I knew him. I think he was trying to have everyone on with that crap."

"No," Rob said. "He believed in all of that. He was a socialist through and through."

Stuart's father, although an avid reader of the *Daily Mail*, hadn't objected to his son being left wing. Stuart said they only bought it to read Fred Basset, the dog cartoon. Before that it had been the *Express*, for The Gambols. After all, his daughters were nurses. After all. Stuart had tried to be one. He'd always believed in the trades unions, like most Scots. An intelligent man, he filled his house with books in order to give his children something interesting to read, should they be interested. Mr Mcleod was in a great deal of pain. Physical pain. He was flushed, overweight and prodded fiercely at his heart, as if he was suffering from dyspepsia, but making sure it kept on going.

"I can't think about it too much," he said, filling Rob's whisky glass, "I've got my other children to think about." He paused. "The twins had a look through his books – they just couldn't connect them with the brother who used to read to them when they were little. It was sad to them and to Orla – they felt they'd never really known him." And it was obviously sad beyond sadness to Stuart's father.

Up on the ceiling Mcleod fumed, but there wasn't a whole lot he could do about his Dad's opinions. He wasn't surprised. He had known very well what they were, always. He also knew that his father had been a dark horse, a brooding man, a fearsome temper. And when he was like that you just had to let him alone. Now they performed the whisky ritual one more time while Stuart's mother, a small, brittle woman, always cheery, always busy, preferred to believe something else about her son. He'd made some poor choices – she'd always thought he should've been a writer or poet. Stuart cringed. Why the fuck had he followed Rob down here to see his parents? But it didn't change the way he felt up there, looking on at this sad scene.

Rob had seen it all unfolding there and then for the first time: the way people coped with such terrible grief, the stories they seemed compelled to put together over something utterly broken. He remembered drinking whisky with Mr Mcleod one Christmas long ago, and how he had told them about his wartime experience as aircrew on a Lancaster bomber. Something like a fifty per cent survival rate, of whom he'd been one, obviously. But the survivors never came back either, everything they might have cherished blown apart in mid-air over Germany. You didn't believe in anything afterwards, none of this socialist wishful thinking. Because you have seen people stripped bare, as they actually are.

After he'd dropped out of Warwick Uni, he had dumped himself on Malcolm and Zoe for a year in Bristol, being quite content to be the pet of his hometown's middle-class types, as well as new friend Jake Rubin, whose father's accountant had wangled him a full grant. Mcleod had also been an exceptionally soft touch, not the miserly Scot at all. In those days Rob had especially liked being bought breakfast in a college refectory, about seven o'clock, just as they opened up and everything was fresh, a beautiful end to the day. Mcleod had obliged countless times. It had always been a situation – in an anonymous space – referred back to as long as their friendship lasted in any sort of place that was … the café in a department store maybe, or when he'd gone down there to visit Rob, one of those old empty cafes, deserted palaces of Formica and mirrors, a row of pearly portals strung up the Lower Cheltenham Road. Hamburger, egg, chips and peas, on a sixties oval plate. Coffee. Rob had learned to be happily alone in those places. First stop on Giro day. But if Stuart was paying, he was more than happy to share the experience.

Rob had turned out to be a human vacuum cleaner. That's how it felt to Mcleod, sitting there insubstantially with his recently repaired head, trying to work out what, if anything, had happened to the labour movement. So much for lifelong commitment: he hadn't even bothered staying alive long enough to witness its demise. But he blamed Rob for his bodiless condition. Rob was still playing him along, or thought he was: a summons here, a consultation there.

This leeching fucker had really taken the whole bag of dog biscuits with added vitamins; he'd wolfed them down and come back for another session of jump and catch the Frisbee. And thus fortified he expected to do the casual tossing while Stuart happily jumped and ran and barked. No more. His eyes danced over the pages of his book. Re-embedding strands of those disembedded broken traditions, which had come loose, like Agathe's great thatch of dark hair; reflexively tailored into a bright sleek bob of modernity: a place of magic and mystery, the eternal now and again.

Mcleod had been the first to go, first through the gate to nowhere, the turnstile of eternity.

Another train dopplered past them in the opposite direction, travelling much faster than them apparently, so that their own train was rocked off its rails for a few seconds by the mournful horn of the light-years express out of the hell they seemed to be travelling towards. The passing train enveloped them in its battering alarm, a long accompanying slurred scream shrieked of terrors escaped, fading out down the line back to London, whatever it was moving too quickly for the weather or the rails or the rapidly deteriorating rolling stock of the Western main line. Most of this section had always been a single-track railway.

Paul, if asked, would have no doubt spouted a load of wishful nonsense. Christmas conviviality, he loved it dearly, way past the sell-by-date of the last mince pie. Through the last few years of his life he had still been harking back. Eighteen months into his role as chief of copy at a small, dynamic agency he had produced no usable words, just sketches of reaching hands joining together in unity, fighting to be heard, which he then seriously tried to sell to his employer, and the bemused corporation client, as the best way to rebrand Milton Keynes.

On the kerb opposite his final West End agency's office, they drank one last bottle of Grolsch ("You can't top a Grolsch!") and Paul had admitted that he was only going through the motions at work. He'd been waiting for them to give him the sack. He wanted to show his contempt one last time. But they'd read his signals alright. No-one in the small but prestigious agency had spoken to him at all for the last few months. It had been a politics of self-righteous refusal, an empty gesture. Then they had sacked him, and in an attempt to milk the advertising cash cow to the end, he had gone freelance, and got no work at all, and died shortly afterwards for real, forever, in his flat on Gray's Inn Road.

Paul pulled out his phone again and started loftily pecking and spinning with his thumb. Soon he was immersed in something, reading on and on, turning the screen to landscape view, blowing up images and videos, to look closer in that peering way in which he so much resembled a pagan god, Apollo maybe, expanding and collapsing worlds between his grubby fingertips. "This is interesting stuff," he said after a while. "I think I've cracked it!"

"Cracked what?" Rob asked indifferently.

"Dragonflies," he replied. "Come on, Rob, Stuart, Marie, I'll bet you know nothing whatever about them. I didn't either until now." He held up his gold Samsung, his newly discovered key to all available knowledge, to the future itself, which had already turned out to be a little different from the advertising campaign which, as a reanimated ghost, Paul was still mentally formulating.

The others showed little interest in whatever he might have discovered. Rob had noticed this about them: lack of grasp of the implications of anything. They all wore masks, for example, but only because somebody had been handing them out at some point in their journeys. They didn't, any of them, seem to know what the pandemic was, and had completely failed to notice the emptiness of the streets, the train, obviously hadn't been watching the news or interacting with others. Ghosts had an instinctive belief in the future, or at least that things were continuing as they always had. They existed in an eternal present of consciousness, but whatever portion of the mind continued for the post-life crowd, it didn't seemed to involve rapid processing of sensory input or making any great connecting leaps when presented with new information.

Both Rob and Paul showed signs of wanting to discover the world again, to relearn it or take it up like a new game.

"Dragonflies," Paul repeated importantly. "Dragonflies."

"They're 300 million years older than us, millions of years before the fucking bastard dinosaurs. They fucking ruled. Before the fucking English. The English were fucking nothing. They were fucking gigantic beautiful creatures." Stuart turned stiffly back to his paperback. "What do you know about fucking dragonflies then?" he spat at Rob.

"One poem," he said. "I only know one poem."

Paul sighed, began to explain from the screen of his Samsung. Dragonfly nymphs were dull in colour. They crawled dully along the beds of rivers for years and years. They were the ungainly bullies of the riverbed, gobbling up other insects and even small fish, everything in their path, powered by this varied other life until finally they shed their old bodies and emerged as adult dragonflies: fast, ultra-manoeuvrable and equipped with a trailing net to scoop up prey, conjoined bug eyes that could see anything anywhere, ruthless predators…

"Why do they always say animals are ruthless," Marie wanted to know. "What could an insect know about mercy?"

Beautiful but to whom? And why? These were always recurring questions for people like Agathe and Rob, but they didn't voice them. Somehow for them dragonflies seemed not to inspire terror.

"…with vicious, razor-sharp mandibles," Paul read on.

But apparently they only lasted a couple of months. Years of preparation all for one bright spurt of continuous consumption, perpetual motion: the ultimate shopping spree of full being, all fuel to keep that incredible machine up in the air.

Perhaps you could say they bloomed in late middle age, they'd finally polished up their act and nothing was going to get in the way of performing it to the hilt. Urrkk! Speared by a dragonfly, ripped apart and ritually, mechanically consumed. Collectors preferred butterflies, because when dragonflies – and their dainty damselfly cousins – died, their thousands of tiny brilliant scales fell off and they returned to a dull dusty brown colour.

"Hardly seems worth it," said Mcleod. "They'd be far better off no bothering in my opinion."

Rob tried to remember encouraging things Mcleod had said in the past. He hadn't always been like this, had he? He'd had a strange reaction to the boys who had hatched into dragonflies in the carriage. They had been bottom feeders for years, those two, just bagging along in their dun tracksuits, fattening up, scoffing down Doritos and KFC. They had been waiting for their moment … to be pressed into service. But they had seemed patient and helpful hovering up near the ceilings, in abeyance but possessed of tremendous power, pulsing fire within their elongated spiky bodies, a pair of matching novelty light-bulbs designed by God to light up for a while and make a spectacle.

"Those two kids," said Rob. "Do you think that'll be the end of them, just shooting up into the air? They just trail off like rockets?"

"No, Rob," Marie said exasperatedly. "They were off somewhere, to do something important."

"Oui," said Agathe. "Bien sûr."

"Like what?" Rob asked.

"I expect they mate up there," Marie said. "How should I know?"

"What are they doing?" he repeated. He felt dull, witless.

"They cling together after they have sex, and turn into hovering wheels," said Paul, holding up his phone to offer them vivid digital evidence. "He clamps her in position by the neck, so she can't get away."

Rob, Agathe and Marie together watched a short video of coupled dragonflies rolling around in the air, laying their eggs still conjoined, through a slender tube, in well-hidden places, within the tiny tubers of curled green tulips. They could just about make out the commentary, voiced in a rich baritone by a trained gnat.

"After she has laid her eggs and been released by her male captor," it went on, "an attractive female is often attacked by legions of other male dragonflies, fighting over her, violently attempting to mate with her. Incredibly, the female dragonfly has developed an ability to feign death in these circumstances, in order to avoid unwelcome sexual attention."

Marie and Agathe laughed. Rob looked at Agathe, tried to catch her eye or something. He hadn't seen her laughing like that in a very long time.

"The devil's riding horse," Paul said. "That's a good name for them. The devil's darning needle," he continued reading. "Apparently if an idle maid fell asleep by a stream the damsel flies could sew up her eyelids."

"Bring it on," said Marie. "I'm ready." She closed her eyes behind her girlish metal framed glasses and smiled an invitation to the Devil, to darn them shut.

"Don't say things like that," Rob said. "You know you want to see your friends."

"One of these days your stupid, ignorant mouth is going to kill you," Marie spat.

"Marie," said Rob. "You don't really want your eyes sewn up."
"True," she admitted.

"Horse-stingers," Paul continued. "Adder bolts. Snake doctors. Satan's nurses."

Marie laughed. Agathe was listening to this too, enjoying it.

"OK, I made that last one up," Paul admitted.
Rob was surprised by how they all managed to engage with this, to take it in their stride. He hadn't seen them happier together, not even in life.

"What were the prehistoric ones called?" Mcleod asked.

"Meganaura," Paul replied. "Some of them had a thirty-inch wingspan. Fat bodies, sharp ripping teeth. There are a lot of fossilised specimens, And there have been some regular sightings in Georgia. They fly in from a different dimension," he added. "So the locals say."

"Nowhere near as big as those fuckers were," Mcleod continued. "I thought they were going to kill me with that fucking ray thing."

"You seemed to know them," Rob said quietly. "You seemed to know who they were, what they were doing here."

"Not really." Mcleod lapsed again into silence, continued reading.

All of a sudden something made Rob feel sorry he'd questioned Stuart about this. As to what the actual recent dragonflies were, if that's what they were … but the others didn't seem to know either, and were easily distracted.

As he watched them settling into their seats, looking obliquely away from one another as if natural shyness and a feeling for solitude had isolated them, Rob wondered if the ghosts were also something like greedy, shabby dragonfly nymphs, slowly advancing. Unaware except when there was something immediately to be chomped on. None of them had any sort of glow, not yet anyway. If anything defined their common physical appearance, it was a brownish, heavy, papery look.

Stuart, of course, hadn't always been mad. But now he would be, Rob thought, for evermore. Whereas he, through all of this had retained the calm rationality which he felt had been lent to him by an unknown source

100

of mental funding. Why was it that, to himself, Rob seemed so richly nuanced, at least, but these other friends of his were functioning on little more than a few routine tics and scenarios, which were, incidentally, just about all that he was able to remember about them?

Thirteen

Each snow-bee was somewhere in size between a golf ball and a tennis ball, springy and dense with a translucent rubbery substance packed inside, although they seemed to disintegrate rapidly upon impact. They continued to scythe down from the sky in relentless, machine-like volleys. They travelled at enormous speed, but stuck fast like petrol bombs, like glue – and spread a sticky white fire over every surface they touched. But who had concocted them out of dry dust, powder and paint? Unlike any snow he'd seen previously, these semi-animate creatures seemed to have been designed with one purpose and one purpose only: to obliterate the Earth.

They were snowballs, anyway, or maybe snow-pygmies, packed together in the small hands of who knows what profligate celestial shaper of beings. Couldn't she or he just have made a snowman? But there was more malice than good-natured seasonal mischief in this aerial bombardment. The ageless one was definitely playing for keeps, from reserves of youthful stamina that appeared to be inexhaustible, ineffable: a punishing light, its sources hidden from the eyes of men and women. They could only submit to relentless battering, buried forevermore by a gleeful childlike God.

He wondered if this was happening all over the world. New York. People with turned-up collars and turned-down hats running between tall buildings, looking for shelter in their dark interiors as the snow-bees strafed across Ellis Island and up Broadway, hammering itself over the city in a thick coat of hard shiny white enamel. And how about Germany? France? Africa? Japan? They too would be taking their slim chances.

God's beautiful snow: a clean page for the world, Sometimes you could see it coming, feel it in the air, this frost of frozen rain on the roofs of parked cars, the empty sparkling sky, delicate dove-grey cloud cover.

Rob tried to recall these signs of heaven's bounty, white flakes of coconut to cleanse the world's palate. In transit from the brick chimney stack of the house next-door, stripy vertical lines fading to a lazy meander, a soft caress from God's loving hand. A pat on the head, patronising maybe but also reassuring, then thickening again and growing stronger, then breaking down, and dusting the quiet, supine earth and the prone corpses of dead soldiers with the brightness of heaven, silver rags, and the sun from the fierce mountain caught them and the valley of the shadow of death is full of pushed light, setting off the two red holes in your right side. None of this did Rob remember anticipating from when he'd set out that morning for Waterloo.

Staring across into Marie's face, he remembered sitting opposite her in her temporary flat in Notting Dale. She was miserable, washed out, and one of her favourite words seemed to apply. She was desperate. Post-natal depression. Bad enough, But there was something darker underneath. He had heard no word of reprieve for anybody, not even for herself alone and her dubious place in the daisy chain of generations. She just wanted to be a child playing in the fields, and that was no longer an option. She had been seeing a priest. She had been reading John Clare's poem 'I Am'. There was a stanza of it on her funeral card, along with a laughing photo of Marie in the year of punk rock, the year of Braintree. Not the verse about being the self-consumer of her woes. Maybe it was true about her lovers being stranger than the rest.

Perhaps it had been though. Otherwise how account for her staying around so long. Happy enough just to be an example of an Irishwoman rather than the whole delirious shebang tied up in one delicious little package. Marie had continued to be there, shadowing him like Jiminy Cricket. Marie had kept him – and Stuart – involved in the campaign for Troops Out of Ireland.

But it had been there, in Notting Dale, with the wee scrap asleep in her stilted carrycot in the next room, where he had last talked to Marie, explaining the situation with Stuart. It wasn't the way she had thought between the two friends. For some reason, Rob had been trying hard to get her to take this onboard, to see its implications, as if it mattered any more. Stuart had died long ago. Obviously she had her own problems to consider. Rob sensed then that she was in danger. He'd been trying to show her that she could trust him. That he might have the power to help her. But, he thought, he had possessed no such power. At any rate, he had been unable to rescue her from her murderer, father of her child. Perhaps she could move into the Acton flat with him, he thought aloud. He saw her interest quicken, but she shook it out like a match.

He had never been to County Derry, but he'd made one trip to West Belfast and Armagh, in other company. Monika Wrona, an Irish-Polish-Australian friend, and a couple of comrades, on an International Women's Day picket of Armagh women's prison. They'd stayed on Twinbrook estate, home of everyone's big brother Bobby Sands, the Republican prisoners' leader, then still alive. A tidy place, built on a rolling slope, it was respectable working-class, peaceful, or would have been if it hadn't been for the British Army walking in through your nicely framed show-off window. The woman of the house had called him into the hall, where she opened a drawer to show him a selection of wooden trinkets he'd carved in the H-Blocks, things a boy would make. But he was a man.

She just wanted him home, from a war which from her point of view was pointless whether justified or winnable or what. The boy's father had wanted to know what Rob really thought. That they had to get into the political arena. That it would take a long time. That it would end in power-sharing, But, he added, suddenly lucid because he had to be, for them, a United Ireland would eventually be achieved. They were a genuinely nice couple, but not particularly convinced by his ad-hoc attempt at prophecy.

Crossmaglen was battle-scarred, predictably enough, but there was nothing like seeing it for yourself. A community centre only to be approached at a crouching run from the car, helicopters overhead. Rob and Monika had danced close together to a band of local punk rock kids and he had felt the heat of her. Everyone was happy, the place full of visitors, English feminists, American lesbian activists, while local nationalist women tried to create a celebratory atmosphere. But it had crossed Rob's mind that he and Monika – a dark beauty, done up to the nines – shouldn't be flaunting any intimate moves on the dance floor. It would have been in rather poor taste in the circumstances. Somebody might cut up rough. They sat at the front, out of sight, and kept their heads down for the remainder of the evening.

Monika had been a real hit on that trip. Everyone had assumed they were a couple. West Belfast Sinn Féin were most courtly. Marie, he reflected, wouldn't have made much of an impression on them. She wouldn't have wanted to be there. She could hardly say she was on a fact-finding mission from Derry. All, the same it was a pity, a pity. A pity she hadn't been the dancing queen. But she was only a farmer's daughter who'd lost her mother early to cancer and grew up in a house full of demanding men. According to Hopkins, stationed in Dublin at the end of his life, Home Rule was a betrayal, Gladstone a disgusting traitor.

Rob listened carefully, picking apart the sounds of the moving train. There was no engine noise as such, unless it was a sort of faint duotonic whine that might have been tinnitus: a nothing sound broken by occasional high-pitched brake squeaks, and below these a constant low rattle of old sleepers. Snow-bees continued to rain down like cats and dogs.

Halfway across a patchwork plain of gimballing fields, he laid his head against the glass and, without any sense of panic or feeling of unnaturalness, began to move out and upwards into another world that arched above him. It was some sort of militarised heaven of dragonfly angels and huge vaulted ceilings, seemingly painted on an extensive sky that twisted out of true, yielding impossible perspectives; the angels carried messages over great distances, departed on errands and missions according to a lost book. Rob had misfiled it, he knew, just chucked it on a shelf that led into an occult room somewhere in the past. These details had the muddiness of a ream, but they drifted away, and the space into which he'd been projected came into sharper focus.

They rose higher and higher in a series of linked intricate conical shapes arranged in a vast circular dome of light, and at the apex the invisible seer of all faces was hidden in plain view: too intense, too unspeakable, too glorious to behold. And linking the great turning cones in processions of iridescent beauty, legions of dragonfly-angels ascended and descended on a series of great ladders, each at least a hundred miles wide, and what might have been chaotic was revealed to be ordered and true and complexly harmonious. Great consorts of angels arrived and departed, spilled across the firmament in dripping chains of coruscating light, strands of luminous seaweed lifted from the ocean and thrown against a dark hump of rock, apparently random – except, he noticed, these were braided together in legions of ten thousand, which it turn multiplied and bifurcated, spilling upwards, outwards.

Again, they were like racing motes in a torch beam thrown around a dusty attic, but these were immense streams of pure energy directed purposefully by God across the infinitely complex loom of fibres which He was continuously and actively weaving into a thousand-million constellations, collapsing some and forming and new stars and, on the quoins, satellites of these newly-created celestial bodies, each attended by the dragonfly angel armies of the Holy Spirit – that field marshal of the armies of the Father, directed by His love for the multiform beings He created singly, one by one, during a single workman's week, and by the infinite compassion of his Son for mortal men and women in whose features He saw reflected His Son's own beautiful likeness.

Running the whole ongoing Creation, Rob understood, was a considerable and labour-intensive enterprise, and his own role in same was likely to be negligible … and his beautiful friends, what could they remember of their old, unhappy lives? Which weren't so bad, really, just too short. For him, anyway, they would always be the papery masks they left behind, the shed imprinted rinds of these beings. Just a clutch of short, confused lives of people who never quite found a centre of gravity, never quite jelled.

They had been treading water, so they discovered, perhaps too late, over a void that would swallow them all up. Life had turned out to be less than they thought, they themselves shockingly flimsy, not quite what they had been led to believe. They had been lied to about their own possibilities, and each had made this discovery in his or her own way, an absent faculty, a smudged area of the circuit diagram which never cleared, a series of holes that dropped in empty spaces, compressed and decompressed all the words into nonsense syllables, and you discovered in the end that you had after all been designed for a simpler purpose.

Rob awoke with a start on the corner of the edge of his headrest, wedged into the window with a nasty crick in his neck, and as quickly and effortlessly as it had assembled itself, his vision darkened, crumbled, vanished. However, he remembered Stuart's sister, and the way she'd shamed him, shamed Rob himself in the name of what to her was the obvious truth of things: that nurses were there to nurse, not to make some sort of political point. But the pay for nursing assistants hadn't exactly been brilliant, he pointed out to her, a vanishing figment of his confused dream.

Mcleod had pulled away, refused to be comforted, to have his elbow taken – minimal, awkward physical contact that was too late, too little, too preposterous somehow. And then there was the coldness of his refusal to speak. All these had been symptoms of shame. He had taken it all – all something – upon his shoulders. He knew that shame was real enough, not necessarily just put on as Aristotle seemed to suggest. It was because you'd done something wrong you acted ashamed. He was guilty. Guilty of something – but what? Instinctively he knew what his friends thought of him was probably right. They should know, were sinners themselves, after all.

And for somebody who could only behave according to the illusions he had helped to sow, who was willing to forgive anyone who-knew-what (including himself of course) Stuart felt only a distant contempt. Rob simply hadn't woken up to his own nature. Mcleod had given him one last look at the door, half-pretending to have been persuaded to live. Rob hadn't known what was going on at all. And he was the first to move away, at last to take up his own life, whatever it might turn out to be.

OK, things got tough, but that didn't mean you could just step away from it all with a shrug. You were bound to others by a thousand threads. The food was in the pudding. The proof was 150% absinthe. Just gulp it down but don't forget to blow out the flame. The anger of the gods shows when your vowels lengthen and dip out and a low whining tone replaces everything you had been thinking about with an error message. Was that what this was? The dragonflies were winking at him. That's enough now, that's enough. But what could he ever do except keep bouncing the ball until somebody joined him?

Bring it on, bring it on. Mcleod's attitude showed in his continual reading, which could only be academic. Marie's head tilted uncertainly. Robbed of speech, she seemed to have no reason to care if the world ended or if it didn't. Paul continued in his bubble, hoping for the best. Rob wondered what it all would mean in the hidden, inaccessible future. Everything or nothing. He believed he had seen it all coming, all except this.

"So, Stuart, how's the intergalactic revolution?" Stuart's sister, a charge nurse and a member of the no-strike RSN, had shot at him across the Sunday dinner table.

Stuart mumbled, humiliated. Didn't reply, kept his head down. He glanced at Rob. See? he looked. This is what I get every time I come here. But he didn't say this.

His sister had elaborated more on Stuart wasting his time, living in a fantasy world. Rob was moved to defend his friend. Although they'd met before, he didn't really know her. "Stuart is a serious, intelligent person," he said. "You should respect what he's doing, even if you disagree." He and perhaps Stuart's sister were referring to COHSE, and to Stuart's trades union activity.

She chortled in contempt but everyone settled down. Rob, who'd had a few tots of whisky, felt flustered, overheated. It had felt right to defend Stuart from his sister (and the rest of the family, who agreed with her) but he felt he might he in the wrong; faced with them around the family table they had a collective weight and coherence that was undeniable. Stuart could only squirm under its incontrovertible rightness and Rob could only follow suit. It was their judgement of him, their terrible, implacable judgement. But they were only trying to make him see reason, see sense. No, not really. He'd already been humiliated enough, and they would never back off, his big sisters. Stuart had told Rob how they used to humiliate him with their sailor boyfriends when he was thirteen and they were seventeen-year-old slappers. Cruel to the end, that was sisters. How grateful Rob was not to have had any of his own.

Agathe and Marie had followed one another at a two year interval in the procession of his loves. Sensing his gaze, reading his mind, both looked back and smiled at him, incongruously dissimilar sisters. There had been others, following in swifter succession through spring and summer, dying off with autumn's withered leaves, leaving his solitary withered stump to stand in a field's elbow. Agathe had knitted him the blue jumper and sent it in the post to England, and it became the patched jumper he repaired over the years with different wool and wore for years until it fell to pieces, as a talisman of who he really was.

Now he sat alone in front of the screen of his laptop, dispensing English tuition to faceless, safeguarded teenagers, his only human contact. These kids were a coda to the career of a well-meaning loner who'd once fancied he understood women. He listened to their confessions and offered bland, specious advice. One girl, sent home from school for hitting a classmate who had poured flour into her bag, thought it was a racist attack: the flour meant she was trying to be white. The other girl had denied she meant it that way. A Ghanaian boy seemed to believe Black Lives Matter was founded by Satanists. A small girl with a Birmingham accent had bravely suffered his jibes about the city's screwdriver mechanics.

Outside, in hospitals and care homes, people were dying. Elsewhere the streets surged. Black Lives Mattered. Nothing could be heard in the empty streets, bowed sleepily around the bottom of their hills. A distant helicopter occasionally, no sirens in the empty roads, perhaps the distant wail of a keening mother, kneeling over the body of one of her teenage sons, but they were little reported nowadays, these markers supposedly of a spiralling urban endgame.

London had heard a lot more about George Floyd in Minneapolis, and a group of young women, one of them a councillor, had taken the knee outside Hornsey's sold-off deco town hall for the precise number of minutes and seconds that the police officer had knelt on George Floyd's neck Rob had been touched by this action, as much as he was agonised by the stabbings and shootings of young people, the way they guttered and flared, although it had nothing to do with him. And then the hated Shoemaker, beloved by many, had apparently been defeated by forces of light and yet the world drifted on in semidarkness, playing out its cards, threatening terminal chaos.

Everybody seemed to know the same things, although not everyone was having the same experience. Being shut in alone was different, he thought self-pityingly, much worse than being shut in with your family, depending on what they were like, but neither of these were anything like working on the front line in a hospital or a care home. What had been exacerbated slightly was the feeling that reality's realm was taking place just beyond reach or comprehension. Political events not directly by the Covid pandemic continued to break through elsewhere, as if looming out of an overlit national fog of the routine soap operas of pocket lining and sexual corruption in the upper echelons. Muppets on heat. America appeared to be careering out of control, on the brink of a racial civil war: a character out of Mark Twain at the helm of a careening paddle-steamer, the mighty tread of the Shoemaker shaking a prostrate, terrified land.

Rob and his fellow teachers were deemed exceptions, even at the height of the soaring infection rates, and in pursuit of such a lockdown assignment he had travelled to Bowes Park on the train only to find the vulnerable boy in question was out making deliveries from 8.00 am. A lovely boy. He had said that if the school or anything it might lead to could provide him with a comparable income, he would be only too glad to return to his lessons. "He loves wearing a mask, key worker smilingly explained.

"I'll bet," Rob said.

The young woman smiled at him under her mask – the nicest he'd received in a long while – and signed his tuition form. He would be paid anyway, but Rob disliked these waste of time goalless pseudo-assignments.

The other boy, he realized, in Walthamstow, had been a big fan of The Clown, probably still was, a franchise serial killer, even worse than Crusty or Freddy. The boy had shown him a couple of clips on his tablet, hollow laughter echoing around night streets, his wicked blade forever running with the red gold blood of innocence. The Clown's victims were fodder, the earnest boy had seemed to accept, and that was all, and The Clown couldn't stop himself from killing them, executing them. He had his own reasons. Whatever, whatever. The boy hadn't been too sure what they were. But he couldn't stop watching them die. What had that boy been doing, in the end, except cackling over evil deeds, over crimes he himself would greatly like to commit? The Clown served no redemptive purpose whatsoever, he wasn't punished.

Racing away from town, down the tracks to the West Country, Rob hoped the virus would dampen this particular forest fire, at least temporarily, although he suspected that being locked indoors would only lead to full time immersion in the antics of the Clown. Everything would be wiped out by this once and for all, he had thought, in the end. The instress was indoors now. His global fame opportunity cut even shorter. Just another trick of our forward motion in time, if that's what it was (an illusion really) – a game of infinitesimal replacements, displacement of the past by the present, yesterday by today, the day, the hour, the minute by the second. In the shush and drift of the last days, this overall similarity.

Mathéo would have to come in somewhere, Agathe's schoolfriend in Charleville, facilitator of their friendship, sometimes of their long-distance love affair. Mathéo had enjoyed quite a career in the French educational diplomatic service, spent quite a lot of time in Morocco … but he had become a disciple of the idiot Georges Perec, the sad language-clown with his trivial puzzle-fanatic's approach to literary form: a clever schoolboy who trivialised everything he touched, in Rob's opinion, but Mathéo was still very much alive, buzzing along in Paris, Rue Fabre d'Églantine and its surroundings.

"You're miles away," Marie said. "Away off with the fairies – you always were … are."

"Just thinking about work," he said. "Just boring stuff."

"You're desperate, so you are." Marie said it by rote, a ghost reading off a card.

Even the most sympathetic listeners to Marie's monologues had often glazed over and toppled in stupefaction from sheer attention deficit. Her lips were still pursed in readiness to spin a yarn, but either she'd worn out her stories or this faculty wasn't part of the equipment of ghosts. Marie, he recalled, had been bored if she wasn't holding forth, and completely unable to detect a restive audience behind polite English smiles. She wouldn't have cared anyway. It would have been her pleasure to bore them.

But she had been right to keep talking. He missed it now. Possibly it was why he remembered her so well. And there she still was, in front of him, still tilting her head from side to side in neutral, just as she had in life. He'd made such a mess of his life, was such a clown. What a pig's ear he had made out of his own silk purse. And entirely due to his own stupidity.

Again he drifted onto something else, about *Randall and Hopkirk (Deceased)*, the sixties TV series about a detective agency where one of the partners, Marty, was a ghost, a man in a white suit who appeared on sofas, leaned against walls, emerged from the kitchen. Jeff was never surprised to see him. Marty could zoom around and spot criminals in nefarious acts, and Jeff would meanwhile protect his young widow, Jean. Jean couldn't see Marty but she remained chaste and helpful. Reruns of it in the years after Mcleod died had been a sort of comfort food to him.

Fourteen

After Rob went home, Agathe found work as a tour guide at the medieval castle in Sedan, a nearby ancient town built in a loop of the Meuse. Everybody had thought her too shy for this but they had been happy to be proved wrong. The week before she started work there had been a series of violent rainstorms, and the river was in full spate, threatening to engulf the centre of town, tearing its guts out, rushing broken boughs, insufficiently nailed down sheds and crumpled prams around a crowded peninsula of narrow-shouldered old buildings. It was the heavily fortified scene of many humiliations for France; where the Prussians always came, where you signed the treaty. As far as the river was concerned, you just had to let it hammer past you, and not stand too near the edge.

It was quite a journey every morning on her mobylette. There were a lot of things to learn, but it was a challenge and a hop away from home towards independence, a trial for when she moved to Paris to begin university in the autumn. Sedan was a town that, although picturesque to an extent, was haphazard in style, slightly rock and roll in atmosphere. She enjoyed its surprising angles in the sunshine, sat by the river to eat her sandwiches, when it calmed a little, and on duty tried to answer the questions of old fools who arrived to look at the hideous, slab-sided castle which had so strikingly failed to defend the Ardennes. Mostly she sat quietly at her desk; there wasn't much to do. Not many people came. She wrote a long letter about it all to Rob. She was looking forward to seeing him in England.

Behind her desk she read a novel about a beautiful puppet who controlled her master. It was good, this book. There were scenes in it she found arousing, written in an old style, the style of an old children's book. She had read it a few times before. It was a favourite of hers. She was no beautiful puppet, nor did she especially want to control anyone. But she didn't want to be controlled either. As she worked her way back and forth through this nineteenth century erotic novel, there were those exciting scenes of enforced paralysis, of restraint, of submission, but there was also the play of this conundrum of being a woman, a play of control and release, hiding something or just being cruel for your own shimmering pleasure. She liked this story. She liked it but it was bête.

The story with Rob had taken time to get started, but she liked to think of that one too, daydreaming in the long afternoons before she had to lock up – *la clé était vachement énorme* – and ride her mobylette back to Charleville and Hameau des Chênes. It had started when she was thirteen and a half and he was fifteen, a pretty boy with a guitar, a real idiot so it seemed, but she had stood back and laughed. Nevertheless, she had enjoyed laughing at this English idiot would-be pop star with her friend Mathéo, his *petit correspondant*, and wrote to him herself after the school party returned to England.

At a party once she had asked him to translate the lyrics of 'Moon Shadow' and 'Papa's Got A Brand New Bag', and had even danced a little with him to 'Get Up (I Feel Like Being a) Sex Machine'. But the trouble in those days was that she was so small and skinny. Her breasts in those days had been like bee stings, as she'd overheard his friend Steven, this Steven she didn't like, say to Rob, glancing at her – a child! – as the two boys leafed through trente-trois tours at a miniature cream and red record player in the basement of Nicole's house. Bee-stings. Tits like piqûres d'abeilles.

There had been another horrible adolescent at the party, named Alain. He wore heavily-tinted glasses all the time, cool and silent in a tan leather jacket; he invited himself everywhere and was for some reason considered by himself to be dangerous. And during the course of the afternoon in which they had consumed a whole bottle of cassis, at that infamous party in the teenage annals of Charleville-Mézières, he had spoken confidentially to Mathéo about Rob.

"I like your friend," this slimy Delon had said. "Tell him I am going to fuck him."

Agathe would have to wait until she had proper breasts, to which she had resigned herself, but they were a long time coming. After Martine faded from view, she persisted. On a return visit to England she placed herself near the front of a group photograph of them all on a lawn somewhere in the boring countryside, quite nearby. She was playing to the class, upending an empty bottle into her gaping mouth as she stretched back to catch any drips and to show off her not yet breasts. And when Rob had returned to visit Mathéo a year later, she arrived next day on her Solex, fifteen years old, a smile as wide as heaven, bled out into white infinity, her large brown orbs too dark to be over-exposed. Agathe was getting more beautiful alright, but too shy to speak.

When she arrived on her bike Rob had taken photographs of her with a borrowed 35mm camera, which he printed himself and sent back to her, images in which a long exposure time had revealed her angelic radiance, burning out into pure white light around the dark lines and stark shadows which etched in her exquisite features. If she knew what she had she showed no sign of it. She was still a child, and Rob was a child too, acting grown-up with his borrowed camera and his endless lousy poems. Clumsy successions of mundane words she would try – and succeed – in bettering in her own notebooks, in prose-poems which she kept secret, to herself.

Mathéo arranged an outing for them into the countryside, where there was a deserted old farm he wanted to investigate. He thought it was probably similar to the Rimbaud family farm in Roche, which he'd never seen. Rob used up the remains of his film taking shots of Mathéo and Agathe, materializing like spectres amongst ruined cowsheds, a crumbled, gutted farmhouse with windows at which they might appear, a dark tunnel into the past with Agathe at one end and Mathéo in the foreground, wearing his old faun duffel coat. A position he liked to remain in, she told Rob years later, because he always had to win everything, had to come out on top. But, after all, her father would have said, there is nothing wrong in this. If he can always come out on top he should definitely do so.

He had sent her all these ghost pictures, hand-printed on photographic paper, as a kind of insurance against the day they would all be ghosts themselves. It wasn't fair though, she knew it wasn't. Broken shadows, flat grey light. Agathe teetered along the shafts of an abandoned plough. Mathéo, in a double-exposure, looked up at a grey slatted blind over a wide window with daylight behind. Agathe appeared in a doorway in an apartment where they'd spent a strained afternoon, as though bringing coffee from a kitchen into another room: a shady modern furnished apartment to which Mathéo had borrowed a key.

But nothing had really happened between her and Rob. They had never been left alone. This time too it had seemed at first that Rob was just too dense to understand what was required of him. Perhaps he didn't like her, she thought, as she sat night after night in his attic room, and nothing happened. He'd arrived with his friends, in a big old English car, and these new friends seemed different to the old ones. They set up an elaborate pagan altar in their tent on the camping, said they were white witches. They were long-haired, cool, and full of confidence. After a couple of nights they carried on towards Morocco. Interesting people, they seemed almost adults, his friends.

It was Mathéo who had found the attic room chez Rozoy, an eccentric doctor with a wild daughter who daubed feminist slogans all around town, and negotiated the (cheap!) rent, and they had all cleaned out the filthy place together, and eaten a cheese fondue to celebrate, and Mathéo's older sister had found him a job cleaning cars at the Peugeot agency in Mézières where she worked in the office. And it was her own sister, Lisette, who had written a note to Rob and arranged to meet him on the Quai Rimbaud. Lisette was extremely beautiful, the same age as Rob, and she had won a concours for reciting 'Le Bateau Ivre' in a regional schools competition. Agathe knew Rob would prefer her lovely sister. But Lisette had told him that she had found Agathe naked and completely drunk in her bed in the middle of the day. She was pouring wine over her breasts to encourage them to grow quicker. If he liked her sister, he would have to do something about this. She was ready, Lisette was sure about this. Her sister needed to be fucked.

Agathe asked her if she'd said the last words in English.

"Oui, bien sûr, Ta-Ta." Her sister laughed. She had wished to be clearly understood.

Ta-Ta retrieved the enormous key and took it to the gatehouse and found her mobylette where she had left it, outside by the weathered concrete cycle rack. Now she unlocked the chain and hung it over her shoulder and tied her bag to the rack and put on her helmet. Now she decided to ride straight home, not after all to linger and look around the shops as she had half-thought. She rode away, a tall, stately, but stooped figure, always a bit flustered, carelessly flickering out, breaking up in the slanted light from the fields, through the trees, a slightly strange but resoundingly normal young woman he had barely glimpsed two-thirds of a lifetime ago.

"I'm going to produce a living animal from this cardboard box!" an elderly Algerian in a suit proclaimed in the square. It was market day and the Place Ducale bustled with shoppers, fresh fruit, meat, knick-knacks: a regular outdoor *brocante*. Around its edges were some Algerian stalls selling cheap clothes and ornamental pipes, but this man with stubble and stained teeth appeared to be apart from these traders, equipped with nothing except a cardboard carton which wasn't even a whole box but one that had been opened and flattened, so that it could be peered through, clapped together dramatically, tossed down with contempt upon the tarmac surface of the square, to show it was nothing, then retrieved like a bad but unavoidable fate. A small crowd gathered. "A living animal! A cardboard box!"

Rob stood on the edge of the small crowd of Algerians, mainly women and children, who watched him half-sceptically with folded arms. He watched as the old man worked his audience, carefully folding the box together until it was firm and solid, banging it robustly with the flat of his hand. Rob couldn't understand most of the words. He was cajoling audience members to touch the box themselves, to assure themselves of its substance, but any promise that a living animal would soon appear was quickly crushed when, having half-convinced everyone that a creature was inside it, he violently collapsed the box again and began the rigmarole o peering through it and tossing it down on the ground. The audience didn't stir or react much, but they were led fast by his performance. Rob was too. It was the first time he had seen the process of storytelling exposed so plainly. There was no living animal in the box, only the rigmarole of endless delays and evasions and spurious suggestions that a resolution was at hand. The box folded and unfolded, the words rose and fell, the people shifted on their feet perhaps, but sensing they grew restive the old Algerian would try one of his old moves again, and again they were with him, waiting for an outcome.

So he circled the Place Ducale, bought some frites, and arrived back at his starting point to find that he performance was still going on. The crowd was bigger now, and he had to edge in to see what was happening. The Algerian was standing up (before he had been sitting on a chair or crouching), holding the box before him, raising it to the low skies. "There is a living animal inside this cardboard box!" But he knew by now there was no animal. He couldn't be bothered to hang around to be made a fool of any longer. He went back to his attic room, sorry he had spent the money on frites.

For Mathéo it was a simple enough story of a simpleton entertaining other simple-minded people with something stupid in order to trick them, to trick them out of money. He pointed out that Rob had missed the end of the performance, which anyway sounded stupid, It was wrong to watch these things, like laughing at imbeciles. It was for them, if they wanted to believe it. Agathe was more sympathetic. She saw what Rob meant. There was something fundamental, some elemental truth about the Algerian's performance. Rob had been impressed mainly by his quality of conviction, how he had held the passersby in the palms of his hands with this simple idea of his and turned them into an audience.

Mathéo thought they were his family, his relations, at least some of them. But Agathe had gone back on a following market day. She had found the old Algerian and seen his performance right through to the end. In the end, she said, he produced a kitten, a tiny kitten, from the box. Agathe supposed he had had it up his sleeve all the time.

"It was very convincing," she said. "Nobody could see how he did this. Then he sold the kitten – the magic kitten – to somebody in the crowd. Then he produced another one. He was selling his cat's kittens," she laughed. "Very funny, this type."

But an event not long after placed the old man's performance in proper perspective. That evening Agathe headed towards the square where she was going to meet up with Rob and Mathéo for *le grand fête des algériens* as she had called it to herself. She was delirious with excitement, although outwardly, as usual, she appeared as calm and self-possessed as could be. They had looked all week at the stage being erected, surrounded by large speaker gantries. Now it was ablaze with lights and the square was a sea of brown faces, looking up at the wondrous spangled beings that danced and pranced before them, pouring out undulating streams of Arabic melody to the accompaniment of accordions, amplified ouds, electric guitars, drums and synthesizers.

The stage formed the centre of an open floodlit bubble in the unlit square, as though an alien ship had touched down on a whim to entertain the people of Charleville-Mézières. But the white population weren't present in profusion. Agathe and Rob and Mathéo stood close together, stunned by the sophisticated, orchestrated spectacle. TV cameras were present, flanking the performance area, perhaps had instigated this event, which rolled on and on into the night. The singers, men and women, were richly, formally, glitteringly costumed, each of them a huge star, the tuxedoed MC was polished and ecstatic with justified praise for the musicians, who were gods. Their vocal expressiveness, whether in songs of love or oppression, cut through barriers of culture and language and spoke directly to the soul, so that simply to stand there and be with the Algerians who had come in from Mézières and other towns hereabouts was to be on the edge of something half-understood, emotion and yearning, and happiness, at least for as long as the music lasted, beamed in from a futuristic media-land.

Mathéo's friend, Raoul, said it was the closest he would ever get to seeing Jefferson Airplane, The Grateful Dead and Janis Joplin all on the same bill. It was something they all remembered, anyway. Unlikely to mean the same thing to any of them, but nevertheless the same event, as meaning-less as you like. Times of innocence. Genuine hopes. A ray of light breaking through the cynical manœuvrings of half-forgotten politicians, bloated creatures poured into dark suits, who seemed so very old they must surely die soon … and then perhaps things would get better. Portugal was in the midst of a bloodless revolution. Salazar's fascist Estado Novo regime was crumbling after sixty years of dictatorship, new revolutionary governments would soon be taking power in Mozambique and Angola. Malcolm had written him a long letter from a roadside taverna, where they'd been forced to rest the Austin Cambridge until it was safe to travel. Zoe, his girlfriend, had joined them there. They were all going to carry on to Morocco. Remembering this, Rob was embarrassed by their blithe confidence, kids who were looking around at things for the first time. They were near the end of a long period of affluence and expectation which would leave them a bit baffled; but illusory or not, another kind of solidarity, affirmation and community, and all of that, had surely been kindled into brief blazing existence in the Place Ducale.

She was in the back garden wearing a bee-keepers outfit, a protective gauze mask around her wide hat, like a spacewoman. White in the dappled pale yellow and orange and slashes of green and bleached out blues. This had been in Aix-en-Provence, with her first husband. When they found their place it was all walls without roofs, stairs without banisters, doorways covered with moss. Agathe had loved it, forgiven him for a moment. In her mind's eye she saw courtyards full of scratching chickens, browsing donkeys reading the flowering grass. She loved Provence in the early years of her first marriage, saw it through the eye of romance as it always had been and would be, the masses of golden yellow and sea-green fruit in the little market place of the nearest tiny village bathed in dappled light.

It had been strange living there. She'd found she could ignore her husband altogether and see the landscape as it had once been, dotted with windmills, long strings of donkeys laden with sacks on hilly paths, and the millers and the millers' wives dressed like queens in their lace *fichu* bonnets and gold crosses. Agathe loved handling the bees, the calmness, the precision this required, her feelings of reverence, of care, her sense of intimacy and danger and awe. Bien sûr she would carefully steal their honey, which was the strongest, purest honey bees had ever made, picking up all the freshness and delicacy of Provençal wildflowers. And later her husband tasted it, and said "Hmm, pas mal," and licked it off his cruel fingers: a man who felt he truly appreciated these fundamental things of the great French life.

He was often away on business, meeting clients. Agathe and Mono left all alone for ages. Sometimes she had to meet these clients also, but she found it difficult to know what to say to these rich clients for bespoke homes conjured out of rubble but finished, truly finished so that they had a quality which her husband said he did not need to describe. Men and women like these clients of his simply knew what it was. Agathe had preferred the company of the honey-bees. She formed lasting friendships with the workers, and expected no reward except a glass of muscatel at the end of the day.

Often she had lain down tired in a good way, and Mono, a toddler, slept deeply and peacefully in the countryside before her father had started drinking and shouting and bullying Agathe. What was wrong with her in the end? What had she done wrong? Nothing, nothing. He turned out to be mad that was all. Perhaps not actually mad – but nasty, just as her ebullient father had been to her own mother. A dream. A dream of life that hadn't been able to continue, and eventually her husband, a cold man, found himself a socially warmer woman, a hostess for his boring parties. Somebody who could make conversation with these snobby types she had always avoided at home. Who always avoided her, if truth was needed, especially in her years as a student in Paris.

Jacques was different. He had been a far better man for her. They loved one another, a truly physical couple. She knew exactly where she was with Jacques. With Jacques they had all been together and danced the farandole far into the night. Some hope, because life wasn't always easy, but at least it contained some hope, and then you had to admit and find what you wanted or needed to have in order to life your life as sincerely as you could manage. At least, that's what she used to think, not at the beginning but later on. She had found a poor stonemason to be a good exchange for an ambitious architect, although both had been practical men.

Jacques was an honest man. She didn't have those incredibly painful yearnings anymore, nor the whole sense of an endless crushing loneliness she used to get, and with Jacques there had been no need to look outside her marriage for love or physical excitement. It had been a difficult part of her life she had been hoping to forget. But with Jacques there had never been any question of any riding backwards on the Pope's donkey.

Fifteen

Molly was also the name of a woman in his childhood, a greengrocer's wife who, out of the blue, wrote an eighteenth century novel by spirit possession. Rob and his baffled parents went over to listen to her read from it, but her husband had called in a control commission of nuns in case she was being controlled by a demon. Trying to stymie her independence more like, cut her down to size. They were there when the nuns in came to listen, but they'd only said she had an imagination, and that dead people couldn't really come back and tell their stories through a living person. They were in heaven or hell. The disappointment hadn't immediately killed Molly's interest in writing. She'd completed a sequel.

A power seemed to crackle from her fingertips; it flowed through her, seeming to discover voices, or provide them. She felt special, invincible. But it wasn't language in itself that made human beings special. Although important, it was only a symptom, a side-effect of the big brains. What they could do with language was far more important: they made anything mean anything they liked. They thought they were bigger because their language told them so.

Eat whatever you like, God had said to them. Just don't take the life itself, don't drink the blood of the animals, or human blood either. Because later there will be a reckoning of all this blood. The Lord God Almighty had made a binding covenant with Moses. And this was to be the reckoning promised. The end of human days.

A bit late, Rob thought. Anyway, he couldn't avoid feeling that he personally was the target of this particular night's antics. Unless the ghosts were just figments, some sort of peculiar species of guilt-generated avatar idly toyed with by a played-out brain.

Molly Hubbard – she had been real enough, surely? His parents had been unable to bear the sight of her. If they happened to be watching a nature programme or something on BBC2, they would turn over quickly as soon as she appeared.

Rob thought of his own foolish complaints to God. How childish they were at the end of the day; at the end of days there would be clarity for every created being.

You could laugh – ha! ha! – but ... he realized Marie was glaring at him again. "I wish I could remember what happened," she said. "I can't seem to get past Joshua ringing the doorbell of the flat. I'd just put the fucking baby down after a feed."

"That's when you passed on," Rob told her. "Probably a few hours later."

"She did go to Dervla, didn't she? I wanted her to go to Dervla."

"That's right," he said placatingly. "Your brothers respected your wishes. Dervla brought her up in Sligo."

"They respected me! Don't make me fucking laugh!" She did laugh, however, shortly. "They didn't change her name?"

"No," he replied. "She is still Shelagh."

"How the fuck would you know anyway? It's none of your fucking business." She burst instantly into violent tears. "She's alright then?" she said at last. "That's something anyway." But she added: "What about me? I'm done for! There's no more of me left!!" She cried and cried and wouldn't be comforted.

What else could he say? After all, these were the same last words they'd exchanged, back when she was still a living woman, a few months before her death.

"Rob," she said. "You drive me absolutely mental so you do. You think you're so brilliant, but you're just a good-looking idiot. That's who your perfect ideal woman would've been: an Englishwoman, twenty years younger, with the same delusions of grandeur." For a moment victory was hers, but she burst into tears again.

"But they never liked me!" Rob protested.

"Anne, Anne," Paul said.

Stuart Mcleod looked up, stricken, from his book. "Marie," he said curtly.

Agathe started to weep in sympathy, not because she understood anything that had been said, but because she too was an unwilling passenger on this raft of death. Like Marie she had died too young; she hadn't lived long enough to slake her mighty thirst on the innocent blood of animals. Rob looked on in dismay, pinned down between two wailing women.

"C'est bête ça," she said, reading his mind.

"Oui, c'est vachement bête." Rob said. He should've known that someone who had heard a banshee, believed in a leprechaun's shoe, and carved a wicked splinter of glass out of her thumb with a razorblade, had badly needed his complete protection from reality. Whether that same woman had indeed been strip-searched and interrogated by the Brits every single time she travelled back to County Derry was another matter. Likely? Unlikely?

Her brother Patrick had said: "Rob, put it like this. If you were the IRA, I'm not saying I know who they are, but would you be sending your most important secret messages through *Marie*?"

"No," he'd admitted. "But they still could've harassed her for being who she was and where she was from. I believed that."

"Maybe they did do those things. Maybe, maybe," Patrick said. "I know they did those things sometimes. But to Marie? Well, Rob, I just don't know. Marie was *thran*, if that's a word you might know."

Rob did know that word, from Marie's own lips probably.

"You know, Rob," he'd said, standing there in his tweed jacket and his shiny brogues – he looked as if he might have a briar pipe in his pocket – there outside the Old Bailey. "If Jack Kerouac had by any chance gone out with an Irishwoman," he said, "you could be sure it would have been a mad one."

Rob smiled at this man whose boyhood he had heard so much about.

"I'm glad she had some happiness with you. You seem like a nice bloke. Don't take any notice of these spiteful gays –" he nodded towards Dougal "– though I will say this: it's a tragic story alright. I can see how it might appeal to you; it might itch at you, at some time, as a writer. But if you do take it into your head to write any crap about our sister, I can promise you'll have the McIlvoy family on your back. Don't do it, Rob. Please don't do it."

"Hmm," he said.

"I don't mean to sound harsh," he said, "we're not the mafia. But it makes sense. That's all I ask, think about it. We thought about it, and we decided that the best chance, the only chance really, for her little girl, is for her to know as little as possible about her mother. She mustn't know her story. That's her only hope, don't you see? Just to have a normal life – if she hears any of that stuff she won't have, that's always the risk. She'll become obsessed with it later. She'll go down the same route. She'll harm herself. Do you see? We can't risk that, can we, not if we really care about Marie and her baby?"

"Dervla," Rob said quietly.

Patrick smiled again. "Ah, you know about Dervla. Yes, Dervla's said she'll take her on, bring her up with her own family. With full support from us. We want her to know her mother's family, Rob. Not too much about her mother. We don't know much about her ourselves. Well, she told you about Dervla."

"That's good."

"She'll just be a normal girl there. She won't stand out that much. Maybe a bit exotic, but you know."

They were justified, he thought. The less she knew the better. Like her thoughtful brothers, Rob was resolved that Marie's daughter would not, not if it could possibly be avoided, be permitted to turn out *thran*, like her mother. They'd looked into Shelagh's future and what would help or hinder. It was how you thought, Patrick explained, if you found yourself taking responsibility for a life you weren't expecting.

"Go you on, go you on." Marie was still here, still *thran*. She sat and stared and murmured one of her familiar pieces of Irish nonsense, her seventeen curses. Rob thought she'd no longer believed in any of them, hadn't for a long time, except for the banshee, in that she still believed. Rob believed in the fucking thing himself. These were scenes he had often revisited, ground over in the midnight hour, just because they were there. He had worn her to a point. Like the real woman it never wore out, still jabbering and jabbing away, a sharpened dowel of idle malicious wit that meant no harm. No, her daughter hadn't been allowed to turn out like her; he hoped she hadn't anyway.

Paul was feeling left out. He remembered Marie. He remembered her alright. He remembered you talked to her once, and after that she just bounced things off you, if she thought you were okay. He remembered Rob looking at her, so full of love, so full of impossible love. But he was here and now as well. He could see that Rob could never have really loved her, not really. It had just been a sex thing for her, obviously. And for him too, he supposed, until it got too difficult for him to bear all the other stuff about her. Rob had been a coward about splitting with her in the end, but after that he'd never let himself get too involved. Paul could see this at a glance now, but he didn't know what to say. At that point he just started talking.

"OK," he said. "I think I've got this stuff all worked out." He held up his hands in a silencing gesture.

Marie found this irresistibly comical.

"No," Paul said. "I mean it—" he laughed. Marie's mockery reminded him of his sisters. He knew just how seriously to take her. "– I meant it. I think I know what's going on. I know why we're all here."

Mcleod perked up at this. He'd always been impressed by Paul. There was something irresistibly exotic about him. He was agog, all ears. "Tell us," he said. "I'm sure we're all dying to know."

Paul pointed upwards with a long index finger. "Upstairs," he pulled a lugubrious face. "The Supreme Being."

"There can't be immortal souls," he snorted in abrupt derision. "There would just be too many of them."

"They don't take up much room."

"Look, you know it isn't true."

"Just saying."

Marie had shed her long grey schoolgirl's coat, he noticed. She was wearing her bibbed denim sack, the one she'd been wearing when they first met: practical, no nonsense, plus her dark woollen tights, her red clogs. She was highly agitated. Before anyone could stop her she'd fumbled a packet of cigarettes from her pocket and lit one up, trembling between her fingers. "The Devil's playing with us, right enough." She pointed a finger at them accusingly. "Do you really think God messes people around?" She paused. "Now why would that be? Now why, I ask you, would he do that to us?"

"It's a test," Paul said in an explanatory manner. "We're being put on trial."

"It's me that's being put on trial," Rob said. "You lot have already been judged."

"And just why has Upstairs decided to pick on you at this late date?" Marie enquired.

"Whom the Lord loveth he chastiseth," Mcleod intoned from across the aisle. "How different, how very different is all this from the life of our own dear Queen."

Rob remembered this was once a saying of his. He remembered his friend laughing as he told him, from a book he'd been reading, either in the abandoned family home in Thames Ditton or in his parents' attic in Amersham, where they'd moved before he went to university. But now he cursed himself – why hadn't he listened when people told him, over and over, that it was imperative to leave people behind, not to worry too much about their problems. You'd have enough of your own. Different people had told him this at various moments in his life, some obvious rule of existence he'd missed learning. He didn't know who to trust. No-one hadn't turned out to be the answer. But at the time he'd thought Stuart was a fairly reasonable person. He had seemed to know what he was doing.

Paul looked at him with a self-conscious frown, tapping his lips with the edge of his hand. *I chop it down with the edge of my hand.* His favourite guitarist, his favourite song: it was the male rhythm. He narrowed his eyes slightly. "I think you're on the right track," he said, performing a slow, mindful Tai-Chi chop in Rob's direction. "This whole thing seems to centre on you." If aplomb were all that were needed he would have been a winner at any game of seduction: nothing was left to chance.

"It must be God – who else can it be?" said Agathe earnestly.

Rob remembered the film *Ghost,* which he'd seen once in a grainy pirate copy on VHS. In that Hollywood fiction the angelic dead had protected the vulnerable living, and the bad people got sucked straight down to hell before your eyes. It had appealed to him greatly. That's what this was, he realized, a replay of *Ghost,* and those wise innocents Agathe and Paul knew about it all already … but they knew nothing really, he concluded. They were just fragments of whatever they had once been, a few faded tics that were all he could bring back to life, pale conjurings, nothing as spectacular as Molly Norris's loquacious spirit guide.

"You think you've got this totally sussed, don't you?" Marie said sarcastically. "You really think you're something *special.*" She spat out the last word, enjoying herself greatly as she looked for an ashtray in the arm of her seat and found it wasn't there. She stubbed her cigarette on the side and dropped it on the floor with the others.

"Yeah…" Stuart jeered. "God is wise and merciful and nice alright but no way generous enough to bother with the likes of you."

"Well, the alternative is that you're just figments of my mind."

"What mind? I'm not your fucking property, never was. Never will be"

"Eh," was Marie's response. "It can speak! I don't remember you having any of these opinions before, Rob," she added.

"I've been practising."

Paul nodded, a nodding dog of empty agreement, but he'd never heard Rob speak in such a fashion either. Too busy with his own time-stream. Too self-absorbed.

Mcleod looked deeply perplexed. It was as if everything Rob said had once come out of his own mouth, at some point, but now he couldn't recall what or where or how.

Agathe had never really understood him, nor he her, so not much change there.

Paul did his mannered Tai-Chi derived lip tapping gesture again. Grasshopper, it seemed to be saying, I am carefully considering a justly wise reply to your innocent but misguided question. But when he spoke again he was serious. "We are real," he said. "We are as real as you are, Rob, as real as this train is." He tried to tap the table but embarrassingly his knuckles passed straight through it. And all four of the ghosts turned round and glared at Rob with a sort of solemn anger. Paul had spoken for them right enough. They glared at him and shrugged. They hadn't been looking for this after-life, not at all.

Betrayal sprang to mind. DON'T DESERT THEM NOW had been the categorical imperative headline of Paul's newspaper advertisement for the miners, a precisely-wrought, emotional appeal calculated to wring one last donation out of anyone who cared enough to put their hands in their pockets to help poverty-stricken families as the last days of the final strike wound down into deadlock, defeat. For Jim it had been perhaps his son's proudest moment. For Rob it hung there still in a frame in the entrance hallway of the Hubbards' comfortable, battered family home in a leafy backstreet off Clapham Common, next to a poster of Bertolt Brecht.

But if Rob had kept in touch with the Hubbards for years, it was largely because Paul had told him to one night, in the basement of a noisy pub in China Town, a location Paul now abjured. It was after the fits had begun, shortly before he died. Rob had happened to be meeting up with an idiot who'd recently moved out of his flat. It had been a halting conversation, consisting of last words, in which Paul foresaw his death, its possibility anyway, and said he thought Rob would get along well with his father. "Get to know Jim … if you can," he'd said with his final air of mystery.

Rob didn't know what to make of this – although well used to amateur dramatics from Paul. He feared things were getting out of control somehow, for Paul, and within a couple of weeks his generous friend had died alone in his flat of an epileptic fit.

Jim had been a serious journalist on one of the quality broadsheets, in fact, a sometime foreign correspondent who latterly tramped the home and gardens beat, which was more or less how he had put it when Rob got to know him properly. He always had an air of having just touched down from somewhere, or perhaps he lived in some intermediate adjacent empyrean all the time, or perhaps he simply assumed his paternal editorial role on life when Rob appeared.

He told stories well, but the one Rob liked was how the Editor (and the subs) carped about the length of important reviews and articles he'd commissioned. "Oh, not Ray and his bloody semi-colons again. How about a full-stop, Ray?" That had been a truly representative response to a genius of cultural analysis. "Well done, Ray," she said in a Welsh accent. "It ended." They all seemed to Jim to have been employed on some sort of work experience scheme.

Rob carried on meeting up with him sometimes, to hear these stories, from an old man still eager for news from the beyond, news of his lost son, in the corner of a snug in Soho, where Paul had died, or in their Clapham living room, where he had said: "Wouldn't it be great if Paul opened those French windows and walked in right now."

"Yes," Rob concurred. "It really would." And looked above Jim himself at a framed photograph on the stuffed bookshelf, serious-minded, marching along, his unlined face, his eyes glancing to one side like those of Sir Thomas Wyatt, not in fear of discovery as an adulterer, as Rob had first thought, but because he saw everything, everywhere, was the vigilant eye of the king.

"Your mind creates what you need," Jim once said. "If you need a guardian angel," he continued, "one will appear, because your mind will fashion it out of whatever materials it finds to hand."

Jim had once snatched an old coat of his from the pegs in the hall, and given it to Rob to wear. A long, creased up, belted journalist's raincoat from the seventies. Rob had worn it for a couple of years, until it grew too flimsy and derelict looking. Rob felt he was being dragged back into the past by it, way beyond retro and into the wheelie bin. Jim with his round blue eyes a-twinkle, so like his son's. The game had been afoot whenever you met him. Until – a bit vaguer every year – he faded as everyone must.

Years earlier, when Rob had first got to know Jim better, Paul's father had driven down to Brightlingsea, where he'd been living above a chandlery, and took him up to Suffolk, to the mouth of the river Deben, where he had a small yacht moored. Paul had been right. He and Jim did get along pretty well. There turned out to be more to him than Rob had imagined, and long after Molly Hubbard had been dropped and forgotten, Jim had continued quietly with his interests. A genuine scholar of German literature, an amateur philosopher, he was a would-be steerer of his children and the solid rock behind the buzzy phenomenon that had been Molly Hubbard. He had always been an astute advisor to his wife, as well as a comfort to her once the glare of weekly public exposure and the superficial friendships and affairs she'd enjoyed with various media-types had vanished like the dew.

He had been an investor in things, in boats for example, but also an astute financial investor, in futures that bore seasonal fruit for his family.

They cruised out along the estuary on the engine; its channel was busy with a queue of other weekend boaters, and bordered by a flat, bleached out landscape, planes of scruffy fields and paths of skew-whiff vector careening between them through marsh grass, wandering nowhere, out past the edge, the final parting of Felixstowe where they hoisted sail as the sea took them out across its huge dipping bowl, and Jim had looked at him, and could see that his breath had been well and truly taken away. "Good, isn't it?" he'd said.

Paul's father was a man who had found out where the honey in life was to be found, and this great movement out beyond the bay was one great dollop of honey he didn't mind sharing. And for Rob, riding the winds out to sea was a worth-having experience he'd had only once before, on his railway guard friend Mike's impressive 30-foot catamaran.

Jim's boat was a more modest affair, strictly coastal. That's all he wanted it for, to do this and to bring his grandchildren down to enjoy it with him. They zigzagged back and forth in long sweeps, gaining the open sea where Suffolk was just a faintly traced line that dipped in and out of sight, they alternated tacking and holding onto the rudder, which needed a firm hand and kept them on course for a featureless far off place aimed at in the heaving briny, the whole of it straining past you, bulleting you forward along a hard shoulder of heavy water, striding high there, hanging onto the reins of a bucking sail, ecstatic, swinging off, sweeping smooth on a bow-bend, hurling, gliding forward and somehow beating the big backward wind. The sky – banks of cloud high above the wide skies of Suffolk – Jim Hubbard had soared up into it in his day, stepped amongst the clouds, between them, witnessed incredible things, leaning on his long bent stick, surrounded by vistas as terrifying as Caspar David Friedrich's sublime, which at last had truly made his hair stand up on end.

In the distance, something stilted, a low, squat sentinel, appeared to push up over the far horizon as if it had just broken surface. "It's one of those things they built during the war," Jim called. "Shall we head for that?" He added, "Then I think we should be heading back before we lose the light."

As they neared the huge structure, Rob saw there were two or three beyond it, strung out in a long line of defence, stretching miles away out to sea. They were like the heads of gods that had pushed up out of the waves: guardians, forts, risen castles, sentinels, and each one was likened unto a great fortified city. You could imagine them teeming with busy miniature people, impenetrable, guarantors of the ultimate sanctity of the island, of the great interconnected polis. Uninhabited, empty, deserted but still magnificent and undeniable, although in essence it had just been made to look like that, it was the temple of its own appearance as much as anything else, a giant theatre, an example of marine architecture designed to look fierce. But no, as they drew closer, he realised it was truly massive and secure, a symbol of itself that was without fixed meaning. locked against comprehension.

They shuddered and veered back towards the land these giants had once protected. Rob recalled feeling somehow cheated again – the guardians were not really guardians, this was only that, and that was all it was, his travels, of which the upshot was to come later: a quest to eat the sheep's eyeball of the Arab spring with his favourite grandson. Monstrous if you really wanted to think about the relation of this weekend article about skateboarding to the actual numbers of Arab lives lost overall and the appalling role of the West and simply the scale of what was at stake for local actors, those bit parts in this foreign correspondents' jamboree. Jim Hubbard seemed to have regressed to the thirties, era of Waugh and Bill Deedes.

They moored at a pub, drank a pint of Adnams and ate a crab sandwich, and when they got back to the mooring, late twilight, they shared a skinny dip in the marina to wash off all the guilt and most of the salt. This was male fellowship. Appreciated, and what lay behind it was Paul, the one piece of Jim's ably and easily completed life-jigsaw that hadn't quite snapped into place, and had then been lost. His only son, the philosopher prince, who Jim confessed, he sometimes imagined walking in through the open French windows of their South London house, as if he'd simply been off somewhere for a while, unable to find his key or raise them via the doorbell, or had wandered around the back, through the locked gate and into the garden to surprise them. Paul seemed to have caught this intense wishing from his father, but this was one area of primary desire in which the luckiest man on earth was obviously to be disappointed.

Paul had considered it important to try and bring them together. Had it been? And why had he persisted in it beyond first politeness and care? Rob seemed to have little to say to him about his son: he'd liked him well but they just didn't see him a compatible way, through Jim's family myth. The more his father talked about him, he more he seemed the creature and victim of Jim's fantasies. He'd also suffered what seemed a mild defeat in being unable to complete his book on borders, he who had crossed so many of them on a journalist's safe conduct; but at least he had come to no real harm, and so far as he was concerned, had caused none. It wasn't doing good though, or was it? Rob wondered if any sliver of the realities he'd spouted about with such an air of historical authority had ever personally penetrated his well-armoured hide. But he expected they had, and he had gone mad with it all and done it all, and that was what his son had had to try and follow.

He always returned to his old formula when thinking about the Hubbards – to make allowances, to put them in a class of their own, which they certainly were in for some undefined reason, although principally in their own eyes.

"You should become a Buddhist," Jim suggested. "Something like that. Something that leads to laying off booze – or whatever it is – and gets you healthy."

Rob's own father continued to turn the pages of the daily paper from front to back, trying to grasp what had happened, what went on. Whoever you were it all eventually drained away into opaque particles, specks of lost meaning.

Sixteen

Rob and Paul pressed their faces hard against the dark window. Crewkerne wasn't visible. A dim white tunnel now completely encased the train; they were running along a glistening tube of hard compacted snow, boring through it like a ferocious, toothed turbine. Again, reassuringly, the engine wound itself up like a clanking old top before moving on. Now they heard a faint sizzling sound, and the travellers realized at once that the outside of the train had been heated up, perhaps with some kind of emergency filament.

"This is freaky," Marie, her grief forgotten, giggled in appreciation. Live fast, die young—that had always been her philosophy.

But it wasn't the train that had been heated up, not at all. Stuart noticed first. He saw that the moving train, now gliding along at maybe fifty miles an hour, had been sheathed by a pale blue condom of fire. It completely enclosed the train at a distance of about two centimetres, burning its way through dense drifts that had covered up the land in a frozen night more complete than anything known before, although plenty had imagined such freak occurrences and whatever their consequences might be. Were there actually any survivors out there?

"We're going on a big ride now," Stuart said. "This is it." He put down his book on the gig economy.

Paul felt suddenly terrified, beyond anything he could have imagined.

But the lights were unwaveringly lit, the carriage still warm, almost muggy, although none of its occupants had been able to generate any heat or body odour.

Agathe sat still, quietly composed.

In real life they had all the good arguments, and they had talked him down easily. Rob's heart was beating faster. He was alive! He was definitely alive! The others presented themselves to him as a frozen tableau, waxworks posed in characteristic attitudes. It was clear to him that they didn't know what was happening, even less than he did. They seemed oblivious, almost embarrassed, caught out between scenes in a play for which they hadn't been handed eloquent scripts.

Paul, in his anarchist years, had believed in a lot of dope and smoked a lot of it too. The others did also. But whereas they were picketing, demonstrating, worrying about whether the labour movement was really strong enough to defeat the forces of evil, arguing with passersby in the shopping precinct – after a brief period of campus-bound voluntarism – Hubbard had slid effortlessly into a glamorous world of affinity groups, cells, key people who lived and loved together and would stand together in the pinch, at the end of the day, at the beginning of night, and until that day they would be having some fun doing it.

Small groups were more important than the masses, who didn't know how to live or what it was they should want anyway – how could they? – but affinity groups, exhibiting the loyalty displayed by students of Kung-Fu to their masters, would hone the programme that could achieve full being for everyone, bringing it about by means of a principle of attractive example. Masters and mastery were a problem of course, for an anarchist, but a natural phenomenon after all, and so a full open democratic process was definitely essential to the health of even the smallest revolutionary fragment.

Charismatic male leaders were a recurring phenomenon, their propensity to accrue numbers of female sex slaves had been mooted at a summit. This had already led to a necessary split in the organization, in which Paul emerged as leader of the larger faction, and following that it had fallen to him to think of interesting, productive revolutionary actions for the others in the group to perform.

All of this had seemed incredible to Rob, some sort of fantasy Paul had conjured into being. It was certainly livelier than standing around a brazier with some suspicious workers-in-struggle, running off leaflets and handing them out, offering unwanted advice to the more progressive comrades on the trades council – but there appeared to be hidden qualifications of social class and physical attractiveness for membership of an affinity-based cell. Perhaps that was mean. He knew he didn't believe in the right things anyway. He could only be a follower of something that had some momentum other than that provided by his own will or ability to bullshit. At bottom they were rich kids as devoted to notions of exclusivity as founders of a country club. They behaved like a terrorist cell, but without doing anything illegal or dangerous.

Rob and Stuart had laughed about it. How the hell had he pulled this off? "Just you wait and see," Stuart said. "This is only the first stage." It was to him like watching the evolution of an alien creature. Who knew what they could and couldn't do? His friends, those two anyway, had no idea. He was way out of their league and they both knew this to be the case. They didn't know what to make of his ludicrous political antics.

His first idea had been a Plato and Heidegger reading group but he hadn't been able to stir up much interest. For a while it seemed better that they should get to know one another thoroughly, build up more trust. They could join in existing demonstrations which they broadly agreed with, but do it in a different way, as themselves, putting forward a different way of living and being. It was something they could gradually work towards and achieve, and they could hand out leaflets they had printed, explaining in clear terms what anarchism had to offer ordinary people.

But you had to admire Paul – Stuart and Rob had both thought – for finding a way to be fairly powerful and to take himself seriously without anyone needing to be persuaded to vote for him. Paul, tall and lean in those days, statuesque in his Moroccan djellaba, with his mass of blonde curls and his piercing gaze into things ahead, had been a figure of fun amongst the more conventional left-wingers on campus. His consistent attitude was that if you couldn't turn being revolutionary, or even left-wing, into some sort of jaunt, you might as well forget about passing it on except to a few psychologically crippled guilt-freaks.

There had always been for some reason an undercurrent of cynicism running through the student attitude to being at university, which was after all free in those days, but these were far from cynical people, Paul especially. It was all incredibly important to him, even if retrospectively there was an obvious element of him starring in his own show in the coolest place on earth. Nevertheless, he'd always had a direct quality about him, a sense of plunging forward to the next fence.

Rob looked across at the animated shadow sitting opposite with his phone, now reading up on Crewkerne, and felt an uncertain pang. This had been somebody who sprinted though life on tip-toes, leaping from one situation to the next, addicted to transformations. Picking up allies, discarding others, always moving forward, so it seemed, until they had lost sight of him, and a few years later Stuart had died, and Rob got in touch with Paul through his father to tell him what had happened. Because Stuart had been his friend before he had. Rob had met Paul through Stuart, in the aftermath of a particularly heated philosophy class. He remembered them bursting into his tower room, full of high spirited talk of a Hegel reading group, Stuart had led him back there for some reason, but Rob couldn't do much but listen to their jousting, striking poses. He put a record on and stuck one together. Rocky. Six quid a quarter. A bearded guy had turned around and offered it to him during the vice-chancellor's opening address.

"Sounds like a dull place," the idiot said. "Old but dull. Alfred the Great founded it. William of Orange prayed in the church, shortly after landing for the Glorious Revolution in 1689."

"And drop like King Billy bomb-balls in," Stuart chimed from across the aisle. "Until the town lie beaten flat."

"Will you shut up with fucking Yeats," said Marie stoically.

Paul, he remembered, had turned up at Mcleod's funeral in Amersham, his style changed. Maybe it was just the circumstance, but he'd been immaculately if casually dressed, his golden locks shorn in a brand new eighties bob. A coach load of fellow workers from the hospital had attended the Methodist service, and some other friends mingled in the back garden, nibbling funeral nibbles. Paul had been standing with Stuart's father, the old Lancaster crew member, looking red-faced and sweating profusely. Paul' stance, legs apart, and his chopping Tai-Chi hand movements, gave Rob an unexpected, embarrassing lift of happiness, reunion, continuity, as if this was some sort of festive occasion after all at which the guest of honour was about due to arrive.

"I just want you to know, Mr Mcleod,"— chop, chop—"Stuart was a great bloke. One of the best, on the right side, if you know what I mean. I'm so glad I knew him. He made a difference to people."

Mr Mcleod, standing there with a whisky tot trembling in his hand, looked rather cowed by this upright intense stranger. His eyes were swollen, red and watery. Rob didn't catch what he said in reply, but he saw Paul reach out and put a firm hand on his shoulder. Stuart's father had been impressed though that so many people had turned out for his son. He talked to a lot of them; they were impressive people he thought. He would never understand what had happened. It almost made him feel, he said later, as if he hadn't really known Stuart. His mother had been giggling as usual in manic sandwich-preparing heartbreak.

134

Eventually they all left, going their separate ways in cars, coaches and on trains, away to live their marvellous lives. One of the women had been pregnant. They waved goodbye quite gaily, motored off on their long journeys, and it was as if Stuart's funeral had turned into one more somewhat belated graduation party. Rob waved the last of them off, feeling in the pit of his stomach that he had been responsible for his friend's death. Somehow or other he had taken a life that should have been Stuart's … but all he'd taken was a few books by which to remember his friend.

A few faint pencil marks in the margins of Derrida's *Of Grammatology* were all the remains of Mcleod. This tape-repaired copy was in Rob's possession; always close at hand though he'd never yet read it. It was certainly well-worn. Stuart seemed to have studied it like a bible. What a pity he'd made no stronger impression on the world than those faint marginal strokes. A pity, and yet that is how it is. Many called, few were chosen. A long rest of your life to let it all go. Not so hard for most students, after all: the hunger faded, the ideas never lodged. Looking at it though, Rob felt himself to be in communion with that calm, concentrating movement of Stuart's living brain. Out of those barely touched in traces he made a presence, a reciprocating auto-affection. He had certainly impressed himself on Rob. There was no doubt of it – he was the most vivid ghost, the one who was still alive inside him.

After a while Rob had put the battered paperback aside, ideas he'd managed to pick up battering around his half-baked brain. Picking it up again he saw that the book was a 1980 reprint, published two years after Stuart left university, which showed he hadn't given up on philosophy after graduating. He'd applied for a job at Essex Hall, the old hospital for imbeciles, where all graduates were taken on, and some, according to ability, rose to be managers. Reading day and night, spending his wages on brand new shiny books. But all the same the marginal lines in *Of Grammatology* were faint, and petered out entirely in the last two thirds of the volume. The too hard book, the book which broke your heart. They tried to hand it to you as you walked in through the door. You realize fiddling the intelligence test isn't going to work. Either that or he'd just been kidding himself, and going through the motions.

Rob thought that Mcleod's heart had already been broken, in some other way. He never understood how or why. There was at least a sliver of mystery about his short life. Rob remembered running downhill at midnight on New Year's Eve with him through the dense wheat of Amersham, in the corner of which field nestled the square obelisk monument to the protestant martyrs. The children had been forced to light the pyres their parents had been burned on.

The monument had at one time become a point of attraction for himself and Stuart, a place where innocent Lollards had burnt at the stake in 1521 for worshipping and reading Wycliffe's scripture in English: a creepy spot with its own built-in refrigerator; a place to sprawl on the grass with a couple of tinnies and a joint or two, with only the slightest thrill of apprehension that one day they might be manhandled into the flames by self-righteous parishioners or even worse themselves be called upon to light the faggots.

And as for his own poor heart, that had obviously been wounded, wounded, followed by a sort of intractable numbness, an inability to accept the reality of Stuart's death, then dreams of return, compulsive conjuring up of ghosts, which had started right then, amplifying a pre-existent refusal to take the rolling present and its alleged consequences too seriously.

Seventeen

Agathe stirred against him in their sleeping bag. It was perhaps early evening. The night before, alone, he had walked down to Le Rimbaud to buy cigarettes at two in the morning. Amazingly the place had been open, and despite its ill-repute he'd thought he would come to no harm there. As he stood at the old copper bar he noticed a small dice throwing game, a bowl lined with baize and containing two dice, at his elbow. He idly picked up the yellow dice and a woman sitting on a stool beside him said: "Tu joues tout seul, chérie?"

Rob smiled, paid for his Gauloises, and left, embellishing the tale as he walked back to his attic room.

It was cold in the attic room but they had the bar-fire on, and were snuggled up warmly in the bag. Agathe had arrived straight from the Lycée Chanzy, lifted her Solex through the wooden gate and wheeled it into the Rozoy's tiled vestibule. Rob had been scarcely awake at the time, so it had been a good way to face a new day. She'd extracted chocolate cake wrapped in foil from her satchel and they had eaten it together straight away with coffee.

Last night when she had been baking the cake for Rob, Agathe had put her bare arm into the oven to see how hot it was. Very hot! She felt mounting pain immediately, but was able to detach herself and float away from it. She had left her whole arm in the oven for a long, long time, and when she pulled it out, her skin had been completely black, her flesh split open. But it had healed up quickly enough in the fresh air.

"Do you want some ravioli?" he asked her now.

Agathe stirred again. They'd been bundled up in the sleeping bag for hours, asleep in one another's arms. "Avec quoi?"

"Du pain?"

"Oui," she said drowsily. "J'en veut bien."

Rob slid out of the bag, pulled on his clown's trousers, and hobbled across to the camping ring, trying not to pick up another splinter from the filthy floor. He opened the can of ravioli and dumped it into a small saucepan he'd fished from the tiny sink. He lit the gas, agitated the meal a little with a spoon, and selected slices of everlasting bread from the packet he'd shoplifted from Monoprix earlier in the week. Voilà! They ate from bowls, dipped their bread. Agathe hadn't got out of the sleeping bag, which rested on a rickety camping cot, so he sat at the table, watching her eat languidly, then scrape the bowl clean with her spoon.

"Bon?" he asked.

"Yes," she'd said. "It is very good."

But was it really good enough to warrant jerking the poor woman up out of her alpine grave? Making her traipse around and do his bidding? Separating her from her husband and child? But there the separation had already happened, apparently. It was permanent, irrevocable. Just as their partings at Charleville-Mézières railway station had been for good. It had been difficult for him to settle to any other life. And even then, it was only on condition of it being provisional, temporary. There was always this other life, an unlived, always potential life, waiting there, over there in the land of parallel, of horned croissants. Someday they would find their way back to that beautiful attic.

It was an outright lie, impossible to believe in once she'd plunged off that road. Rob felt incriminated by her presence here on the train. She was an embarrassment. One knot he would never pick apart properly. He should have respected her grave, but here she was: back on a train, in a blizzard, saying foolish things. She knew she shouldn't be here, but on the other hand she seemed to have nowhere else to go.

As a matter of fact, in a disintegrating cardboard suitcase in the corner of his cupboard, he still had every letter she'd written to him. From the age of around fourteen to however old she'd been when she died. No, no. That wasn't quite right. She hadn't replied to the last one, unless those papers strewn in the footwell of her car had been an answer she was putting together, flown out of the glove compartment, part of an unfinished letter she had been writing to him.

"I still have your letters," he said to her. "I kept them all."

"Oui," she said. "Mais tu n'as les lu jamais, tu n'as jamais compris ce qu'on disait."

"I missed you."

"Tu me manques."

"I loved you, Agathe."

"Ah, bon?"

Agathe looked away, a tear in the corner of her eye.

Plainly she didn't believe him. She had loved him, but he hadn't loved her, not really. Agathe had thought about it a great deal, back in the days of her misery, and that had been her conclusion. But Rob, the idiot, was determined to contest this even as they plunged headlong on an out-of-control ghost train towards the gaping gates of fucking hell. Vanity lasted until the last possible moment: that was his conclusion. And those workers whose labours we hold most precious and reward the least, are well aware of this. Nobody wants to know, so they're forced to keep quiet about all the things they have to do to ease our crossover into the unworld of death, where Gilgamesh and Enkidu still lived, not on gold thrones but wandering among catacombs, layer upon layer of crumbled skeletons in a land of darkness and crumbling bones and choking chalk dust. The Land of the Dead.

Rob had read this in his first term at university, not long after they'd parted. And he'd thought, oh, so this is what they had by way of religion and myth before anyone thought of anything better. Gilgamesh was a grim tale indeed. They hadn't minded telling the truth about the afterlife, but was this the best humanity could come up with? He'd been frightened by its brutality, supposedly great mythic characters, made out of cardboard, painted with crushed scarabs, washed away in the river of forgetfulness. It was too much for him, too pitilessly indifferent to the myriad lives of beetles and ants, to people such as themselves: he and Agathe and Marie and Stuart and Paul Hubbard, who still thought he was in charge of them all somehow, or if not, he definitely should be.

Rob remembered speaking about it to his personal tutor.

"So what do *you* think happens after we die?" the neatly bespectacled lecturer had asked him.

"I don't know," Rob said. "Does anyone? It's just somehow I don't have any response to this, I really can't relate to it." He didn't remember if these had been the awful words, but it was some crap like that. He just remembered his deep blankness, a sort of horror because he thought these old clay tablets represented the truth of existence, before there had been enough time to forge so many convenient lies out of the breath of ongoing history.

His exasperated tutor said nothing. Who could blame him? Rob squirmed in the rattle of his ludicrous narrative. What the fuck could anybody have said to that sort of crap?

And what was the nature of Gerard's friendship with Robert Bridges? It was long lasting, but there were gaps. Bridges ended up being poet laureate, ended up sounding like a more, sentimental, easier version of Gerard, his long clonking lines rimed with London snow and an atmosphere of tweeness about his busying schoolboys and flummoxed workers. Bridges' light branched in another fork at the quoin where their energies had touched closely and parted company. Robert went for science, Gerard moved with what seemed a terrible logic towards the life and thought of a religious. So close, they were almost never on first name terms.

At this point they no longer had much in common. There was the misunderstood friendship with young Digby Dolben, an infatuation confessed and forbidden, although Gerard the floor before a picture of the Virgin Mary in each morning in his memory; his feeling when goaded by Bridges with Walt Whitman's ample verse, that this mind was more similar to his own than any man's, also that he appeared to be a very great scoundrel. Whose verses limped off into big prose, Not trimmed and tacked like scrupulous Gerard's. Still, he'd been unable to carpet the world with them, unlike those big guys. It was a pity, Rob, thought, that he didn't write to Whitman instead of old Coventry Patmore, mooning on and on about the dead angel of the house up in Highgate.

All this he remembered from introductions to the Oxford and Penguin editions. The clever young Oxford editor particularly detached and lucid, although seemingly on the side of the kind Jesuits. She laid it all out for you, strategically wincing away from what to a modern sensibility shrieks from every page he wrote. Perhaps he remained pre-sexual, never tested, circumcised by Welsh Jesuits, deterred from all extraneous interests and attachments seemingly shunted around,. It is essential to practise detachment from other created beings, St Ignatius whispered in his ear on retreats. Your primary relationship is with God, who has expressed himself through the church of your maker. A cruel discipline for a frail man, but one the crippled Hobbit embraced with pleasure, with joy.

According to a modern editor it had been the so-called 'Communist' letter that produced the long hiatus in their always affectionately bracing correspondence. Gerard's tenor had been that the Empire was so immorally run and to such little benefit to the working-class man, that he couldn't blame him for wanting to tear it down. He couldn't of course condone destructive methods, like those of the Paris commune where fathers had in fact been executed. Aside from this, he himself was fully in accord with the ethical principles of communism. Hopkins qualified this in a hasty postscript by the following delivery. Neither letter was replied to by Bridges.

And yet the breach eventually healed. Gerard was irresistible, and Bridges cautiously plotted his posthumous career, prevaricating for a long time because he thought his friend had been a failure, wasted his life. Rob knew competitive conflicts in his own friendships had led them into deep, foundering waters sometimes. But you wanted the old familiarity to continue

As a youth Gerard had replied to 'The Convent Threshold' by Rossetti, and to Richard Garnett's 'The Nix', a short poem of a raven haired sprite who steals the glowing blonde locks and azure eyes of a beautiful rival, leaving her to wail imprisoned underground in her crystal grot locked in Nixie's darkling skin, imprisoned behind her wildly darting eyes.

Perhaps with poets this fear of being usurped by having your beauty stolen was particularly acute, although it could apply to anyone; perhaps in the case of a religious and an ambitious secular sensibility, the friendship would inevitably lead to a *contrafactum*, to a run of counterfeit songs set to another's tune, to some uneven and difficult exchange.

Eighteen

Mathéo came in carrying several bulging carrier-bags he had picked up in the street, at the corner, beside the small chemist's shop which faced out onto Rue Victor-Hugo. The dumped shopping bags were jammed full to bursting with wallets of uncollected photographs that had been brought in for processing. Mathéo was excited by this find and spilled them out onto the carpet of his and Gisèle's apartment in Reims. Some of the black and white photos reached back to the late fifties, many were from the sixties or early seventies, and the three of them (was there another, Rob tried to remember, a co-operative guest ghost or two hovering around?) sorted through the snaps, packet after packet, sometimes mechanically, but more often stopping to look closely, so it was soon evident that a certain amount of indifference was going to be necessary if they were ever going to be able to examine every set of photos.

But what, then, was the point of all this looking? When you paused you began to speculate. After all, why had so many images of loved ones, captured in so many special moments, been abandoned by their owners? You couldn't help but think they'd died, before they could retrieve their property, but perhaps there were other possible reasons. The photographer had merely forgotten to pick them up, had run out of money, or else the people they recorded in interaction, often posing in front of local landmarks, a fountain depicting Louis XV, a gold-winged crowning angel, and sometimes a small but imposing religious sculpture that stood in front of Reims cathedral, had only been slightly acquainted, and those moments hadn't, on balance, been treasured sufficiently to pay for the reproductions.

There were many photographs of family groups, including children of different ages, and these you'd think would have been worth the keeping.

There were also photographs of empty rooms, perhaps taken to show off new cheap furniture in a small flat, an immaculate, freshly-installed en suite, or simply for the sake of an impulse to capture something not ultimately worth preserving: absence, loss. Few had any erotic content, and even in these few there was something shy about these glimpses of skin. The photographer had been too embarrassed to show his face again. By leaving these memories for the pharmacist to deal with, they had left them behind. Whatever reasons you applied, cumulatively the experience was one of a loss of meaning, of death finally, tidied away, forgotten, and they were only sifting through ashes at the backside of a municipal crematorium, expecting to discover something apart from their own ghoulishness.

Rob sat back from the task with a stiff neck. "I can't bear to look at any more of them," he said.

Mathéo ploughed onwards, flipping through them at lightning speed, throwing them down on the carpet, an undifferentiated heap of body parts. Gisèle had dealt them deck after deck onto the same growing pile. They obviously felt that Rob wasn't doing his share of sifting – What was the point? One last witness? – and so Rob picked up another wallet, and another, at least replacing them and respectfully folding them down before tossing all these never-known forgotten lives onto the same low mountain range of scattered limbs and lost smiles from long ago grown up children, adults.

One way or another the people had moved on, and this unintentionally tidy if random compendium of certain aspects of their intimate lives and modest pleasures, those of the city's poorer people, whether native French, from the Maghreb, or elsewhere, had been unearthed, discovered, consumed and obliterated once and forever in the same moment. But what had they actually found out? A research project worthy of the idiot Perec: a blinder which emptied lives of their actual meaning, a gestural allegory of disappearance just as his lipograms had pointed at and discarded the disappeared Jews of Paris. But who did Rob Goddard think he was anyway?

After they had looked at every single one, Mathéo piled them all back into the carrier bags and quickly carried these away to replace them, where he had found them: outside the chemist's shop on the corner of Rue Victor-Hugo. If it had been Rob, he thought, he would have kept them to ponder over, to analyse, to savour; or perhaps, he thought again, wasn't it more likely that he wouldn't have bothered to pick them up at all for fear of committing some contemptuous, intrusive act? Even the pharmacist had only fed them through a machine, or perhaps more likely had sent them out to a photo processing plant somewhere or other, probably itself staffed by ill-paid immigrant workers, like the infamous Grunwicks in North-west London, where there had once been a well-remembered strike to unionise the place. The defiant, expressive face of the strike committee's leader, diminutive Jayaben Desai, had been photographically imprinted on Rob's brain with a vividness that eclipsed any of Mathéo's stolen images. "We will black them!" she had cried, "We will black them!"

The door at their end of the carriage slid open once again. The guard stepped though abruptly, braced his stocky body between the aisle seats and looked down at them. "Looks like we're running this service just for you, tonight," he said with strained affability. "Not far to go now." He turned to Rob. "Where was it you were heading, sir?"

Rob noticed that his collar was open. He had loosened his necktie. "Sugarford," he said calmly.

The man looked at his watch. "About half an hour's time," he said, "barring any further misadventures. We're running an hour and a half late, I'm afraid. Filthy weather, isn't it?"

The ghosts murmured assent.

"Next stop, Axminster," he said. "Fifteen minutes or thereabouts. "Sugarford afterwards. But I expect you know that already." He chuckled in half-apology. "As for the rest of you am I wrong to suppose you'll be travelling on to the end of the line with us?"

"I find it amazing that you're still running this," Paul said with an odd, leading politeness. "Given all this nonsense we keep hearing about strikes and whatnot."

"No strike tonight," the guard replied. "No more Bob Crow, that's why."

"Who's Bob Crow?" Stuart perked up.

"You don't know who Bob Crow was?" the guard laughed in cheerful contempt. "Where have you been buried?"

Paul too looked blank. Rob realized he had been bluffing earlier. None of the ghosts knew anything that wasn't over thirty years old, if that recent. He was the only one who knew. "Leader of the RMT," he said. "He died a few years ago. Bob Crow was a working-class Essex guy from Hainault, the man the *Daily Mail* loved to hate. A good working-class leader – one of the best in fact. I met him once."

The guard looked surprised but pleased to be having this conversation. "Not everyone would agree with you," he said. "But he obviously did us a lot of good. Not only train staff, but track-workers as well, all maintenance crews, everyone on the railways and the whole London transport system."

"Wasn't that what he was originally?" Rob asked. "A track worker?

"That's how he started, yes," the guard replied. "Trackside worker. Big bloke as you'll recall, a bit of a bruiser in appearance. People had always listened to him, I expect. " He faltered for words, baffled as anyone else by the mysterious phenomenon of Bob Crow's success, his folk communism, his steadfastness, his working-class straightforwardness, effectiveness. "I'll say this for him – he never forgot who put him there." The guard added.

"And he's dead you say?" Stuart said glumly.

"I wouldn't be surprised to find he was on this train," said the guard.

They all looked around hopefully. No Bob Crow appeared.

Marie cracked a laugh at the sheer ridiculousness.

"Anyway," he retreated, a little embarrassed, steering back to his original subject. "The weather. It's not something anyone can bargain for, is it? Well, in this case it's so extreme that the term 'Act of God' might well have to be used in future negotiations." He paused, loosened his collar further. Now Rob knew why. "They've closed down the entire network until further notice," he continued. "Until it rains or the track workers can dig everyone out. I'm sorry to report it's the same right across the country, apparently. To tell the truth, nobody knows what will happen. But anyway, we were going to terminate at Salisbury, but the driver got a call from up top to carry on down to Exeter as a normal journey." He smiled, upbeat at the last. "Which is absolutely fine with me and my good friend Derek the driver, because we happen to live there, don't we?" He chuckled. " Soon we'll be home, tucked up in our beds."

He seemed an optimistic sort, this guard. Rob wanted to ask him his name and shake hands with him. The ghosts looked at him. Paul especially wanted to pursue a proper conversation but he felt humbled somehow by his own ignorance, and hung his head. Rob's grandfather had worked for the railways, his great-grandfather a station master, but although he burned to say so it seemed impossible to mention now without seeming a fool. Stuart wanted to know more about Bob Crow, but he too said nothing. Agathe was looking at him too, a nice man this one. But it was Marie who spoke first.

"Wait a minute," she said. "Are you the guard or the ticket collector?"

The guard laughed, delighted by her accent. "I'm both!" he said. "Usually there are two of us," he twinkled sadly, "but tonight we're running this service with a skeleton crew."

And with that he left them, ambling down to the far end of the carriage and through the sliding door. He was headed down to the bottom of the train, to his place, his guard's cubby hole, where he would take on his other identity and soon be able to open a door and poke his head out again, just to check if anyone wanted to get on, and, if possible, to blow his whistle and waggle his paddle, at Axminster.

Nineteen

Agathe was too old for these things now. They were best left to the little ones. Jacques was a good sculptor, a real one, and a skilled stonemason. He earned their living by the strength of his arms and the skill of his own two hands. He was more proud of this work of his than of his sculpture. People looked away when you said sculpture. They smiled when you said stonemason, gravestones, inscriptions, repairing the walls of old houses and great hotels, and they thought you were alright.

Jacques had held up his two large, bony, encompassing hands, which looked hard, and clean, cleaned by stone, because you didn't want to leave any marks on it, like your own blood for instance. Jacques laughed his long, smiling laugh with his wide mouth, his strong handsome yellow fangs. Everything about him had been strong, capable and handsome.

Rob blessed him, blessed his blonde eyelashes and everything else Agathe had loved about him, his long body, and his long, lonely pain without her and Mono to complete the circuit so that a current might flow out of his fingers, through his mallet and chisel, into the stone. Now he had had only the sculpture. You couldn't say it wouldn't age, because what he had made of Agathe was already ancient, crumbling like her flesh. In fact, he had thought bollocks, it was nothing, nothing at all, his sculpture of Agathe's long, stretched out back. It mocked him with his own vanity, his shallow preoccupations, all the stupid, childish things on which he'd wasted his foolish days. All the same, he might decide later, it contained all his love, all he knew about it anyway. Jacques was destroyed by her death … for a while.

Did people destroyed by grief actually die? Rob had heard a report via Mathéo via Agathe's big sister that he was drinking hard. Perhaps after a year or two you gave up. Agathe was meanwhile looking for him and Mono, looking to get back and resume her life when it had ended and they had moved on years ago.

Between the Charlie Hebdo and Vincennes supermarket attacks and the assault on Le Bataclan, Rob got in touch with his old French pen-friend, and visited Mathéo and his family in Paris. Unfortunately he'd come down with flu on the way there. After a couple of days snivelling and misery, Mathéo suggested a return trip to Charleville-Mézières, as if intuiting that this is what Rob had come for, although perhaps himself looking for some encounter with a nagging past, a tense present.

They'd slid out past the Paris suburbs, places of infamy tucked away from the carriageways in darkness, names notorious but unknown to Rob, indicated by large feeder signs, and then they were beyond them on a vast plain of wind farms where giant white blades scythed the night-fields on either side of the motorway. It was as though Paris itself was just a small carefully curated backdrop, while France itself, the real France, had been replaced by this nightmarish spectacle. Memory sliced to ribbons by whirling bomber propellers from a retro-future. "It is necessary," Mathéo said, sliding a CD into the dark powerful car's player. "I like this when I am driving, do you mind? Rameau."

Rob needed his ghosts to bite him, but Mathéo was no ghost, not yet anyway. Mathéo was solid, real. He perceived himself to be moving and acting in a recognizable, commonly understood world-environment, trying to show him something about the way things really were. Mathéo had acquired a resolutely bleak view of humanity, but also retained the positivity of an enthusiast, an obsessive. But it was definitely Rob's unreasonable and awkward flu-smitten recurrence, his apparent quest for the past (which didn't exist, it was Mathéo's own quest) which had prompted this impulsive, peremptory return journey.

Mathéo had earlier been kind enough to hand him the secret key to his tangled love life. "They were bad women," he said.

Rameau's music laid out pristine grids of logic, and these processes of planning and execution were what kept this modern systems-world running, these interlocking propellers between which there was so little room for manoeuvre, and error, if such error occurred, would be immediately apparent to everybody: complex precision, a crazy world. This was believed in by Mathéo, whose work required him to be stringent. Mathéo, a highly successful teacher, of Khâgne, at a prestigious lycée where Stéphane Mallarmé once taught, always swore by such ordinary things.

Rob tried to keep him talking as they drove, feeling for subjects like a medium poking around for triggers, for lost loved ones. The years in Morocco, his not too troublesome daughters, teaching Khâgne, harking back to his time in Jakarta, where he had undertaken his first assignment as a teacher, during his national service, his first real challenge.

Rob's streaming cold, which felt like flu, had been laying him low since his arrival. It had come on during the Eurostar journey, wiping out his neglected language abilities, and his hosts had been therefore avoiding him for a double reason. He choked and wheezed and coughed and produced buckets of snot which a king-size box of tissues on his knees could scarcely accommodate. They seemed to have somehow approached the periphery of long-suffering hospitality. Rob wouldn't have been surprised if Mathéo had wanted to push him out of the car at speed on L'Autoroute de l'Est.

They stayed overnight in a large grey stone house in the Ardennes, a hameau where his wife had grown up, which also gave an impression of being presided over by an ancient municipal order. It had a well scrubbed look, an elegant chateau, and traces of Flemish influence in the architecture, Mathéo said, although it reminded Rob of the more well-preserved parts of the English North and Midlands. Rob leafed through Martine's childhood books in her ancient comfortable room.

The following morning they swooped into Charleville for a whirlwind recap of a past that was still palpably twitching. It had already infected Rob, racking him with convulsive sneezing and coughing fits as they approached, places familiar from long ago swimming up in a hallucinatory blur as Mathéo climbed up to and pivoted past his childhood home – a whitewashed house with green blinds, a whitewashed wall, a concrete garden with narrow strips of flowerbeds, in a row of similar houses.

This whole area of a few dozen linked streets seemed to be the essence of France somehow, because it was the first example he'd seen: a baked-out-in-the-sun appearance, a sort of weathered, improvised feeling about it, of just waking up, the newer housing on the opposite hill scattered and coloured like child's bricks, even though this was all completely untrue and they were a long way from any Mediterranean sun. They passed the corner café, the tabac, and the volleyball courts. They were just things to be found in a part of France he happened to have visited, but he hung on doggedly to such central definitions, while Mathéo – who knew, since he owned an elderly Labrador bitch – better than to try and dislodge his friend's ineradicable impressions, merely shrugged them away.

They turned down the steep hill where Mireille used to live. Rob had drunk a glass there with her parents in a small living room filled with gypsy-style ornaments. Modest, friendly people. Mireille, the pretty girl of whom Mathéo had said mockingly, "She plays with car tyres in the street."

The whole area had a roughly hand-painted appearance calling up the forties, the early fifties, working-class, lower middle-class, house-proud: a network of roads Rob had wandered around for hours when he'd lived there, pausing to examine bowed rusty tubular iron loops planted in a concrete wall, drinking it all in, trying to retain some essence of the place and why its skewed ordinariness gave him pleasure.

They passed out along the indifferent road skirting the beautiful estate. Rob was briefly shown a dream landscape for the last time, torn off his eyeballs with considerable pain as he looked out through his passenger window, unable to connect, huddling in his own snivelling skin, hiding from it all as they passed though Place des Droits de l'Homme, and entered Quai Rimbaud from the far end; on their right the cindered boules courts no longer existed along a stretch of ancient town wall, les vieux had all apparently died, and to their left the Meuse unexpectedly appeared with an elegant squirm, an eddy of brown light with a cloak of weed flung over its shoulder, a green caul drawn over half its width so that it turned, a Moebius strip, a murmuration; the river's green snake, bordered by flies, crawling past them as they plunged along its length, past what had been Le Rimbaud, and the ancient tumbledown house where the old woman had lived, the very old woman who knew Arthur Rimbaud, who had failed to come to the door when Mathéo called politely through the letterbox, a woman who would have remembered nothing.

Rob recognized the old, crazily sloping concrete benches upon which you could only perch uncomfortably on the edge for a few minutes, or lounge back and look up at the sky, gaped at by quizzical passersby. The trees were large and indiscreet, densely planted and packed full of rustling, concealing leaves. Not many streetlights, but he was sure there had been once. A sunny day. This time Mathéo was determined to hammer on the door of the past until it opened wide and admitted him. Rob melted down in his flu symptoms, sniffing at an open window like a dog in transit, as his friend's frustration mounted at his hometown's customary pig-headedness.

First stop was Rouget de Lisle, the secondary school. They sat in the car outside the low buildings, linked by a semi-covered walkway down which they had all scuttled long ago. M. Klein, Mlle. Desroches, Mrs Ford, and the delightfully eccentric history teacher who had lived in the new flats and invited them in to drink a special liqueur and listen to his Mistinguett records. J'ai fumé de l'Eucalyptus. Mathéo was absolutely certain this man had been a pervert, but could offer no evidence, he just knew. Charming, thought Rob. That's what you got for inviting a few boys around, for being friendly and hospitable to English visitors. Mathéo's version of the ugly truth.

Mathéo wanted to drive out to Hameau des Chênes, to try and visit Agathe's mother, who still lived there according to the town directory. Rob remembered her as a small, ineffectual woman, cowering in the shadow of her ebullient husband, but at least she had survived him. Rob had found this out by Googling Agathe's name and discovering her father's obituary in *L'Ardennais*, along with a note that his youngest daughter had predeceased him. He had known Agathe was dead, but he had devoured this report of her celebrated father's demise, a slender connection to his own past. He only wished she had lived to bury the bastard.

On the way out there, before Charleville ended and the road opened out, there was a small bridge Rob didn't remember, with a small tree-lined stream running under it. Mathéo stopped the car for a moment so they could look along the path beside this stream. It led all the way to Mont Olympe, he explained, and once he and Rob and Agathe had walked along there on a hot summer day with a picnic basket, he thought. Rob could recall none of this, but Mathéo seemed to be watching their adolescent backs disappear into the distance towards Mont Olympe.

Mont Olympe, a steep wooded hill on the far bank of the river, above the camping. Rob remembered walking along some old canals on the outskirts of town; it was the day he had learned the word *écluse*, lock, and for some reason it had stuck, formed a small gate in his mind. This was further along, up behind Mont Olympe, and he wondered if this stream ran from up there. Mathéo said he thought it did somehow. But it must have been another day, another walk perhaps. He was unsure whether Agathe had been there or not. Raoul he did remember, usually present on all other jaunts. Mathéo had arranged to meet up with Raoul, once his closest friend, although no academic competitor, in the Place Ducale.

They crept in through the estate of larger dwellings where Agathe's family had lived, older now but still imposing. Rob recognized Agathe's house as they rolled up to the gate, mainly for the large garage door in the ground floor. He had no wish to see Agathe's mother; it would be an excruciating experience to be sure for both of them. He wanted to flee immediately. Mathéo got out of the car, but the sign by the doorbell had been torn out. They looked past the gate, but the house had a deserted look. There was plainly nobody home. Agathe's mother had died here. He wondered about her sisters, her younger brother. Had they looked after the old woman?

Rob remembered discussing the common market with her father in order to prove he was an intelligent boy, and Agathe and he bathing together once when everyone was out, and a deckle-edged black and white photograph taken beside the tall fence in the back garden, of himself in a blue bow-tie and a striped cotton blazer, long centre-parted hair, and a huge happy grin to be there. Still the same would-be pop star. Its small size and old-fashioned format meant she had taken it on her tiny plastic camera, her little brother's, and specified these prints to some ancient pharmacist she had located. The same edges were found on the first photograph of herself she had ever sent to him. It was years since he had found it again, slid it out of a faded letter in her schoolgirl's handwriting, around three years old, smiling out at him in swimming costume from the bottom of a slide at the seaside. He had slid them all away for good long ago, and had no wish to remember them now. Nevermore. Repose dans la gloire, mademoiselle.

Mathéo was willing to give up fairly quickly and drive back into town to meet Raoul, but he thought it had been worth a try. She would have been delighted to see old *p'tits amis* of her daughter, of course. Agathe. Ga-ga, ta-ta. Rob's whole body seemed to be weeping, trying to expel his memories all at once; he grabbed another handful of tissues and tried to mop himself down. Mathéo was quietly contemptuous of his weakness; he had seen it all before and overridden it with no special qualms. Besides, it was just as hard for him. You had to face up to these things – it was good for you.

As they sped across the fields back to town Rob managed to catch a further glimpse of the barely trodden path beside the stream that perhaps led back to *les écluses*, to the locks, to their opening, to Agathe. Mathéo, seeing him trying to look, started talking about how run-down the place seemed to him now. There had been no economic miracle of any kind for the Ardennes, and outside the scrubbed up, refurbished streets in the tourist-orientated centre, it was plain that a lot of the people weren't well off and the buildings they lived in were in ill-repair. Charleville rubbed along somehow, perhaps it was a dead end town for some but Rob thought they would probably have to admit it had is points.

They parked in the little square beside the old library where Arthur Rimbaud had written so disparagingly about elderly librarians, or perhaps in those days it had been a school from whose first floor classroom he had stared out into the sun. But, Rob wondered, had Arthur heard the same pretty eighteenth century melody assembling itself painstakingly day after day? He had been surrounded by the chaos of war, corpses of dead Prussian and French soldiers littered countryside which had been a strategic site of wholesale slaughter in two subsequent world wars, this gentle, half-enchanted place where, as teenagers, Mathéo and Agathe and himself had wandered about with their chocolate cake, their picnic baskets, mobylettes and overcoats and small cameras, their guitars, in a land overlaid by municipal grids, safe from harm except at the tusks of marauding sangliers banished by now to a few profitable farm-corrals in the surrounding forest.

They ate a boar-free hot dog from a van. Mathéo led him halfway across the bridge to Mont Olympe only to tell some irritating story about how one of Agathe's sisters … They stopped at the midpoint and turned back to get to the Place Ducale to meet Raoul at the appointed hour. The green river of memory moved sluggish beneath them, small boats and barges clung to its banks; Rob glanced down at the tiny narrow islet beside the museum, la jette from which a boy had once launched his frail, homemade craft into the sad, scented twilight.

As they strode towards their rendezvous, Mathéo stopped short in the middle of an alley, pointed triumphantly over a high stone wall into a secluded courtyard adjoining some tall old houses. "And in there" he said, "it's where, in Les Poètes de Sept Ans, he has bitten the little Indian girl on the buttocks."

Raoul, when they found him in the square, hadn't changed a jot. He was still the curious boy to whom Rob had explained the lyrics of White Rabbit. Looking a little older, but then the same could also be said of Mathéo. Rob wondered if he seemed to them the same idiot they had once known in passing, if at all. Raoul was a nice, unassuming man, olive-skinned, Spanish-looking. Unlike his friend he hadn't fallen far from the tree. He'd married his childhood sweetheart, whom Rob remembered, and now he had sole care of their daughter in a village a few kilometres away from Charleville.

Raoul worked as a teaching assistant. He also made money out of selling records from a stall in the town's indoor market brocante, or sometimes from racks under the arches here on the Place Ducale. He still liked the English and American rock music of his youth, and whilst he spoke little of the language he understood a lot through music. Although simultaneous multiple points of reference didn't always made for easy conversation, for him the stars were still the stars and that was something. He knew the names, the tunes and the life histories of every American, English or French musician who ever picked up a guitar and warbled on les vinyls.

Today the square was denuded, hosed down, and bisected at several points by incident tape. There had been no incident so far but a small police car was circling to ensure that none took place. There were flimsy, box-like contraptions, sort of cars, also floating slowly around, mobylettes of the future. The statue of Charles de Gonzague, the town's founder, which had once raised its angry sword towards Paris from the centre of the square, had been replaced by an ordinary, boring fountain. Nothing too incendiary. The Duke, he was informed, had been exiled a few years previously to a small island in the pedestrian shopping precinct.

Rob bought a few more cold remedies, but he could tell by the defeated expression in the eyes of the helpful young woman behind the counter that none were going to be strong enough to make an impression on whatever he was suffering from. Back at their outside table he alternated swigs of cold beer with deep draughts from a bottle of sugary cold syrup from which all the life-enhancing drowsiness had been removed. Mathéo and Raoul rattled on as though they'd parted only yesterday. Rob had difficulty following their conversation.

"Oh, do you remember than incredible festival of Algerian pop music here?" he managed to ask during a short lull. "It was amazing. The whole place was taken over by Algerians, a big stage, big stars, doing this stuff like you never heard before."

"Oui, bien sûr." Raoul spoke seriously. "I remember this well. It was great. It was another time. It can never happen anymore."

"There used to be a lot of Algerian stalls on the market," Rob remembered. "Sometimes street performers."

"Not now," Raoul said. "They dare not."

"It's the law?"

"No," he explained. "They would be in danger. The police stop Algerians from coming into town. For their own protection. They have to stay in their own areas, in Mézières. It's the same all over France, I think." Raoul looked sad, a bit ashamed to be reporting these facts.

"I haven't heard the clock yet!" Rob said suddenly. "Does it still play the same tune?"

"Non," said Raoul. "It is broken, out of order." He laughed quietly. "But they say they are going to fix it soon."

Mathéo looked away over the hosed-down, vacant square. As least it was still standing, surrounded by those tall, elegant narrow-shouldered buildings which Charles de Gonzague had commissioned; a model town, a planned town constructed on design principles of classical order and harmony, not perhaps a new kind of polis, as they had claimed, but it and other French towns like it had endured, would continue, as far as he was concerned, forever. He didn't want any kind of an ending. He wanted a continuation, a follow up, a next move. Depending of course on what it might turn out to be. The central thing always was to defend this French way of life which had taught the world so much.

They set out together for another walk around Charleville – past Charles de Gonzague on his new plinth, past the municipal sprawl around the post office, a cafe that had once been called Le Gonzague, a florist's shop he remembered, cascading with fresh blooms; another old shop, immaculately preserved, selling old fashioned children's clothes, sandals which looked like they were designed in the thirties or earlier, but were obviously fresh and new, still in style.

There were several Rimbaud vape-emporia, a large brasserie which had once been a cinema where they had seen the French equivalent of a Carry-on film, a comedy with fully exposed breasts, and a hatch opposite Monoprix where you could still buy frites. L'Univers, a café near the station, immortalized by the town bard, was a place where they had got drunk on pastis as teenagers. Nowadays a no-go area, Mathéo and Raoul insisted, although it looked sleepy enough. Mathéo said there would certainly be trouble if they went inside. Guaranteed. Instead they took a photograph underneath the ever youthful bust of A.R. in the Sunday bandstand park where he had scored Merde à Dieu on the benches. The base of his statue was engraved on each face with a different achievement: Poèmes, Les Illuminations, Une Saison en Enfer, Explorations en Afrique. Rob looked particularly old and bloated and terminally ill. He didn't want to be photographed dying under a statue of fucking Arthur Rimbaud. This picture, they had all agreed, was one to instantly delete.

Heading back to the centre they passed the tall Church of Saint-Rémy, from the broad steps of which he had once rescued a sparrow whose tail feathers had been clawed out by a cat, he supposed. The bird had hopped around his attic squawking for hours until Rob had been forced to return it to the church steps, to its proper fate. Now they were in front of the Rozoy's door in Rue du Petit Bois, the heavy ancient wooden door of a castle, the small door set within it through which Agathe had once lifted her mobylette now locked fast, brown paint still flaking, and Mathéo was banging on it determinedly with his large fist until it shook and boomed. There were several bells and Mathéo rang each one, a good long blast, shouting his violent polite enquiries into a dead intercom, but there was no response of any kind from inside.

Anyone who happened to be in there obviously knew better than to answer the bell. "Leave it!" Rob called.

155

Raoul looked at Rob in agreement. "It is a crazy thing," he said.

Both of them stood back and watched Mathéo until his strange fit passed.

"While we are here," Mathéo said over his shoulder, finally turning away."We should do this."

Finally it was time to say goodbye and climb into Mathéo's car for the fast drive back to Paris.

On the way out they stopped at the cemetery, which was closing its gates in half-an-hour, and looked briefly at Rimbaud's and his mother's graves, restored now, tarted up, railings repainted. There were none of the notes by teenage poets Rob had once seen there, so similar to Jim Morrison's grave in Père Lachaise, where youthful outbursts and plastic dinosaurs continued to pile up next to the glass of whisky and the unlit spliff positioned temptingly in a Ricard ashtray. Rob didn't blame Mathéo for being disdainful of such nonsense, although it appealed to him that poetry's favourite teenager was as enduringly popular as any dead American rock star.

Rob would have been happy to die in that car .He was completely unbothered by any inconvenience this might cause Mathéo, who in his turn was preoccupied at that moment by his own memories: of his late sister who had at one time worked on a dodgem ride in Charleville, had passed on worn out singles by Johnny Hallyday, Sylvie Vartan and Les Chats Sauvages, which Rob remembered listening to with him, one after another; memories of his mother and father, older brothers he never saw, a retired gendarme and an industrial paint salesman, who had no understanding of his job and no sense of its importance. Education, at least Mathéo's version of it, was purely for the benefit of the snobs. They earned proper money and were just as good.

Rob remembered Mathéo's sister with warmth. Now he remembered suddenly that one of the mechanics in Mézières had been an African. He used to prance around the workshop whenever reggae came on the radio, holding a broom across his chest like a bass guitar, well liked by the other mechanics. "He is funny, Jean-Christophe," said Mathéo's sister one day as they'd driven home from the garage in her old silver Peugeot 305.

As they now drove back to Paris at high speed he told Rob about his Belgian father, who had grown up in an orphanage, joined the army and struggled hard all his life to make a decent showing for his family. Mathéo had managed to trace distant relatives in Charleroi and Brussels. They were, in his opinion, the Belgians, a beautiful people. His father had known something about how to live, about what was the right thing to do in any situation – Mathéo was grateful for whatever in the way of a reasonable outlook he had succeeded in passing on to him, the youngest by ten years, the cleverest of his four children.

Rob sank into his misery, but there had been a moment on a street they had walked along rapidly, looking up at the row of houses he didn't properly remember, when he had almost willed himself to catch sight of Agathe, still moving around behind the green, rusty shutters of a room they'd once shared.

And that, apparently, had been the end of France. Rob had only ever been a visitor, after all, a carrier away of sideways impressions, and now he was not even attuned: a permanent exile from a country that had never existed, the name of a nervous disease, strewn in the ruins of the Bataclan, soon rebuilt, and all the unreconstitutable bodies had vaporised, drifted away into the black hole of the past. That, he thought, is what Raoul might have said, if he had known him better.

Twenty

Daddy-long-legs arrived every year to cluster in great tremulous armies around the entrance to the flats. Sitting targets in their tens of thousands, the sheer numbers were obscene, disgusting when you contemplated them. And they just sat there doing nothing, their very fragility an offence, an invitation to kill in large quantities.

"They don't live long – let them live," said Mr Herd, the cantankerous old caretaker whom the kids goaded and tormented. There had been a certain antagonism behind his words, which made you think this stooped, elderly stick of a man wished he had a pirate gun himself with which to splatter a few boys.

Rob understood this and stopped splattering them with his rubber-suckered pirate gun. He felt ashamed and always let them live after that, noticing their gangling beauty in flight.

Already curling inwardly from the slaughter, he felt its nauseating excess, its logistical impossibility. Reloading the pirate gun with its bolt, pushing down on the spring until it clicked, had made each of their deaths individual, an execution of the entire race, if that were possible, a cull which had soon accelerated to a frenzied merciless pace. After this he had left the insects in their own place, and hadn't wanted to know anything much about the mechanical simplicity and warrior virtues of the ant, the recklessness of the wasp, but always respected those lost stately bees who sometimes blindly applied to him for guidance.

Yeah. It had been doddery old Herd who had stopped him, he remembered now, and his mother who had explained why. Herd also had a right to live, unmolested. Rob himself had understood all this already, by way of his passionless mechanical execution of the daddy-long-legs tribe. Zulu had recently been on television. Providence would say God had provided daddy-long-legs to teach boys this lesson. Providence referred everything back to humanity: it was an egotistical line of thought. *Tipulidae.* Flitting about the house in summer, gangly, brown daddy longlegs is familiar to many of us. The larvae can become pests of lawns and crops, but the adults are a valuable food source for many birds. God provided them for the birds. The common crane fly: a harmless second cousin to the mosquito.

By now the snow-bees had bombed the words out of their mouths, covered up the world with a substance as opaque as liquid paper. Ghosting mistakes, leaving a clean matt surface. But underneath was an even worse mess than before. Large numbers of people had been killed, and soon … soon what? Would they hatch too? He thought of the Dartmoor ponies, all dead and buried, no longer peeking shyly out from behind their wild fringes, not changing into anything, they didn't need to.

But who, he knew they would be asking at the end of the day, is this Rob Goddard? A weird kettle of fish, hard to pin down. Does he like to watch, like Andy Warhol? Is he just a cold jellyfish who stings when you touch him? Is he pure cod, doughty haddock or rock salmon: a dog fish by any other name? He would have liked to oblige but it died out long ago, long ago behind the temporary hoarding that came down where the bus station was demolished and presently rebuilt, so that survivors, if any, could only gape past it at what once was there. Rob hoped they were living well in that drowning town of a certain uncertain charm he had left behind. People had a way of saying a name – and saying, Oh he (or she) was a long way back, a long time ago, but for Rob that was hardly ever the case.

You might see me on the corner, he thought, but it won't be true. I won't be there any longer and nor will you. Pass on, vaporize, chase out the last tendrils of this particular unhappy being of people smoke and delaying tactics (or his own valuable moon shot, kicking a ball around with a student outside a kitchen in Avon Way, trying to make a sort of connection with a younger self, who wasn't, that was it – always worth a go but always futile. You're weird, not like us. No, he had to argue. I am not. Yes, a little weird I most certainly am. Mad as a starched flare.

He remembered a colour photo of Mcleod standing above the railway tracks in the tall grass behind the crooked house twisted by a Victorian earthquake, stripped to the waist, his chest thin and bony and pale to the point of translucency, standing in an orange light, grass waist high. Around him at his extended fingertips dragonflies were feeding. At a party once he wore dark green nail varnish and a stage Regency jacket, and was humiliated by the host for his ludicrous appearance, which was only freakish and embarrassing to the other guests. But he wore the nail varnish, dark bottle green, until it chipped and wore off completely, finally picked off flake by flake, during his shifts at the hospital, Essex Hall.

Repetition – recurring memories and scenes, swamping earlier versions in an ill-matched palimpsest. All memory seemed to be like this: obsessive, just the recurrence of ordinary things that are there: a man who can't let go of an old girlfriend, a pigeon settling on the same ledge. We tried to rub it out, but it came back. We turned this automatic quality of neural experience into meaning if we could – but eventually we knew that we would have to blot it out. You will remember them until you can remember no longer, long after memory itself has come to seem pointless, until it frays, capsizes and turns to the darkest phantasmal firmament. All the same, you remembered them better than the traces of your own toenails, your dead skin, sluiced away blood and mucus.

Trouble is, there weren't any more people left, not like them. Wouldn't it be good if … wouldn't it be good if all this had been agreed: if we already knew everything. He was so relieved they were still alive, still conscious, in a way, and so grateful to them for giving themselves to him, for offering him so much good and bad advice, for being so right about his many failings.

Thisness = *haecceity* = specificity of beings, their individual qualities. Aquinas said the processes of ordinary being could only be said to be 'analogous' with God's, whose being is fundamentally other to that of the creation. But Duns Scotus reasoned on behalf of a univocity of being: existence may all be named as the same thing. Creation is part of god, an aspect, a showing forth of Divinity, but is of course finite rather than infinite. That's why Hopkins feels able to find all his homely comparisons, to find his likenesses in unlikeness: because with child-like literal-mindedness he sees the Almighty's relation to his creation can always found to be paternal. His kingfisher sonnet explained all this, his nature journals with their detailed mathematical drawing instructions, elaborate this unity of created beings, their relatedness, and evidence of God's designs. Good = being. God is visible everywhere. Merely the subject of an analogy, he is the bald opposite invulnerable term.

In Hopkins' case it had been there from the start, in his prize-winning boyhood poem 'The Escorial', in which the cruel martyrdom of Saint Lawrence by burning over a gridiron is according to Manley's books sublimated architecturally into a grandly beautiful building, a World Heritage Site, an official monument to royal sanctity, designed by Toledo, headquarters of Christianity, and in a less ghoulish, more casual effort Gerard had dashed off what seemed to be his first dragonfly poem, written after observing a ripe nymph opening and the being hidden within emerge painfully from its dun armour.

He played his wings as though for flight;
They webb'd the sky with glassy light.

He had been a persuasive writer at first blush: *she schools the flighty pupils of her eyes.* Indeed she does, her first charges. He is full of spring and restraint. His whole life's battle had been to perfect those early poems, to build on them, to lift his powerful native insight clear of clichéd language and diction.

Rob wasn't going to give in to easy despair, that would be … too easy. He wasn't going to jeopardise his precious humanity. He'd never say 'no more' like cowardly Stuart Mcleod, he'd never repudiate the gift of life. He could always hope day would come again, which it obviously would, and for other problems he could always wish, always hope for a better day.

But why was the Almighty always planting his enormous boot on poor Gerard's neck? Smacking him down to earth with a great fist? Looking hungrily at his bruised bones? Blowing him around in mighty gusts from heaven when all he wanted to do was get the fuck out of there?

Ireland and Liverpool were, to Hopkins, precincts of Hell. He just wanted to shuck it off, his old dutiful skin, and sow his beautiful seed somewhere, retire to the country perhaps, but somehow he managed to work on in the fields and kiss the rod of endless duty. His heart still rose up in praise, but of whom? And why? Perhaps, he allowed himself to think, there were two forces at work and play within him – the great one who had created him, and the false God of his own desires which always kicked back in. Poor old patient God couldn't altogether get the best of him. Hopkins could neither triumph nor surrender. He could be nothing, do nothing but drag himself back into the ring for another fierce drubbing.

The faults we find in others are our own. We accuse them of things of which we ourselves are often guilty, but more so, even more so. Hopkins knew this well. Sometimes he felt he was probably the worst person in the world. And he knew it was only going to get worse, worse than any pathetic grief he felt he might have experienced. This pain would have sadistically learned from his earlier suffering how to make itself worse, an agonising virus that mutates in order to become more effective. Where was God's comfort for all of this? Or mother Mary's consolation? They'd fallen silent long ago, so that his endless piteous pleas straggled like a herd of lost sheep unheard over the hills, or just clung together bleating unappealingly somewhere. It was always the same old complaint he had, the world-sorrow of all creatures which battered him like a horseshoe on an anvil, longing for some dispensation he didn't deserve, some exemption from suffering that the almighty was doing his level best to load on him tenfold.

All he could do was beg almighty God for a fucking break, a lull, something like the tea-break in hell where for five minutes they were allowed to stand in excrement only up to their necks. But God was not so merciful as the Devil, because there was always such important work to be done. In his mind he had been climbing a mountain that led only to a sheer cliff above a fathomless ocean, and now he was hanging there in agony. But he was too weak to endure this punishment for long. All he could do was creep away and hide under the reliable rock of sleep. Death ended everything, and every night he welcomed the rehearsal of death that curtailed a suffering creature's tormented interval of wakefulness. Poor sad fucker. Disillusioned! He never admitted it though. Rob admired that stubborn quality in Hopkins. It was his own attitude writ larger.

Rob was travelling on a train of mixed rolling stock, of couple-colour, ploughing onwards through the too early night. First dark and then light, a chameleon, a flashing thing: now red and blue, now blue and green. Rob had never been able to get Stuart Mcleod into focus. Now he observed him more exactly and saw a sad, dark bluish-green. That's the way you always were, he thought, you sad dissector of your own joys.

Twenty-One

Stuart said a last goodnight, buttoned his grubby orange lumberjack jacket and headed out into the sharp night air of Colchester. He was well insulated by alcohol. His friends had practically had to force him out through the door. He'd obviously missed the last bus but didn't really mind walking four miles to the village on the other side of the university.

He was feeling warm and discombobulated from five pints of lager. He didn't mind walking. In fact, he preferred it, on the whole. That night he found everything funny and he could laugh as much as he wanted on the road to get his head down for a few hours before his early bus took him back to Essex Hall. It was ridiculously, ridiculously ... he thought of the hospital bosses in their sleek vehicles, paid for out of his wage packet, while he and those of his section he could mobilize personnel the picket line and handed out their leaflets to a few unsympathetic passersby down on the station roundabout at the bottom of the hill.

What was so fucking funny about it? He knew damned well they were going to lose; that it was likely the entire hospital – a former station hotel – would be privatised, then completely phased out as all the elderly misconfined virgins with phantom pregnancies died off one by one, those hopeless lives and the sins which had led to their life-sentence incarcerations forgotten. Nobody had ever given a hoot about them. The managers snarled past in their Mondeos, unassailable land yachts whose captains occasionally glanced to port at striking nursing assistants and auxiliary staff as if they were a cluster of blow flies hovering around something dead at the hospital entrance.

Now they were back at work, industrial action completed to nil effect, except it livened things up briefly. It was a legitimate excuse to doss, like union work, because one thing was certain, he fucking hated his job. One day it would be over and they would all be living better than in the draughty Victorian wards, with their ancient iron beds, processions of Goya-like refugees in thin over-laundered nightdresses migrating from one end of a ward to another. Blind-led, clinging together as if inching along in terror on a terrifying mountain ledge. They would all be in bungalows, on the Turner Village model, or something, in a future nobody had envisaged – although already planned higher up – in economically independent units.

Meanwhile the nursing staff could only try to defend their livelihoods, for which shop stewards, if they wanted to do it, had a limited amount of support, in the knowledge that really they were pissing in the wind, which the residents of the hospital didn't know how not to do, their steam rising from the laundry tower to rise and mingle with airborne crematorium dust and fall as weeping rain on the urine-swept platforms of North Station. Heh heh.

He walked down through New Town, past those attractive crescents of terraced billets such as he would never own, past other closing pubs – The Artilleryman, The Royal Mortar, The George – stumbling along the fence of the darkened park, and as the hill began to fall away down to the Hythe, Mcleod began to run in a headlong, gangling, windmilling way, laughing aloud to himself as he soared off the surface of this shabby wee planet and into the higher crystal sphere of the upper air.

Everything was babbling through him – everything he couldn't say in political arguments, intellectual debates – they just didn't get it really, never could, and neither could he … happiness? He hated the whole stupid fucking concept. He'd never known anybody who was happy, or wanted to be – except Rob, gone to London, who thought the utmost of happiness but would never get it. Stuart knew this was the truth, absolutely, but he couldn't say why. Only this was happiness to him, a few drinks and taking off from the surface of the earth at a high skip back home from the pub … and then he fell over. He'd missed his flying feet on take-off, his legs crumpled under him, and he was tumbling downhill – and a lamp post detained him like an abruptly restraining constable, and he slid down it.

Stuart picked himself up: condition, groggy. He stumbled against a wall, took inventory of the damage. Knee of jeans torn, wrist bruised, starting to throb … was that a lump on his head? He was literally seeing stars, which weren't literally stars right enough … Alpha Centauri, Betelgeuse. Weekend removal, he remembered. He was supposed to be out of the crooked house by the weekend, when Femi and Jean were coming down – not to see him really, but to see each other for a weekend, oblivious to his sobbing plight.

He felt a bit soberer, very briefly, and hobbled on. He was shocked. His knee hurt but he carried on as best he could, over the Hythe bridge, past the culverted Colne, the lock beyond, the little old pub there which stood alone there, a rickety Gothic signal-box just away from the level crossing. It hurt him to walk but he had no choice, no option but onward, onward. Standing still wisnae really an option. He'd been hiding from this, he knew he had, but there you are. It was never easy for him to make plans, let alone to carry them out. His ability to make plans had led him to where he was today. He laughed and laughed again, shouting a few words that weren't words at all, well hardly, he wis fucked, in pain, but fast-walking did the trick right enough, loosened ye up, and the great ragged gulps of night air helped him rise up above his sotted state. To mount into the bald air once more with a clearer, an eagle's beady eye about him.

As he turned onto Greenstead Road he looked up at a new Benson and Hedges advert freshly pasted on a giant billboard at the corner. Which reminded him: he smoked. He pulled his own packet of Dunhill from his lumberjack's pocket and rattled it unsteadily. There was ought within. He pulled out one of the long slender cylinders and placed it between his bleeding lips, where a flame fired it easily. Stuart swayed like a chimpanzee besotted at a great tumbling waterfall of signification, contemplating the new billboard. A tiny packet of B&H nestled in a jewelled egg, a Fabergé egg if he had known the fucking name of it. Roland fucking Barthes. The cunts had been reading that cunt Barthes alright. Eh eh. Barthes had been one of his early favourites. He swung his bag across his narrow shoulders and hobbled on down towards the roundabout. Deserted at this time of night but for the odd minicab traversing the ancient wall of the estate: ACAB: COPPERS LIED. FREE … and then the tall, perfectly executed letters of a name known to nobody. This inscription was his proudest moment. His name died forever on your lips.

He began to chant to himself to assist the rhythm of his walking, his mechanical jerky gait, concentrating because when he didn't his feet would shoot out in opposite directions, towards the mown borders of the well-tended university pavement, which was lit in such a way as to falsely suggest some kind of fucking civilisation went on there, and a song burst from his cracked orange lips.

Stuart's pace slowed as the brooding congeries of dark, twisted energy and black tower wind approached, froth in the night of goodness when he had once transmuted nay transubstantiated intae womanhood right before the amazed eye of Malcolm Rivers. He couldae had that fucker right then and there if the acid had been a wee bit stronger. Next time. He laughed. "Next time!!" he shouted at the top of his lungs as he passed the dark, shrouded towers dotted with lights. "NEXT FUCKING TIME!!!" the words failed to echo across the hidden campus squatting there between two shouldering hillocks, the hexagonal hub of his days for all these fucking useless years. What was he good for anyway though? Just this. This was it really, was good, the best. Shouting yer fuckin' head away on the boundary road of the university.

How very fucking much he'd loved that fucking place. Still did. It was his own personal discovery, a slice of future he had staked out for himself, just to live near it was enough, or had been, using the library still for his browsing in theoretical sociology, anthropology, piss-demonology, what have you. He knew he was a failure alright alright, but so fucking what? He was in his proper place, cradling, a dark womb, humming with thousands of unlived lives, lives in transit. It was a bit like living beside an airport.

Perhaps they'd give him a job there one day. Anything. Cleaner. He would have loved to be a cleaner at the university. Quite rightly they never wouldae had him. He was such a useless fuck up after all. And Rob. He loved Rob. But Rob should shut the fuck up forever about what he or anybody else should do. He didn't fucking know, that was all. He just didnae ken he was fucking born, that guy. But he was going to have problems, he'd find it out soon enough.

He slanted these thoughts away down the long sloping meadow, banished them into nameless mud, into the darkness, into the muddy Colne. He tramped on silently for a while, to a beat. *One step forward, two step backward – down inna Babylon.* But as the University lights retreated, he started on an Irish rebel song or two. End to end, howled them at the top of his voice all the way up around the bend, past the Lamb and Flag. There were men from Dublin and from Cork, Fermanagh and Tyrone. But the leader was a Limerick man, Sean South from Garryowen. Seamus Twomey was exhumed for fresh battle on the village's perimeter. *An' a big burd drapped doon from the sky, an' it took away the boys...* Stuart sang this with stony conviction all the way down past Ivy Bank, where behind her bedroom curtain Monika heard him approach and recognised his slurring, incomprehensible tones.

She remained motionless as he passed, noticing his voice grew louder as he looked up at the window, but marched on along the green and lovely lanes of Killeshandra down to his rest at the bottom of the village. A nutcase, she thought, laughing, a lovely mad person. Like her father, come to that. Like her sister. He made her laugh and she had a warm feeling about him, that he was at any rate harmless. A good friend, if you didn't mind his popping round for a cup of tea. What became of people like him anyway? She supposed they carried on being whoever they were, however they could.

Outside in the darkness, Mcleod plunged on past her with barely a glance to left or right, down to the bottom of the dead-end village where his roomy room was to be taken from him by the landlady in a fairly short amount of time. Mrs Everett was selling the crooked house, his base, his home.

...These were aspects of his friend which Rob often glossed over, and in himself ... he always found the residue of a point of view in which none of this stuff had actually happened, or if it had it didn't matter much. It had appeared that only one of them would be able to escape – not that there had been only one available place aboard the actual salvation train but that only one of the two friends had been there at the station to get on board.

"You always seem to get through at the last moment," Mcleod said. "You pull it together somehow. Not me."

And he hadn't been far wide of the mark. Rob also remembered that, as years wore on, tacit no-go areas had grown up where armoured pigs patrolled, a this-is-yours, that-is-mine parcelling up of interests and intellectual goods between him and Stuart. Science fiction, for example, had belonged to Stuart. In Bristol once, where he'd been on a recce with Femi who was planning to move with him to St Paul's, Rob bought presents for Stuart. Two issues of a science fiction journal and a copy of *Monday Begins on Saturday* by Arkady and Boris Strugatsky. He maintained his friend's spirits, his addictions, even as he prepared to move away from him, perhaps by way of an apology or because Stuart had once passed him a copy of Delany's *The Einstein Intersection* and said, "Read this!"

Mcleod had been his red-haired android, and he would never let go of him.

"Why am I necessary for this idyll?" Stuart asked him when Rob had tried to explain how he would like to live his life. "You could do that sort of stuff anywhere. If you're going to let a woman like Monika slip through your fingers, you're totally fucked. Monika was for you! Ye fucking idiot."

Rob knew she hadn't been for him at all. "There'll be others," he replied.

"Yeh, the wrong others," Stuart insisted. "Not classy people like Monika, women who've really got something to offer. You never seem to look ahead, Rob. All I can say is try it once or twice." He spoke wryly, bitterly. "See, you can do it too."

That silenced Rob. But what had Mcleod seen coming with all his phony scrying?

Stuart looked too far ahead, that's what Rob thought. He also thought Monika and Owen Johnson were ideally suited, and the fact that Owen had been shouldering his way in from the wings had been a good excuse to make an exit. He'd felt he was being magnanimous, offering them a portion of happiness of which he might have some to spare, seeing what had to happen. He'd never been surer of anything.

Midnight games of Alice in Wonderland chess played with enormous wooden pieces on an acid-inspired Dr Who set. Tripping through the early bluebell woods with Femi, threading through, up and over to the roofless ruined church at Alresford where she would relive being at her father's funeral beside a stranger's grave. There was nothing much like this place, and nothing to do with the rest of your life except remember it, to try and get back to those delusions and paranoias as the big man beside the artificial lake moved the levers that turned everything around and around in scribbled cartoon-strips, demented parodies of power run off on the S.U. machines. Diego Rivera meets the Fabulous Furry Freak Brothers.

But the students' union would never really out-manage Alfred Doughman, who only had to wait for the next contingent to sashay in through the turnstiles, and so it all seemed just a game, until the university dream folded itself away with the memories of the departed. Returned in the mouths of others, things you had been taught or once believed came to seem shallow and not worth pursuing in the first place. But no, Rob thought, you never forgot the things you read about.

One day it was always going to be crystalline and clear and all these granny-knots would be unpicked, resolved and redeemed into a great building. It was the Holy Ghost building which the snow-bees and the dragonfly-angels had been helping to construct since the beginning of time. The place had looked fairly ramshackle for a while, but that had been an illusion: in truth it was all taking shape, resolving into a design greater than any human attempt. Did this come out of some forgotten conversation? Did it matter anymore? Drifting threads of broken gossamer, discarded husks of nymphs, newly hatched squadrons of *odonata* lined up right now for their assigned tasks in heaven's relentless economy.

Twenty-Two

Axminster, when it came, was covered over by an all-encasing whiteness, a tunnel which bounced back the emissions of their pale blue heated filament, bathing the interiors of the carriages in a bright aquarium light, so there were no possibilities of any leanings out, paddle-wavings or whistle-blowings: none whatsoever. The train of couple-colour paused for a moment or two and moved on, but what began to occur as they rolled out of the not merely carpeted but completely engulfed settlement was even more singular.

Agathe noticed, glancing up, that the whole ceiling of the carriage seemed to have become slightly twisted out of shape. Then it was the walls: they buckled as if subject to tremendous pressure and torque, and whole nests of seats began to be popped out of position as rivets gave way. They were bucking and flying upwards as if with an intention of throwing the passengers into the aisle, onto the straining and splitting floor of the carriage. She screamed out in terror, reliving the last moments of her life.

Paul stood up with difficulty and stretched his arms out, as if to hold back the walls. Further down the carriage one of the double seats popped out of its mountings and cannoned into the ceiling. Strangely the lights were still blazing, then the whole carriage, the train itself, seemed to liquefy. The metal was bending more easily now, rather as if it's shape had never been particularly fixed, at least no more than dried-out plasticine, and now, heated or moistened, the carriage stretched out into longer shapes, melted and turned, until, in a final violent paroxysm, an ordinary train of mixed rolling stock dissolved and shot upwards from the track in a rotating fiery rocket, rising into the sky: a corkscrew of densely striated coloured light.

The five travellers instinctively reached out and joined hands to steady themselves, but this gesture soon became irrelevant as it was clear that their bodies had begun to shed substance. They could see through each other, but at the same time were disintegrating further, into clusters of dancing pinpricks of intense white light. Paul was reminded of a particularly spectacular laser show at an underground dance club he had once attended at the YMCA on the Tottenham Court Road. They were turning into eighties holograms. Half-formed thoughts were snatched away, and anyway he no longer had a mouth with which to utter them. All of them, still joined at the wrists they had clasped, shot upwards through the gaping roof of what had been the train, piercing the ceiling of the white tunnel (whose blue sheath had been turned off) and up into a clear, empty sky, glittering with bright stars.

Ursa Major, Orion, his sword dangling from his belt, Castor and Pollux, Betelgeuse, the fluctuating red giant on Orion's shoulder ... all far closer than he'd ever seen them before, looking through his brother's telescope. Stuart – now just an orange-reddish rhythm of irregular dots – felt a sense of liberation, of dissolution. Agathe had grown even taller, before separating out into a similar cluster of lights. Marie, hard, irreducible, appeared to resist this process for a short time, until she too exploded out of her dense ghost-matter into the dancing light-being which she, and all of them, in actuality, were.

The resultant star wheel, revolving around a scintillant Rob at high speed like spokes around a hub, shot up into the higher atmosphere; as they rotated faster they converged into a single spinning globe. This was composed of dark reflective fragments, held together by centrifugal forces. Now they seemed to have lost any sense of being distinct personalities, although it was impossible not to recognize some of the jumbled motes which tumbled together, discarded clothes tangled in a launderette, as belonging to one or the other of the friends. They were shards, jagged splinters, joined together but narrowly avoiding collision, as impersonally collective as a murmuration of starlings, and yet even the smallest fragment of Agathe gave off a certain distinctive note of baffled sorrow.

Marie buzzed with restless agitation. Paul was elusive, emollient, harmonically imprecise but with an undertow of ... whatever remained of Rob's mind didn't recognize what it was, perhaps a kind of hopeful passivity ... something from the person he'd known. The dispersed motes of his own tremulous being seemed magnetized by the others, to approach and be repulsed by them, to take on their jangling colours without having any proper identity of their own. Even in fragments he felt himself as a kind of binding agent between them, an instant and unreliable as super-glue. And the strongest field of all was Stuart's, a darkly savage melody, stubbornly dissonant, speaking itself in an unmistakable accent that declared its true character, abolishing all attempts to touch it in reassurance, incorporated only unwillingly, finally drowned out by the need for unity.

At a higher elevation the revolutions slowed, and the five beings again separated into four discrete clusters, revolving around a central pivot of whatever Rob had become in this centrifuge of light. Finally, they came to a halt, and although there was no furniture or voice of command to suggest it, they had all arrived in a closely-defined no space, a kind of courtroom, and were ranged around a central defendant, Rob. At last, with a crushing sense of his own stupidity – and prior guilt – he knew precisely what he was being accused of.

His trial didn't take place in words. There were no arguments of prosecution, no provision of a defence counsel. Here there was only evidence, presented by some dark invisible angel, and you couldn't really argue with it. The angel – or whatever it was – flashed imagery from one cluster of dots into the central core, from whence it was channelled out again, distributed down the four spokes from the hub, multiplying and gathering force, to be supplemented by a further shaft from the next cluster, until each had discharged its pulse of evidential imagery into his bursting heart. When this had been done he exploded in pain and recognition of his culpability. In one way or another he had been responsible for each of their deaths. Surely that didn't add up? And yet why did he feel so guilty? The proofs were obviously flawed!

But that didn't end the proceedings, not at all. There was more to come before the final verdict. The five light-beings hung in space in the precise configuration in which they had been placed. They submitted themselves to it, as they had to, robbed of volition out in the matrix of the eternal stars, but it was good for them nevertheless. This reflective process was known as the harmonizing, he seemed to know, a reconciliation which lay on the far side of truth and justice, imbrications of harmonies which layered us all together at our edges and made it possible to survive in concert, even though it also contained the root of human evil, of our brutal transgressions of nature, of melody, and the accent which had first aroused our pity, muffling its sharp particular cry. At last he heard their voices:

"You didn't love me, not really," Agathe hummed softly. "Not the way I loved you. It was all a game to you then, using me quickly, for your own pleasure."

171

"Remember when you slapped my face, so hard, in the corridor outside the disco. You hurt me. You enjoyed giving me pain." Marie spat the words into his paralysed brain. "You were no better than the filthy man who killed me. "Two of a kind."

"You pretended," Paul said gravely. "You pretended to be my friend."

"You were a fucking parasite, a self-indulgent blow-fly." Stuart laughed. Laughter in the court of heaven. "You saw me failing and you didn't give a shit."

"Be honest," they harmonized in his head, "you just didn't take us seriously. You didn't. Not really. And we didn't take you seriously either. Not at all. Arsehole."

Were these harsh, dismissive words the real voice of Almighty God? Only a miniscule spot of sin, perhaps, their shared fragment: but it was deadly original sin – the kind that had infected and destroyed an entire fucking planet.

The five travellers returned suddenly to consciousness with no immediate memories of what had occurred. They looked across at each other, They were back in the moving train, rumbling along fairly slowly now, a mundane conveyance, with no sign of anything out of the ordinary, except for the abating snowstorm they could now just about see through their windows. A lunar landscape.

The train was approaching Sugarford; this message crawled across the electronic display in the middle of the carriage: Rob's destination. His father would be waiting at home, as he had been last year, sitting in the small chair behind his walking frame. Rob's brother usually picked him up from the station, but he realized there was no possibility of that tonight. The sidecar-racing career of Florian Camatheus ended at Brands Hatch in 1965, he remembered. Nobody else remembered that, not anywhere. They would be snowed in without doubt. Jumping into an alternative time-stream for a moment, Rob climbed slippery iron steps to the skip labelled 'cardboard' at the recycling centre, and tossed in the small now empty grey box which had contained his father's ashes. His father's voice floated from the box as it drifted down, sounding in Rob's head. "We're alright now," he said mildly. "Together again. Not arguing anymore."

The train stopped, snow banked at the level of the windows. "Sugarford! Sugarford!" the guard called from an open door at the rear of the train, but he didn't wait any longer than usual for a passenger to get down. Rob half-rose in his seat, and sat back down. Wherever his ghosts were going, he was going with them. Exeter, at least as far as Exeter, because that had been the destination stamped on their tickets. The flag waved, the whistle blew. It was too late. The decision, if there had been one, had been made. The ghost train departed for Feniton, creeping along a miraculously cleared single track.

It was difficult to escape the immediate thought that everyone had been killed. No-one had survived, that was the overwhelming likelihood. As their gaze drifted back and forth from the windows to each other the same thought occurred to all of them. They imagined families trapped in their homes, impenetrable tons of ice dumped on top of them, planes smashed from the skies, motorway pile-ups, a mass grave as far as the eye could see. They were desolate, silent, baffled. And yet glimmerings of their celestial journey remained, the inhabitation hadn't left them, and they felt somehow purified, purposeful, although none of them spoke of this.

"It's the wrong kind of snow," Rob said suddenly. "It's not the kind that hurts anybody. It's the good snow, which heals and protects."

"You have to admit," Mcleod said. "There's a fuck of a lot of it."

"Maybe Bob Crow's out with a crack team of titanic track workers, digging people out, clearing it all away, on massive overtime," Paul suggested. His phone was still receiving a signal, and he'd read up on the deceased railway workers' leader following their conversation with the guard.

"Bob Crow sounds like a good'un," Stuart commented. "I'm sorry I missed him."

"Yeah," Rob burst out angrily. "You missed a lot, Stuart. You missed most of it, good and bad. There weren't too many Bob Crows."

"I saw it all coming," he said. "It was fucking obvious, once you thought about it, once you realized you couldn't even live your own life properly, the one you'd been given. I hated working at that fucking place."

But there was no excuse, Rob thought, for walking out on your weekend visitors, Femi and Jean, buying a one-way train ticket to London and throwing yourself off the express before Kelvedon. What the fuck had been going through Stuart's head? What perverse, ultimately cruel impulse to wreak the utmost havoc on everyone who cared for him? Perhaps he'd been unable to think about consequences; maybe that was part of it. Blinding anguish. Maybe he hadn't been able to talk to them, nor they to listen. Just a cold clear heartless decision made early one morning while your visiting girlfriend drowsed beside you in a wide bed.

"OK," he said. "I was wrong. I was angry. I don't fucking know."

"Feniton, Feniton," cried the guard. The word was swallowed.

When Rob first met up with Paul Hubbard again in London, Paul, he discovered, had taken firm hold of his own life – and lived it to the hilt on the sword of Orion. At that time he'd been a full-time worker for the SWP. Well-dressed, respectable-looking, he'd been hired by the leadership to persuade comrades to shut down the Rank and File groups, jettison Woman's Voice. Just back from Coventry, he'd explained it all to Rob in the kitchen of a sub-let council flat in a Vauxhall tower. Rob had noted the slow persuasive movements of his Tai-Chi hands, following the curve of Tony Cliff's straight line. Between them, Rob thought, his parents had made him into a kind of philosopher prince. Possibly Marie was right – they'd done him in with his fantasy identity, the too easy difficult path of being a famous person's son. But Paul's qualities had always been his own. Anyway, it wasn't good to try and square this wonderful creature with the bloated, deluded, failed copywriter who'd been found dead in his film-location art deco tower flat on Gray's Inn Road. Discovered by his most antagonistic sister, who'd popped round to see how he was doing. It had been a recurrence of childhood epilepsy.

Anyway, Rob and Paul had remained friends, although he'd always been the kind of friend who couldn't be told the truth. And what did he know about it anyway?

"Whimple! Whimple!" the guard called.

Nary a whimper at Whimple.

Marie was lolling her head from side to side, dipping it towards first one shoulder then the other, a mannerism which Rob had always found irritating. It made her resemble a small bird who couldn't decide what to peck at next. Probably she thought it made her look attractive. She was considering, weighing things up. She was dead. Her favourite job, he remembered, had been after her marriage to Mar, poster boy of respectable Icelandic Trotskyism, had broken up. Mar looked great on television as the presentable face of the Fourth International, but he'd turned out to be a wife-beater.

She had managed to get herself a job as a vegetable buyer for a supermarket in Reykjavik. The Icelanders knew nothing whatsoever about vegetables, they habitually paid though the nose for imported rotting cabbage. Marie, on the contrary, a farm girl, had known everything there was to know about fresh veg. She was a success there, but there had been nobody to talk to, except for Gudrun. What a waste of a life her death had been. Same for all of these four ghosts. He wondered why they had been earthbound for so long. Now she was on her way to heaven, he hoped.

Unless her pretty face was going straight to hell – in a bespoke handcart he had once been spotted enthusiastically pushing

"Cranbrook, Cranbrook!" the guard announced.

Cranbrook was an off-the-peg sounding name for a new town built over a stream which had once run red with the juice of succulent cranberries growing along its margins. Again, there was little or nothing to be seen there tonight. The shoulders of a giant warehouse beside the tracks were just about discernible, the new-build paradise beyond was buried under a silent expanse of dunes. The guard whistled them on abruptly with his emergency whistle.

Agathe! Agathe! who said suddenly, "I think it is you judge us, not the other way. Why can you judge? How?" She shrugged, not indifferently now but with some hostility, as though she'd at last seen through his arrogance. "I am a simple person," she said. "Do you remember when I am keeping bees? I am very happy doing this sort of thing."

He remembered, from one of her letters. She'd worn a mask, a bee-keeper's hood, harvesting honey in Aix-en-Provence, living in a remote farmhouse with her first husband. It had been here that her daughter had been born. He only wished that she had been his daughter, and he had yearned to be with her, to ride up on the pillion of his brother's Triumph Bonneville and snatch her away. But the electronic ignition had failed just before Clermont-Ferrand, they'd been forced to stow the defunct Meriden bike (so much for workers' co-operatives) in a barn and hitchhike all the way home. Surely, that's not how it had been meant to be. His brother had bought a 750 Yamaha next year. Rob had been so fucking stubborn about Agathe – much good it had done him – and what good were such fixations anyway? No good at all, not for anybody.

Why was Agathe even here? She'd had a perfectly good life, a life like any other middle-class French person's, along with its problems, its unsolved secret desires, until she'd taken her eyes off the road for a moment on her way to work at the *maternelle* in the Alps. Fuck it! She was less than delighted to be here, that was certain. She scarcely remembered him. He'd never really known her, but you think you do. At that age you're at least halfway determined to make things turn out the way you wanted, Rob thought.

"Pinhoe!" said the guard as the train slowed into another featureless station, swaddled in random meaningless death. The Pinhoe camera had been a sensation in the later middle ages, but insufficient light had precluded its use to document tonight's extraordinary weather. The train moved on.

Stuart and Rob looked across at one another. Forty years ago, they'd sometimes held conversations which lasted all day and all night. Sometimes they'd fought, sworn, or just wrestled. Rob had usually done the cooking. They were so used to each other everything about their friendship was taken for granted. Rob had perhaps fooled himself, but it had been like being some sort of blessed twin. But of course he'd been fooled – they were totally separate beings, obviously enough. Not really much alike. Trying to share too much with somebody else was unhealthy; living in each others' pockets led to … less understanding, not more. How little he'd known about what was really going on in Stuart's mind. He remembered the glances other friends had shot across them. Sometimes advice or warnings had been offered. Still, he'd known for years that he must project himself against Stuart.

"You bastard, you fucking bastard!" Mcleod would cry, and hurl himself at Rob, a flailing bundle of sticks, fists flying, and they would have a mock fight on the dusty old sofa, but Stuart would always be sure to land a few punches which hurt and Rob would be forced to retaliate, and afterwards they would probably watch *Blake's 7, The Martian Chronicles, Buck Rogers in the 21ˢᵗ Century … Star Trek.*

It was largely an excuse for physical contact, a form that affection took between them, spilling out sometimes, but it had never gone any further. It reminded Rob of picking Stuart up from the floor at school; he was often the instigator of these bouts, knowing exactly how to trigger them, the right goading remark. Stuart's description of his teenage epic poem had been: my three-pronged fork to jab the sleeping dead. Rob still found his phrase funny. Stuart's violent proclivities had always made him laugh, but of course the impulse was real, and he knew in these fights that his friend would carry it through to the very end somehow. Jabbing had been his mode: a long jabbing finger in a lost argument.

But it had been great watching science fiction. Is was as though each programme was a fragment of the true cross of the future, imperfectly apprehended, flimsily enacted by American imposters, but something like a prophecy, heard at the crack in Delphi where the oracle whispered her directions. That's why we liked Blake's 7 so much, the home-grown version shot on old Crossroads sets and in Oxshott woods. Servalan was Margaret Thatcher of course, that sexy witch, but Blake, the missing leader, and the raggle-taggle army of rebels in a stolen ship – they were the would-be revolutionaries; but what a shifty crew of incompetent but brave space pirates they had been! They didn't know who to trust. They trusted nobody, especially not each other.

On this particular journey they had barely spoken, yet it was coming to an end. A party at which the person you most wanted to speak to was avoiding you. Rob though had believed in obtainable happiness, which he'd always identified with moving on. Stuart said – on the phone once – that he'd been frightened to realize that, when other people spoke of being happy, he didn't know what they meant. Only the English believed in happiness, or something like that, so Friedrich Nietzsche was supposed to have said. Like everything else he came out with it was a load of bollocks.

They stopped once more, at Exeter Central, but this time the guard stayed in his cubby hole. He was sorting things out for disembarkation just as he did at the end of every shift. Exeter St David's was situated at the bottom of a hill, which surrounded it on all sides. Normally a busy terminus and embarkation point, tonight's blizzards had created a whirlwind down there which had completely filled up the wide hollow like a whirled meringue. The station was submerged entirely, so that as their train managed to plough into its final destination, it was like running into a soft gigantic pillow of crunchy-fresh nothingness, through which their blue heated filament sliced easily.

Twenty-Three

After a few seconds the lights went out. It was pitch black. No announcement was made. They sat there wondering what to do next. His companions, of course, could have walked, or glided, out of the carriage anytime, Rob thought resentfully, but he also found their presence around him reassuring. Ten minutes later a glimmer of light appeared behind the sliding doors. A small man in railway uniform opened the inter-carriage door and walked past them unseeingly. He wore the uniform well. Rob noticed he had two parallel lines, like railway tracks, shaved neatly into either side of his head.

He was carrying a torch and, over his shoulder, a flimsy-looking shovel: an emergency tool, part of the train's equipment. He continued along the aisle, heading for his partner at the back of the dead train. Before the spark of his torch could disappear altogether, the travellers got up, retrieved their luggage and followed him down to the end. He had an emergency key for quickly springing the doors.

"Errol? Errol?" the guard called.

"Alright fella," he said. "I'm on me way."

The guard also had a torch, a fierce electric fog lantern, and his own emergency shovel. "We'll have to tunnel our way out, Errol," he said as the driver walked up.

"That's what I was thinking."

"Only how do we get the door open?"

"Can't be done," Errol said shortly. "I reckon if we can get the window down, we can dig from there."

"But where's all the snow going to go?"

"We'll have to fill up the train, bruv. That's all we can do. It's the only way we'll ever get out, I'd say – fill the train with snow." He laughed shortly at the elegance of this solution.

The two of them levered at the window, managing to slide it down to reveal a wall of compacted snow. Slowly it began to ooze through the window. Rather than wait to be swamped, the guard and the driver, holding their shovels at waist-height, proactively dug at the snow and carried it by the shovel-load into the first carriage, whose door soon Derek wedged open. They began to throw it, not on the floor, but onto the seats. Rob and his friends pulled back to the opposite side of the vestibule to let them pass.

"Can we help?" Paul asked feebly.

"No, it's alright," said the guard. "You stand out of the way." He laughed drily. "This could take some time."

Errol ignored the travellers, whether because he couldn't see them or because he didn't do public relations, impossible to tell.

They worked around the door through the open window, piling the seats at the near end of the carriage with snow, and after a time they'd created enough of a gap around the door for it to be forced open and back. Then a larger, creeping wall of snow confronted them. Both were exhausted. But after a swift blow, elbows on knees, they resumed. The beginnings of a tunnel, or at least a recess, began to form but then collapsed, leading to more desperate digging to save it. The travellers were onlookers. They felt like a bunch of spare parts.

"If you lot know of another way out of here," the guard flung at them savagely. "Like through the roof, for example. I'd advise you to take it now."

Paul stepped forward. "There's something we could try," he said. "We can all hold hands. We may be able to carry you out."

Paul herded the guard, the driver (still holding shovels and torches) and Rob close together, while the four ghosts held hands in a ring. The ghosts began to move around them in a circle, forming a star wheel, which accelerated of its own accord, disintegrating then reforming into a spinning gyroscope of intensely coloured lights, which tilted forwards, elongated, and hurled itself at the tunnel the two workers had begun to dig in the snow.

The ball of whirling lights generated extreme heat, rapidly burrowing deep into the compacted snow before carving a sizzling upward path. This seemed to go on for ages. They were stuck, the ghosts were underpowered, they would drown or be crushed; but then the radiant starwheel burst through into the open air, disintegrated upon impact, and left all of them sprawling on a huge white expanse which stretched off in every direction, rising before them into what looked like a range of hills, out of which the top branches of trees could be seen poking. A vixen veered sharply, trotted away at speed across the snowy plain.

Errol brushed snow from his driver's uniform. "Thankee for that," he said, chuckling in near-hysteria, dazed.

There were tracks, they noticed, picking themselves up. Animal tracks but also human footprints, criss-crossing pathways. They weren't alone. Somehow others had escaped the storm which obliterated all landmarks, all boundaries. Not all were lucky enough to survive. As they clambered out onto the snow plain most were left alone, to find their bearings, but to his horror Rob saw, apparently at random, giant kingfishers blinking into being above them. They seemed to catch fire in mid-air, swooped down from the empty sky and gobbled up juicy specimens like fresh larvae with their vicious curving beaks. "Oh the mind, mind has mountains." If the dragonflies were God's right hand, Rob understood with sickening certainty, these hideous, powerful creatures were his left.

"Better get out of this lot," Errol advised. "Soon as possible, like."

The guard who had shepherded them from London was scarcely demobilized – but no longer on rails, he stood differently, more loosely, as he turned and looked around him. "I reckon that's the park up there, about forty foot down, backing onto Melville Road. Over there's the town centre, if you fancy any last minute shopping." He turned again. "Over there's Heavitree. Can't see the river –" and then "– oh yes I can, look! It rises up and falls over a cliff down there. Maybe the Exe is still running underneath. Well, that's where I'm heading." He held up a hand. "Alan's the name by the way, Alan Brightman, should you wish to remember me. And this is my colleague Errol Ford." He waved a nonchalant farewell to Errol and their remaining passengers.

They watched as he tramped doggedly across the ice towards Heavitree and the executable Exe, out of which some future thaw or flood of might ensue. Small figures moved on the ice, showing up in the clear moonlight: somehow people had already crawled up here somehow, through bore holes and fissures made from the roofs of taller buildings, using whatever was to hand to dig upwards, trying to escape freezing suffocation.

"How about you, driver?" Paul asked.

"I live up behind the Uni," Errol pointed vaguely. "There'll be signs of life up there alright. Let's hope so. I hope they can get the old people out okay."

He was about to leave when, above them, a noisy police helicopter approached, flashing a bright searchlight over them. Rescue! But, after a quick look at the stragglers, the dark dragon-copter, its occupants impassive behind closed visors, shot skywards and banked quickly away in the direction of a scarp behind the museum.

When Errol left the five friends realized that they too must part and go their separate ways. But not too soon! Not this time! Rob wasn't too sure where he was going. He needed to get back to Sugarford, to Drunkenhell, to find out how they were doing. He had gifts in his shoulder bag to deliver; tomorrow was Christmas Day. He felt a twinge of anxiety about how they would be received, carried over from previous years, a sense that he was an interloper. He pulled out his Samsung but couldn't get a signal. Perhaps if the helicopter came back he could flag them down, be taken to some information centre for displaced, unwanted people.

Agathe's hands were thrust deep in her pockets, her coat buttoned to her throat. She lifted her large, unhappy head. "How will I find them? How will I find Mono? Jacques??" she cried despairingly. "They must be dead I think." She shivered, who had no right to be cold. Tears filmed and flooded across her sharply tilted eyes. "J'aimais tellement la neige," she said flatly. "It has killed me."

"You'll meet them again. I know you will, Agathe." Stuart tried unexpectedly tried to reassure her. "It will be difficult but it will happen. I can see light jumping up around your head, one of those cones above you." He remembered her on a train to Edinburgh fifty years ago: a faun. This haunting, angular woman was still beautiful. You'd say anything to please her!

"I will walk to the other coast," she said. "From there it will be easy." She began to twist and turn this way and that on the packed surface, as if direction finding by means of some built-in sat-nav. Rob was still terrified, scanning the skies for one of the fiery kingfishers.

In every direction the new dune-like landscape, rolling, almost featureless, stretched away as far as he could see. How far did it go? That was the question.

"Goodbye Rob. It is not –."

What? It is not what? Her final message echoed sonorously in his head and he shivered to his emptied marrow-bones. Agathe didn't say anything further to him, simply turned and walked off without looking back, but as she strode angrily away she broke down in the featureless terrain, into planes, into lines, became nothing more or less than a galloping creature of light, gathering speed as she raced away: an energy blur, a fleeing deer, a silver stag, a greyhound, finally a moving pinprick in the moonlit night.

Paul and Marie stood close together in the snow. They made an odd pair. Paul was large, bear-like, rumpled, and even if a bear made out of newspaper, somewhat solid; Marie, a twitching wire, tiny, depleted now, her battery pooped: she looked burned out, in need of shelter. Paul put out his hand to shake somebody or another's, left it hanging there. Somehow they looked good together. Paul would see she looked after herself, ate well. She would strike out at him but he would easily contain and absorb her many blows.

At their last meeting Paul had said – seemingly expecting to die – that he hoped they would both survive to know each other's grandchildren, but that it might not happen. In a basement bar crowded with carousing young earners on the edge of Chinatown. He'd also announced that he'd been seeing Rob's supposedly heartbroken ex-girlfriend.

"Goodbye, goodbye," Marie waved to them. "Remember me, forget me. Don't let them wipe me out entirely."

With that they turned and walked away together in a straight line, Marie leaning into his bulky side. After a while she jumped up onto his back. Rob and Stuart watched him walk forward a few paces, stagger and fall over. They were laughing, rolling in the snow. They got up, got up and continued to wherever they thought they were going.

"If I had my way I'd send them tae hell," Mcleod said. "They fucking deserve it anyway. Sins of commission and omission. Bad acts. Paul, for fuck's sake! Marie: you know, both. The full hand of mortal sins."

"She didn't kill anybody," Rob said.

Mcleod flinched as the thought struck him like a final bullet. He swelled, rose up, burst out of his skin, unfurled his wings and mounted angrily into the air, a gigantic hovering insect with a green segmented carapace, the most beautiful pale compound eyes, and twinned pairs of wicked razor mandibles. He was poised to strike at his unwary friend, to kill and tear him apart and to ingest him immediately through a stout dangling feeding tube. This is what he deserved. But he didn't, the creature just hovered there and twitched, an enormous armoured dragonfly angel, which is what Stuart had been after all, as it turned out, all along. The creature seemed to be observing him closely, then it seemed to grow, to charge itself up somehow, and with a single convulsive movement of its pulsing, segmented body, flicked itself higher into the air; then it shot upwards rapidly at another sharp tangent and Rob finally lost sight of the large, fearsome insect that had once been his friend: it had vanished, gone.

Rob looked away across glittering dune-scapes on which more moving black dots could be seen in the far distance, clambering into the light from fissures and burrowed shafts. At last the four ghosts had departed. This year he had been determined to enjoy a proper Christmas dinner with all the trimmings. He trudged off in search of this small memorial happiness: a mutant file extension of nature's empty gift, perhaps, but one everybody deserved.

For some time he tramped in what he took to be the direction of Sugarford – intuitively he knew his family were still alive and that's where he should go. A seven-hour journey on foot, his phone told him, but that had been on the roads. The signal blinked in and out. The surface was fairly solid here – he guessed it had something to do with the sheer ferocity and density of the snow-bee onslaught but it might be unpredictable, powdery, further on. Somehow, he knew, it was much too far to walk. He might die, tumble down into a freezing rift, succumb to exhaustion and frostbite; might even decide by himself just to lie down and sleep in the silent snow, seduced by its ancient song.

Rob seemed to be dreaming on his feet. There was party they'd been invited to attend. A do they were honoured to be invited to by someone who owned a house. When they were inside, a pleasant journalist offered advice to a group of admiring young activists. "Avoid newspapers," he'd said. "You may dream of getting your own by-line, but you can never really say what you want. They'll get to your mind. They'll twist you out of shape." This advice seemed stupid. The host was only telling them his own experience, like everyone did. *I wrote a letter. I wrote it in the air. You may know from that I have a friend somewhere.* Blues lyrics trickled out of a wall socket. Men gathered in the garden, preparing to steal everything they'd ever owned. He tottered, recovered.

As he walked he sang a song to himself, more than one, first one then another, to keep himself awake. He was reminded of how Agathe and he had once sung to each other as they walked along the roadsides out of Scotland. He was shivering violently now, his teeth chattering like those of a battery operated laughing skull. He tramped onwards. It was difficult to lift his feet high enough to clear the powdery snow that was still falling over this new white country that had been built so speedily over the messy old one, too old, too new, too full of ghosts, too much ramshackle unplanned dumpiness. He wondered what the new new would be like. Under heaven's rule. Any better? He was dying, he knew. He would have to lie down soon, and that would be the end of him. It had been alright for the shy generous ghosts. They didn't feel the cold. They could zoom off where they liked, but they'd certainly left him in deep shit this time.

Just as they had previously. Rob couldn't help continuing to piece together his memories of them. It was automatic, like raising his numb legs and planting them one after another like wooden fence posts measuring out the blowing whiteness, which was freezing harder and harder by the minute. And when he had lined up his lead soldiers in neat rows he knocked them all down and then lined them up again in ranks. He wished he had some farm animals. And when he had lined up his friends in the right order, he moved farther back, he tried to think of some moment when it all began. Not his life as such but his understanding of the world in which he had lived his adult life. This was another good game, but his brain kept losing pieces of it.

In delirium he remembered a nice, shiny boy in the television lights, gazing up in amazement at the studio giants. He hadn't turned out to be one of them. Refugees from the country with no rights. The dead had no human rights, he had always thought, except they obviously did. You existed. If anyone knew about you, you had your shout out for compensation. Look at the shadow people. Didn't they get a big pay-out consideration thing for being defamed for sliding down walls, along pavements, when they'd never had any choice but to be trodden on? Loops and hooks and eyes pulled the thread along the curtain, folded it all away in the wardrobe, never mind what for or to be seen again. Never-no-more. The shadow men were standing up on their own two feet, underfoot only at high noon, they are sloping after you in the sun.

Then he found what he was looking for. He began weaving loose ends together until he had made something splendid. It was what people used to call a castle in the air, a fairy castle made of glittering ice shards. Rob was exhausted, just too cold to go any further, on the point of final collapse. He would finally be able to see himself from above, a dark lozenge, a leaking ink cartridge dropped in the snow. He would be covered over, barely a mound. Why them? Why not me? Such were the thoughts he turned over most as he staggered along, because he was alive and therefore guilty. But evidently that wouldn't be lasting too much longer.

> Aug 10th (1872) – I was looking at high waves. The breakers always are parallel to the coast and shape themselves to it except where the curve is sharp however the wind blows. They are rolled out by the shallowing shore just as a piece of putty between the palms whatever its shape runs into a long roll. The slant ruck or crease one sees in them shows the way of the wind

– Rob looked away across the sifted shapes of the newly settled snowscape attempting to trace the instress of its apparent lability, and the lines that ran across revealing its feathery structure, to see one direction of travel under this dimpsey starlight at the end of what might never end: this endless ordering of geometrically related planes, the foreverness of design.

> ...the regularity of the barrels surprised and charmed the eye; the end behind the comb and crest was as smooth and bright as glass...

Gerard had described a sea that looked this, in his journals. Rob remembered it sharply, clearly now for a moment.

> ...It may be noticed to be green behind and silver and white in front: the silver marks where the air begins, the pure white is foam, the green / solid water. Then looked at to the right and left they are scrolled over like mouldboards or feathers or jibsails seen by the edge...

But to Rob the inscape remained vague, broken up, although high above him clear signals were indeed breaking into bolts of electrical instress. They were connecting the upper firmament to the earth in a zig-zagging network of shining filaments, as the dark dragon-copters continuously searched for human life, returning again and again across wide white striated wasteland.

> Feb. 24th (1873) – In the snow flat-topped hillocks and shoulders outlined with wavy edges, ridge below ridge, very like the grain of wood and in projection like relief maps. These the wind makes I think and of course drifts, which are in fact snow waves. The sharp nape of a drift is sometimes broken by sharp drifts and channels. I think this must be when the wind after shaping the drift first had changed and cast waves in the body of the wave itself. All the world is full of inscape and chance left free to act falls into an order as well as purpose.

His feet too numb to feel anything beneath them, Rob trudged on for a no-time until he came to ground that was sheeted with taut tattered streaks if gritty snow. Green white tufts of long bleached grass like heads of hair, or the crowns of heads of hair, each a whorl of slender curves, one tuft taking up another. For a dizzy moment \Rob thought he had come to the end of the snow, to land. But when he turned painfully he saw that he had merely traversed the filled in gigantic verdant bowl that surrounded the Blackdown Hills. He was standing atop one of them, perhaps somewhere near the Culmstock Beacon, sadly engulfed. It hadn't been lit in time tonight.

Until another dragon-copter came and hung poised over him like a big black bug, blinding him with its twin searchlights.

Instinctively, he put up his arms to protect his eyes.

A harsh, barking voice cut through the din of chopper blades, "Don't move!" it boomed. "Don't move!"

"I'm innocent! Innocent!" Rob shouted up at them. "What am I supposed to have fucking done?"

His voice was drowned out by the thrashing blades. Water from the wind flooded into his dry eyes. The long, bulging machine twitched a few metres above the snow, creating a whirlwind of ice flakes, which cut at his flesh and almost blinded him. He buried his face in his elbow in a desperate gesture of submission. A sturdy harness was lowered down from the gaping fuselage door. Rob managed to drag himself up, and step into it, and fastened the thick nylon straps across his quaking shoulders.

Twenty-Four

They must be the police force of Heaven, Rob realized. He was lying on the floor of the helicopter, partially disentangled from his harness. He wasn't in good shape. He was shaking from head to foot, too exhausted to even tremble, darkness closing in. The female looked down at him with large pale compound eyes. What he'd taken for her helmet, he realized dimly, was some sort of chitinous dark blue carapace. She lifted one of her feeders and a beam of her healing radiance arced between the claws of her raised mandibles. She shot it at him casually, and it splashed over his body, bathing him in an excruciating, scalding heat.

He sat up immediately. He felt brilliant for a moment, and then pain enveloped his chest. He collapsed. The policewoman held up her mandible, indicating he should lie still. Which he did, very still indeed, feeling every atom of his body coalesce as the heat of the beam slowly subsided and the healing completed. The lower part of the policewoman's elongated body, he noticed, looked as if it had been drawn out of molten glass, like the swans and fauns and shepherdesses in his late mother's cabinet. It was aglow with a fiery blue light, the source of her incredible power.

He raised himself more gingerly and looked around. His rescuer's partner was piloting the machine, only the back of a similarly carapaced head visible, wings folded neatly under a uniform. A window to port offered the wide expanse of whiteness, raked by the searchlights of dozens of similar dragonfly helicopters. People were still pulling themselves up to the surface via shaft-like sink-holes, black pinpricks which had already begun to add a certain industrial graininess to parts of the landscape. Rob looked towards the rear of the machine and was surprised to see three of his ghosts sitting along benches against the fuselage. They were a sorry, bedraggled bunch.

Paul and Marie huddled together on one side, aluminium-lined blankets draped over their shoulders. They looked at him, abashed. Paul offered a wave of greeting. Marie looked huffy, sunk into a small cocoon. Opposite them Agathe was wrapped to her neck in a similar thermal blanket. She looked back at him half-curiously, but seemingly without recognition, just as she had when he'd first encountered her on the train.

"Hi!" Rob waved at them, "you didn't get far then!"

"Far?" Marie keened. "*Far?* We've been walking for miles and miles. We should be fucking dead. We are fucking dead."

At an abrupt direction from the dragonfly medic he went back to join them, and sat in a vacant space next to Agathe, who stirred slightly in recognition. From the blankets they wore he guessed that they hadn't had the heat-treatment. But it seemed only minutes since they'd waved goodbye. Rob guessed he must have experienced some sort of time-distortion out on the virgin snow-field. Boarding the Waterloo-Exeter train, almost like a memory of early childhood. He didn't remember anything much before walking down the platform. He tried to remember if it had it been snowing at that point, or earlier on when he'd left the house. He didn't think so.

Suddenly the ambulance chopper shimmied violently, changed direction in mid-flight and tilted forwards, its searchlights blazing. Rob and the ghosts grasped dangling overhead handholds and turned to look out through small round apertures lining the fuselage, through which the mountainous white landscape tilted away, darkly, into the endless night.

"That's all there is now," Rob said in a hushed voice.

The ghosts looked towards him. "Not all," said Agathe. "There is somewhere else – they are taking us to this."

"Did they say where?" Rob looked at Paul but he was abstracted, lost for words. Physically present, a film of sweat on his broken face, but he had retreated from them.

"They said something about a hatching shed," said Marie, her face screwed up in disgust, as though she had shared a particularly tasteless joke.

The dragon-copter stalled and tilted again, they lurched. Rob saw that their searchlights had picked out something below on the ground: a large green dragonfly, apparently smashed to pieces, a scar of debris scattered across the snow. He realized it was Stuart, or the creature he had become, broken up in a crash landing on the snow. They hovered for a moment more, and then the helicopter shot vertically upwards at enormous speed. The ghosts hung on for dear life. They're leaving him behind, Rob thought, tears flooding into his burning eyes. They're angry with him. They gave him a chance but he just couldn't make it as an angel, not for very long, not on his own.

But like a ball that has been shot to is zenith, the twirly-bird began to drop back to earth, plummeting through the wide firmament. The craft's fuselage began to glow around them, to turn to translucent fiery glass. The bodies of its pilots were pulsing, lit up. The ghosts, being weightless, managed to keep their seats, but Rob was flung upwards, hanging into his handrail with difficulty. Then the blades kicked in with an immediate cushioning effect, slowing the craft as the ground rushed towards them. The pulsing of the chopper and its pilots increased in intensity, and as they approached the scattered debris of Stuart, a great bolt shot from the craft's underside and bathed the entire area in orange light.

Rob and the ghosts watched as the wrecked green dragonfly was gathered together, reassembled, healed – until it twitched on the snow, slowly righted itself and rose into the air on battered wings. The chopper 's rapid rise and fall had been a way of charging itself up for this release of energy, Rob realized, which it had drawn into itself from the atmosphere. Stuart faltered, wobbled, but regained equilibrium, hanging there quite helplessly, it seemed to Rob, unsure what he was supposed to do. The chopper hung motionless in the air before him, watching, ghosting his nervous movements, until finally Stuart turned and flew away at speed, skimming low across the snow towards a distant point on the blotted, murky horizon. Rob wondered what was happening there, and if Stuart would be able to find a part in it as he needed. He hoped so. Yes, he thought. They are patient, these creatures. They know what they're doing. He will be alright now.

"You're not going to believe this, Rob," said Paul. "But I always knew it was going to be something like this in the end. It seemed so clear to me – the signs were all around us, if you think about it."

Marie looked at him with incredulity. Agathe made no sign of having heard or understood what he was saying, but Rob knew well this type of energy was something she had always believed in. She had told him so many years ago, as they chatted outside a holiday chalet rented on Belle Île by Mathéo and his family. Back indoors they'd all sat around the large table talking about nothing in particular, Mathéo, his wife Gisèle, their combined children playing together boisterously in the next room. Agathe had written her address and new surname in his notebook, and her second husband, a Jacques Brel lookalike who bore the same name, had written down the title, in French, of an American novel he'd once enjoyed a great deal. It was the last time they'd met.

Jacques was a sculptor, a real stonemason whose large hands could encompass her, span her, bridge her, take in her full measure. His large frame, his mop of thick blonde hair – an actor's face. a violently mobile face yes, much in the style of Brel. This lean, lounging second husband of Agathe's had sculpted her in stone, her tensed back, her buttocks, focused energy in primal explosive female shapes. It was considerably too heavy for the kitchen floor, this core definition of her womanliness, his chisel and mallet masculinity. But his great spanning hands had apparently hewn her long back out of a big lump of raw stone from the plentifully supplied quarries of the lower Alps.

They had bounced and jounced into the camping at Belle Île in Jacques's low-rider Renault 12, the car she had died in, its roof crumpled and its boot sprung open, laden with loose equipment, as flyaway as Agathe's hair. Mono, her boisterous single-minded daughter, charged away immediately. She was permanently angry. Jacques had been so patient with her. He loved her like a father, but after Agathe's death her real father had reclaimed Mono. Jacques had lost absolutely everything in one go. Except himself, Rob had thought, having met him. He could build another life with those hands, that lean body. Shape somebody else. But it was a cruel thought to be thinking, particularly selfish, pointlessly redundant in the midst of selfish pointless grief. Self-pity over something that never was, more likely. I loved you," Agathe might have said sometime. "But you didn't love me. That is what I understood." She could only be honest, only say what she believed to be true.

As the draon-copter skimmed along at speed high above the desolate English landscape, Rob wondered where it was they were now headed – but he trusted the heavenly police; he had no choice. In his heart he knew this to be the outlook of somebody who had lived an indulgent, protected life.

It was warm inside the whirring machine. Rob and the ghosts drowsed as the vehicle droned over the great ice plains, each solitary in its safe cocoon above the wide emptiness of the world. Again, a shimmy, and a sudden stalling halt, signalled arrival. Rob was jolted awake; the others roused somnolently and just sat there in a sort of confused expectancy. He saw immediately that they were no longer alone in the sky. Below them was a large shallow white dome, around which snow had been chopped back into a range of ragged cliffs, and surrounding their own craft perhaps a hundred or more similar dragon-copters were arriving and departing, spiralling in long lazy chains around the dome, from which a pulsing radio aerial thrust up into the air.

The machines were descending onto a series of makeshift heliports that were hewn out of snow around the dome, and through a vent in the top which resembled a slowly blinking eye, a stream of dragonfly angels were emerging, each one firing up, sparked into bright luminous life, shooting upwards, performing a joyful circuit of the dome, and darting off in an impulsive, invisible velocity as if being released in a straight line towards some distant point of the compass.

Rob and his companions watched in silence through their circular portholes while their rescuing pilots paid them no attention, concentrated on guiding the chopper amidst dense traffic. Helicopters, all helicopters, Ron grasped suddenly, in a perception which felt as if it had always been familiar, were based on dragonflies. Everything about them was similar, coded into the manoeuvrable human contraptions which had delivered fiery Napalm to the jungles and villagers of Vietnam, and H.G. Wells' Martians, lurching tripods, carrying nets to scoop up the lower life-forms – all based on those harmlessly beautiful beings, which to a Jesuit poet had seemed to draw flame into iridescent dancing shapes and to declare nothing but the joyfulness of each discovery of their own unlikely existence as created beings.

> Each mortal thing does one thing and the same:
> Deals out that being indoors each one dwells;
> Selves — goes itself; *myself* it speaks and spells,
> Crying *Whát I dó is me: for that I came.*

But if the flame and fire of birds and insects was a strong, simple kind of being, and the pied-beauty of earthworms, diseased trout and toolkits was another less-regarded variety of same – what of the truly complex beauty of human beings as they flared forth unevenly in rage, stilled in blinking comprehension, ebbed and flowed, built and broke down? They shone with the ever-shifting light of higher created beings. The Holy Ghost was within them.

And if as Hopkins declared, Almighty God saw Christ, his son, looking back at him from the features of men's faces, it should be admitted that man himself had only been able to copy the superficial design-features of dragonflies, and to harness these to ill-use as weapons in their eternal war against his weaker others. But why hadn't God prevented this from happening? he wondered for the thousandth time. Why did the Lord God still love humanity? Proximity to these processes hadn't brought him any closer to understanding the ways of heaven, although humanity had done nothing else but imitate the rest of the Creation. At the same time they had held themselves apart, disinterested, assuming an aloof and instrumental position vis-à-vis other created beings. And their attempts to conquer death had only led them closer to madness in old age.

All this, he realized, had been predicted, and Hopkins had only been a naïve if beautiful writer of what he called curtal sonnets, and later on a pained describer of the implacable will of God. Or its absence. God's silence. This, Rob thought, was similar to *The Wreck of the Deutschland*, his poem about immigrant nuns fleeing oppression, drowning in the Thames estuary on their way to America. Christ, come quickly! the tall nun had cried, presumably in German, her final anguished affirmation.

The Wreck of the Deutschland had been Hopkins' great test of faith and poetic prowess. How to make the justice of God's cruel mercies spring to life in sprung rhythm. It was this painfully wrought line of fixed beats and irregular feet which had anticipated the American modernists, captivated Dylan Thomas. His contorted syntax mirrored this painful extrusion of impossible truths: it was strict, mathematical and Rob tended to see in it an arbitrary, empty constraint like those imposed by the idiot Perec. Red means run son, numbers add up to nothing. However you tried to cut it, he thought, perhaps for the last time, poetry was the true voice of feeling.

Now it appeared that humanity itself was to be curtailed, or at least edited considerably. The chopper swooped down into a vacant bay. Rob and his companions were soon disgorged and prodded by attendants into the dome. Behind their dutiful pilots they mounted into the sky again without fuss, offering no goodbyes. Hopkins refused the carrion comfort of despair, battled on through the so-called terrible sonnets. He died of typhoid, so happy.

The friends entered nervously through a portal which was like a rent in the fabric of the dome, a hastily erected circus marquee, passing though electronic entrance arches which reminded him of airport scanners. These were operated by a crew of smaller insects in white shrouds, Rob thought they wore them to protect their retracted wings, and while the others were permitted to continue, he was apprehended by two of these shrouded creatures, both of whom proceeded to prod at him with their mandible-held knowledge-rays. Wordlessly, they allowed him to proceed along an outside track which ran parallel to the walls of the dome. Rob knew this meant that he was still alive, still human. He felt a sudden pang, a dull hatred for his own miserable kind.

This was replaced by the words 'Poor Dad!' He thought of his brother and his father in Sugarford, probably buried forever. He had genuinely wanted to see them, but somewhere out on the snow he had mislaid his bag containing the Christmas presents he'd wrapped up for them. His father had recently phoned the police in the middle of the night, the real police, convinced that a team of blokes with white vans were systematically emptying the garage of his tools and motorcycles. Rob's brother had been summoned. The police had been understanding apparently. This kind of thing was commonplace.

His father had continued the following day to talk about images he was seeing on an unplugged television, voices on a silent radio, spilling out of a wall socket. Through the shared wall he heard the voices of his kindly neighbours, accusing him of murdering his wife. They were also plotting his own death, planning to eliminate all surviving members of the whole family.

On the phone his brother had accused him of not believing this, even of thinking that the neighbours really were plotting ... but it had all been a misunderstanding, Rob hoped. These supplements to his usual Christmas anxiety, sad last enactments of rituals which had once been binding, defining them all in some sort of equilibrium of relatedness ... broke his thoughts into streams of babble, failing to hold down the emotions of regret, of remorse, breaking over him again like something he was ashamed to have forgotten, put to one side. He should have got out of the train at Sugarford, he thought, then he would not have been stuck here. He might have reached his own family.

He fought away the futility of these thoughts as he took in the activity taking place in the large open centre of the dome. Ghosts flooded in through all seven portals: sorry, bedraggled creatures, they were ill-dressed, careworn, dazed ... just like his friends. They were of all ages, some young, dressed in the tattered cheap and ugly clothing of long ago, some apparently old, quite well-dressed, but their garments had been reduced to near rags by decades or centuries on some posthumous skid row. Some were praying, some looked terrified, others were shambling forward resignedly to meet whatever. Arranged in a semi-circle in the centre, around the blinking aperture in the dome's roof, were a number of tall hoop-like devices being operated by dragonfly technicians. All the ghosts were passing through these hoops one by one, occasionally two held hands, and all were bathed in blue light arcing from the hoops. From here they proceeded to one of a number of raised daises where what Marie had referred to terrifyingly as the hatching was taking place on a grand scale.

It was certainly nauseating to watch at first. Rob soon grew accustomed to the sight of dragonflies convulsively emerging from the broken, papery husks of half-remembered features that were their ghost-bodies. There had been some sort of a reprieve, he thought: a general amnesty of earthbound spirits. Each being walked up a short flight of steps onto a circular dais where another burst of illumination was splashed over their exhausted, half-corporeal frames. Within a few seconds they all split apart hideously as the last layers of the husks were shucked. Another dragonfly angel erupted into existence, humble but ready as she pumped herself up and spiralled tentatively up towards the eye in the roof, wide open now to let the new creature through into a life of heavenly service.

It was the most beautiful thing he had ever witnessed. They drew a flame, a glow rather than a flash, and seemed to conduct energy from the raised daises. This was drawn from somewhere deep in the earth, he understood, like drawing a smouldering fire to make a flame spring up, which was instantly drawn out into a long bulging cylinder, a needle of dancing, coruscating light.

Rob looked for the faces of his remaining three friends in the throng. For a minute or two he thought he'd lost them, but then he saw where they were. They had stuck together. Paul was holding the hands of both his soon-to-be sisters. They passed along in a solemn line and let go only as they approached the charged hoop of blue dancing flame and its angelic insect operator.

Paul took first place, almost bounding up the steps in his heavy way, but when the light engulfed him and his ghost-body cracked open it was as a delicate albino creature that he emerged, semi-transparent, crinkling like animated cellophane so that he appeared to wink in and out of existence as he hung twirling and twitching impatiently in the air above his hatching dais.

Agathe was next to go, sloping towards an adjoining dais while a stranger stepped up to take Paul's place. Rob saw her throw her head back and gaze intensely up towards heaven, but she was already transforming. When she burst out of her papery skin she was black, iridescent jet black. She shimmied, tilted, squirming in mid-air, her sparkling mourning dress flashed more brightly than any summer's day. She had been reborn into the eternal beauty of night.

Paul and Agathe hung in the sky of the dome, aware of one another but not close together. They were waiting for Marie to join them.

Marie's turned out to be a difficult hatching. It was plain to see that she was resisting, fighting against the whole process, as though unwillingly giving birth. She stalled at the steps and refused to mount the dais. One of the technicians came across to her, bending low so that its large head was close to hers. Taking this final instruction, she climbed the steps at last and the induction lamp was quickly turned on. Perhaps her hesitancy had something to do with the very different creature that soon hatched from the cast-off body of the small, turbulent woman who had been Marie McIlvoy.

She wasn't long and elegant like the dragonfly angels. She was more or less like a snow-bee, a beautiful round fluffy creature of great size and agility and sting. As she rose into the air the other two responded to her movements. They were shadowing her, guarding her, Rob realized. She had become a queen, he thought. A worker queen. Queen Mab. Also they would help her build a house, perhaps, or take her to where other snow-bees were gathering what was left of the nectar and distilling in into the most powerful honey that had ever been made, of eternal loving drunkenness and healing and nutrition and a brand new start for the remnants of humankind who were pulling themselves up through sink-holes onto the freezing surface of the snow. They seemed to confer briefly, an odd team perhaps, but soon enough they disappeared, one after another, through the eye in the roof of the hatching dome.

Rob looked away. He knew he would never see them again and he wondered bitterly if they hadn't all been using him all along. Everything had been already on the slide back then, but hadn't the world been relatively safer? It could never have been safe enough for his friends, he supposed. But he had been judged, by them, he knew. Suddenly he felt abandoned by this world, whatever the fuck it was, just as he had been by the last one. Tears came into his eyes but it was too cold to cry for long. He wandered outside through one of the torn vents, wondering if he might be able to flag down a dragonfly, cadge a ride somewhere or other.

Perhaps he should simply walk out into the snow, where a kingfisher might swoop down and put him out of his misery. But he hadn't seen any of them for a while. Could be they had gorged and departed. But to where? And what part did these beautiful, seemingly vicious creatures play in the celestial economy? If they were there to weed out the really irredeemable sinners, his survival meant that he wasn't one of those. But it struck him that the kingfishers might be gods themselves, or just bigger angels, remote devices by means of which the Deity fed crueller appetites, or weeded the garden of Creation.

Hopkins, he realized, had been elaborating on a belief-system designed for children: a naive person, he had not put away childish things, merely sought to justify them, to explain them again to the child he still remained. He perfected this, and everything, as had the Lord God Almighty, but his own faith had gone down, not with the wreck of the *Deutschland* but sometime afterwards when he could no longer raise his interlocutors, not the Almighty, nor Robert Bridges, his sceptical friend, but he'd carried on transmitting anguished attempts, like the wireless operators of the *Titanic*, one of whom was from Godalming, whose efforts were also duly transcribed.

He had once been lying in a hospital bed: a stroke recovery ward where you either got up and walked out, or were carted off to recover somewhere else, or quite probably not. He'd found himself listening to a volunteer recite London Snow, Robert Bridges' chestnut about snowballing schoolboys, to a stroke-paralysed German man, a resident of Crouch End for thirty years, now awaiting final transfer. He would rather have talked, if he had been able, about the good fresh bread and cakes from Dunn's. Others had found the strength to shake their heads, to waive their last poetry rights. Rob – who was sitting up and reading – didn't qualify for poetry, but couldn't help admiring this twitchy believer, the earnest white lady who haunted the Whittington Hospital.

Once again, he proved to be in luck. The new cellophane dragonfly, the elegant jet black dragonfly, and a gigantic, coruscating snow-bee: all these were hovering above him in the freezing crystalline night air. They'd interrupted their own journeys for long enough to remember him, lift him up. At that moment another dragonfly, dark green, orange-flecked, winked into view and joined the others.

The four creatures conferred, reconfigured, descended around him. They encircled him in their shared blue flame and carried him up into a glittering, diamond-filled skyway. He too would be a worker in the kingdom of the dragonflies. For the time being a living helper. But, who knew, perhaps he might graduate one day. His ghosts, his angels bore him upwards, closer to the hidden heights: to the sun, the whole ace and eye of creation, and destruction.

Twenty-Five

Rob awoke with a violent start, rising up abruptly from darkness. He knew immediately that he was in a hospital bed. He was surrounded by grey curtained screens. He was lying in a calm, shadowy dell, and far away he heard voices calling and laughing outside on the ward; a trolley rattled; warm food smell, gravy; a man's voice singing drunkenly. There was a green-blinking machine beside him, to which he was connected. He was wearing a hospital gown. He noticed his clothes had been piled on a chair beside the bed, his shoes tucked neatly beneath it.

His head pulsated with a dull continuous pain, but he found he was reaching up towards these things. Perhaps moving would shut it off. He felt as light and hollow as a shed chrysalis. He also felt he could sit up, and tried to do so, collapsing back onto his pillow, into the raging pain at the back of his head, which was still there, a vice around his skull.

So were the peculiarly elaborate dreams he had been having. He wondered why he had tormented himself by dreaming such a ridiculously terrifying world. Relieved to be alive, he remembered them and the memories embedded there, and particularly the old Algerian in the Place Ducale, but in his remembered version the man's trick had been a different one: to fold his cardboard box so that it fitted into an ever-smaller space, until it was a cube fitted into an anti-cube, until it disappeared along with the living animal he continued to claim was inside, or would appear there shortly.

It turned out that everything had to be at just the right angle, the cube, the desk, the light striking it in relation to the chair and the edge of the table. Then pouf! The whole thing had disappeared along with a whole litter of kittens. The audience realised they had been fooled, wandered away kittenless, disconsolate. They knew they'd been fooled by his false logic, or the appearance of it, his angles, his lines of sight, and something seemed to blink out of their faces, a light in their eyes extinguished.

But in his dream, and in reality, he thought, the Algerian had had a better trick. It had all been a ruse to sell his cat's kittens, a successful ploy. That's what really happened. He'd seen this with his own eyes, or perhaps it was Agathe who'd told him all about it. Rob wanted to get back there as soon as possible. He lay still, relaxed into his pillow of pain, too weak to move, and tried grabbing out at these severed threads of gossamer, to no avail, and when his eyes opened again a long black time had passed and a nurse was moving around in the small space beside his bed.

"Wakey-wakey," she said in that ominously cheery fashion of all nurses. "You are still here with us, I am sure of it now."

She was a Pole, he thought, East European anyway. "My head hurts," he managed to croak. "A lot, a lot." His voice sounded piteous, pleading.

The young nurse immediately thrust a paper medicine cup into his left hand, and a glass of water into his right. She was wearing a mask and a pair of plastic gloves. The small paper cup contained two pills. Rob managed to raise his head a little and swallow them with a gulp of water. He finished up the whole glass, which tasted as sweet and as pure as anything he'd ever poured through his pursed lips.

"Good boy," said the nurse irritatingly. "We have saved some Christmas dinner for you. Do you want it now or later?"

"Later," he groaned vaguely.

"Take my advice," she nurse said. "Have it now. In half-hour doctor will be coming to see. Afterwards it will be spoil. They have said is alright for you."

"OK, thanks," he said. "Is it Christmas today?" But he realized it must be. "What happened to me?"

"You don't remembering?"

"No," he said. "Am I in the Whittington?"

"You are in Whittington Hospital. You have been here before?"

"Yes," he said.

"You are very foolish man," she looked at a clipboard which hung over the foot of his bed. "Rob Goddard?"

"That's right."

"You must fill in form," she said. "Oyster card ID is not enough information. No address, no date. We don't need you to be here," she added. "Hospital is very full up."

"Was I knocked down by a car?" There was a gash on his knee, which had been dressed, but he'd noticed no other damage.

"You hit by car?" the nurse said. "I don't think so."

"I think I must have just tripped off the kerb and banged my head."

"You banged head," she said. "Yes. Drunk. You was drunk in morning! This is very stupid behaviour!"

"I wasn't drunk," Rob tried to laugh. It hurt him. "I don't really drink."

"Ah ha," she said. Now she was folding back the screens, and he took in a large open ward full of men, small bundles of rag and bone, sunken in rows of narrow beds, some gasping, surrounded by life-giving equipment, others reading blankly. Opposite him there was the man who had been singing earlier, collapsed into what looked like a stupor, a plate of half-eaten food on his wheelie table.

"Maybe I just blacked out," Rob said. "Collapsed for some reason, fainted."

"Ah," she said. "Tomorrow you will have brain scan."

This nice nurse, whom he loved more than he had ever loved anybody, disappeared without a fare-thee-well and two minutes later a tiny Filipino kitchen worker turned up with his Christmas dinner. She smiled and nodded at him so that he could do nothing but eat all of it, which he did, although without much relish. The doctor came on her rounds and asked him a lot of the same questions. He had perfected his answers while waiting for her, but at the conclusion of their encounter he felt reassured that he was indeed still alive, recognised as such by an authority.

Nobody, least of all himself, knew what had happened to him exactly. It had been a policewoman who had found him collapsed unconscious beside the steps of Hornsey police station. One minute he wasn't there, next minute he was. Hardly anyone else had been on the mid-morning lockdown streets. He hadn't responded when she tried to rouse him, and after satisfying herself that he wasn't just trying it on, she'd called for medical assistance and an ambulance.

Rob felt much better in the morning, although his head was still very tender. They let him get up and walk to the bathroom, which he did without difficulty. They took him down to the scanner room, and the band of radiation that passed back and forth over his head reminded him of the technology of the heavenly rescuers, with their angelic insect attendants, but he atmosphere of the hospital remained calm and orderly, cheerful, not apparently chaotic in the least as one might have expected in the wake of a natural disaster. But there were few nurses on duty and the doctor's rounds were often cancelled. They were left to themselves by and large, but they wouldn't release him immediately despite the crazy pressures of coping with Covid-19. He was suffering from mild concussion, but they were still worried by some irregularities in his case, particularly the length of time it had taken him to wake up. They'd feared he was slipping into a permanent coma.

Rob phoned his brother to tell him why he hadn't turned up for Christmas. His younger sibling apologized for failing to notice his non-arrival. He'd had a lot on his mind. Their father's hallucinations had stopped now; they'd turned out to be caused by an infection. Rob wondered how he'd picked it up but didn't say so. His brother was sympathetic, aghast that Rob was in hospital, but there was nothing either of them could do except wish each other well and say goodbye for now. Anyway, he felt better for having made contact. The thought of looking at anything else on his phone filled him with dread: another element of his disturbing, hallucinatory nightmare had been chased away like smoke.

Lying on his back in the recovery ward, Rob found himself hashing over a few memories to pass the time. Anything would do. During a childhood journey, for example, he had been looking out of the car window as they skimmed along the 'A' roads on their journey back from the coast, Brighton or the West Country. The wide carriageway was featureless, boring, but then a strange figure had appeared, trudging alongside the road, on the grass verge. It was what used to be called 'a gentleman of the road', swaddled in layers of ragged clothes, tied up with string or twine, impossibly dirty. "A milestone inspector," his father had said with a chuckle from behind the wheel. "That's what your granddad used to call them."

At that moment they passed the wretched creature at speed. Rob's father said, "Cuh, look at the state of him."

Rob's mother had kept looking straight ahead. "Something terrible must have happened," she said, "to make him lose his mind." His father seemed unconvinced.

Rob wondered what tragic events might lead to somebody taking up such a peculiar job Milestone Inspector. He tended to think of it as having had its attractors: the freedom of the open road; the absence of duties. But it had somehow struck people like his grandfather as funny, so that he'd use that expression. Where had he got it? Rob seemed to remember him talking about it now. The pay was low but the work was steady. Poor devils. Words to that effect.

"Just lazy probably," his father had said after a while, qualified by: "Only job he could get."

"What does he have to do then?" his younger brother asked.

"Just make sure they're still in place. Showing the correct number of miles," their father elaborated. "Sometimes people try to alter them. But that's rare."

Rob liked the idea of the distance between places being precisely measured and maintained, and he liked this phrase of his grandfather. (Had he made it up? Heard it from his own father?) and it seemed appropriate to attach this duty of these trudging, itinerant men. It gave them a usefulness, a place in the scheme of things. Something they could be seen as cheerfully pursuing – but there the problems began. They weren't happy. They were mad. Homeless. Destitute. The phrase 'milestone inspector' made it sound as if they were enjoying themselves.

The radio had been droning, a soporific silence in the steadily vibrating car, a stuffiness and nausea that would begin to mount if you let yourself experience being exactly where you were and what you were feeling, and all these sensations were to do with an unpleasant sense of being contained, moved along, half comatose in Rob's case. And the gentleman of the road, the milestone inspector, now left miles behind, presumably still trudging doggedly along the verge, had also been contained by the phrase immobilized by false description (that always regrettable jocularity of grandfathers!) before it was left behind, still living it all out in real time on the actual road, in his own actual skull. All his father and mother and his younger brother and himself could do was to butt up against something that was absent for them, always would be, forever ungraspable.

And yet, as he remembered the solitary person they had passed, Rob had been struck by his realness, his actuality, a survival of some other way of living perhaps ,of another age, as if the man had been tottering along for fifty or a hundred years. But he knew this was impossible. He had looked out at the uninteresting blur of passing verge, a place just beyond him on which nothing ever happened. After a while he had noticed that the white blip of a milestone did approach every so often, and as soon as he had noticed them he began to count them, acting as an advance scout for the milestone inspector.

But there was another side to all this transcendence, all this transformation. The rheumy, lidless eye of the gloopy lake he had dreamed of stared straight up at the hospital ceiling. Some disordered fronds – or something – were pushing up randomly around the edges, and below the surface of the lake was everything else, everything that had once existed, just the fins visible, now and then, of patrolling anti-creatures skimming below the surface.

If only they had listened to Gerard Manley Hopkins. If only people, plain ordinary people, had bothered to understand what John Duns Scotus meant when he wrote of the univocity of being. One thing. Existence is one ... not substance exactly but an irreducible category. Totally abstract, totally real. The lake, he realized, was composed of anti-matter. It was unbeing, the end of a process, its final waste product. If only we had listened before it was too late. Before our total lack of care, stupid blindness, led to this endless sucking vacuum.

Rob cried bitterly in his hospital bed, and the nurses were too busy, or too far away to come back and comfort him, even to hear his muffled sobbing, which anyway he tried to bury in the clean, puffy pillows on the recovery ward.

As he began to recover he walked out of the hospital onto Archway Road to buy cigarettes. He was gasping, he hadn't had one for days. He reached for a mask before going into the shop, and was relieved to find them still there bundled in his Robet pocket. There was nothing like a cigarette. It was amazing. He decided to go to an internet cafe to check his emails. That would be a blast from the past.

When he got to the first internet cafe on the Broadway it was closed. Of course it was fucking closed. They were in lockdown. He cursed his stupidity in that relentless self-cynical way of his, which he remembered had been getting worse all the time. Nothing unusual about this. He was always a little unglued. He felt a sudden pang for the days when he didn't have a proper phone, only his old cool Nokia. Rob had known he was getting old when an earnest-looking forty-something woman had accosted him on the DLR, in awe at his "cool phone". A compact lozenge of instant black and silver retro. His dark instrument. If that Nokia could talk, it would tell a tale or two; but they didn't have much memory – in the end he'd been forced to delete important messages from the dead in order to make way for incoming life from managers, even a final lover. For a moment of memory they were all there before him texting and babbling and tears flooded into his eyes. He would never throw that phone away. He thought it should be held in a museum for safe-keeping.

Back in the shadow of the Whittington Hospital he turned on his present mobile phone and looked at his unchecked e-mails. It was January the 2nd. There was a considerable pile-up of junk from around the world, none of it particularly Christmassy, but, as if welcoming him back to the world, he saw that a few people had sent new year wishes and an old friend had actually written to him. A couple of days later they discharged him from the hospital and he made his way back to his flat on the bus that stopped outside Archway station.

In the months that followed Rob carried on with his modest life, picked up such threads as were and continued also to deliver online English tuition. But he found he had an acute recall of his Christmas train journey, his meeting with the ghosts, and the near-destruction of the Earth, as well as the great legions of snow-bees and dragonflies. Humanity was still at the nymph stage of development. He couldn't think about his friends, Marie, Stuart, Paul, and especially Agathe, without feeling pangs of helpless love and longing … but there you are. Would the world just run down like a clockwork train? It seemed so. But somewhere inside him a thought still nagged that the cellophane and tinsel of his nightmare had been, in fact, reality.

Before too long, and without anybody to contradict him, he came to believe this version of events. By and large he felt okay, if a little sluggish in his limbs: a pervasive tingling sensation bothered him slightly, alongside normal aches and pains. Then he noticed that his skin was getting darker, thicker. It had begun to take on a crackly, papery texture, although – deep within – he felt more alive than previously.

Twenty-Six

It had been the only job his father ever got for him. A lot of boring filing work and attaching cheap key-rings to cards with those little plastic-covered wire ties in a Nissen hut on the Portsmouth Road, right at the top of Wellands' yard. Rob's father was chief mechanic at Wellands, and it was something unusual for him to stop on his way home to ask the boss of the key-ring company if he needed anybody.

Mr Crawford said he was certainly looking for new staff. Perhaps because he was impressed by Rob's father, or maybe simply because he had been the first applicant, on the first day had told him that he was the senior man and that he was to keep an eye on the others.

Rob was to learn the mysteries of how to be a businessman, become almost like a son to him, and in time he might even take over the reins of the firm. So he imagined. In exchange for this he would be paid £1.65 per hour, which, Mr Crawford pointed out, was more than the others would be getting when they arrived, although they too would be expected to do filing and figure work, and to listen attentively to his instructions about the importance of recording every single digit in a neat, legible handwriting.

A young woman had been next to be taken on. Rob was sitting at a big, scarred desk in plain view of the old man's perch, manipulating elderly lever-arch files, redundantly transferring scratchy figures into a column with a Bic pen. Crawford had left the room for a few minutes and when he came back he had a young woman behind him. She wore scruffy, nondescript clothes which looked a bit like army fatigues: a man's open shirt over a dun-coloured t-shirt, a pair of olive cotton trousers. Hanging in her eyes was a shaggy mane of jet black, slightly greasy-looking hair. She was tall and loose limbed, or would have been if she hadn't damped herself down somehow, assuming a bobbing, assenting manner. There was something both guarded and confident about her movements.

"This is Hadas," said Mr Crawford, an ancient man, who towered over her, but almost deferentially. She nodded and flashed Rob a brief curved smile before sitting at another scarred desk to be introduced to lever-arch files, graph paper and ballpoint pens. He hadn't been able to easily keep his eyes off her.

Crawford moved slowly in an air of old-fashioned middle-class decency. Rob thought of him as an exemplar of the play fair mentality. At any rate it was plain that the whole of his life was bound up in these lever arch files and he had brought up his large family by means of this on-going business activity. It was equally obvious they weren't there to care about this at all – not even Rob, although he had been immediately offered the senior man position. Once there was more than one of them they were going to do as little as they could manage. They weren't going to take his problems very seriously at all. They were there to idle away the summer, as far as possible, and they were going to rip him off at every opportunity. Such was the effect of the other workers.

In the afternoon they were sent to the packing room, where they chatted and listened to the radio. Radio was great in those days. Plays by Samuel Beckett and Tom Stoppard and other good writers graced the afternoon schedules and even on Radio One early seventies dross was occasionally interrupted by a glittering diamond. David Bowie's Life on Mars? had just been released as a single and it came on at least once a day, at which point they would lay down their key-rings, their cards and their plastic-covered wire ties and listen to it all the way through, from first tremulous piano phrase to last exultant sawing shriek of violins. How well he understood how shoddy everything looked to them. Hadas loved David Bowie. So did everyone.

But he'd never met anyone like her. He almost thought he'd never met anyone Jewish, but inevitably someone else, a Hungarian school friend, sprang to mind; an allegedly crazy but fun, friendly girl, a frizzy-haired outsider who was always laughing at nothing. Not like Hadas. He'd never met a woman close to his own age as confident as her, and, she clearly thought, so much more intelligent than him. Middle-class people to him were a couple of uncles they never saw, teachers and a fairly nice woman his mother cleaned for, and of course, his more recent school friends.

"You think you're so intelligent, don't you?" she was soon jeering at him, with her half-smile, on that first day, after she'd been pumping him for information for an hour or two.

"Fairly intelligent," Rob had confessed with a smile.

"You're not," she said. "You're nowhere near as intelligent as you think you are – as David Bowie is, for example."

Rob had to agree with her there. They'd been telling one another their dreams, but she obviously hadn't read that Yeats poem about treading too softly on anyone else's. Her dream, her ambition, was to go to Jerusalem and study her religion. This meant she would have to join the Israeli Army for a while, do her national service, and prove she was a proper Jew and not just along for the ride, which she thought was a fair enough condition of the law of return.

He could just see her in uniform, toting a machine gun; possibly because of the way she was already dressed, in her dress rehearsal rags. She would look great too – as wild and romantic and committed as the Jews he remembered seeing hurtling across the Sinai desert in jeeps during the Six Day War: a real freedom fighter. Rob had supported the Israelis as a twelve year old. Now he was beginning to understand it wasn't so simple, but he didn't want to argue with her directly.

"You should meet my friend Stuart," he said. "He'd give you an argument. He supports the Palestinians – he likes that woman Leila Khaled."

Leila Khaled was a hijacker, a freedom-fighter, a poster girl of the PLO, usually photographed with an AK 47 and a wide, beautiful smile, which remained even after she'd had her face altered by plastic surgery. Stuart Mcleod had an incredible crush on her

Rob expected Hadas to be angry, but she actually softened a little.
"He sounds clever, this Stuart," she said. "Cleverer than you anyway. Why don't you get him a job here? I'd like to meet him. Go on, Crawford's looking for more people – he told me so himself."

It was a good idea. So good he should have been allowed to think of it himself: actually, he already had. He was the senior man after all. Stuart was his friend. Hadas was a power-tripper, even a bit of a bully – clearly a member of the chosen people, at least of some social grouping who thought themselves automatically superior to the likes of him. But he forgave her – after two years at the grammar school he was used to it. She was interesting to talk to, opinionated, sharp. She also liked sparring. It was her way of finding out what was what, who was who. This was common enough, but Rob had spent years of his childhood cultivating his own strategies of avoidance, sideways movement and redefinition. He found they assisted his maintenance of a good self-opinion. And he had been often enough a partial winner at those games to still think he was really something. He had his little ways of getting along. Hadas always saw right through them and kept on coming until she drew blood.

Stuart Mcleod always had the beginning or end of a cold sore on his cracked lips, which he repeatedly dabbed at, recoiling in angry non-surprise at the blood on his handkerchief. Red wine stained his lips dark purple and the inside of his mouth turned into a cave of blood. He had that kind of skin, delicate, almost translucent, sensitive and, in his case, not particularly attractive. He was always wincing with tooth pain or some other ailment, as though he had been issued with a body that was already falling apart – there was nothing he could do about it except carry on for as long as possible. He was a scrawny little Scot with greasy red hair: an odd, misfitting person, a brittle bag of sticks shaken by spasms of a convulsive, violent energy. His family had lived in the south for five years, but his accent remained nearly incomprehensible. He was shy, very defensive – and it was difficult to get a non-abusive word out of him, probably because he'd been taunted a great deal.

At lunchtimes they'd play darts in his mother's kitchen on a board hung up on one of the cupboards, Rob and the other Cobham boys, up from the secondary modern. Stuart turned out to be a kind of soft entry point to the grammar school world: a disaffected misfit, a vociferous nay-sayer to everything English and middle-class. It's perplexing how different social groups seem to throw the same shapes at you: misfits are often the friendliest to newcomers. But they were friends at a deeper level than any shared, and, in Rob's case, unwanted, outsider status. He wanted to fit in. Girls looked at him. He'd also made another couple of friends, one through playing guitar and singing; another an outsider who'd arrived from another direction. An instant insider, so it turned out. Another boy from Cobham, or Stoke D'Abernon, a middle-class one, who'd been expelled – he was justly proud of this – from his public school: refusing to be caned for smoking Disque Bleu. Malcolm was impressively large-framed, tall, dark, long-haired and bearded. He dressed up in a swirling Dracula-cape, adorned himself with blue eye-shadow and drove an early sixties Austin Cambridge. Hadas immediately thought he sounded interesting and wanted to meet him.

Mcleod had been trying to learn to drive in an unwieldy estate car owned by his father, but unfortunately his coordination was poor. The doctor had put him on Valium to cope with the stress of the driving lessons. Swallowing a handful before one of these, he'd driven straight across the middle of a busy roundabout. No-one in his family could drive either, except perhaps his father, who'd been a bomb-aimer during the war. They weren't really car people. Zoned out on tranquillisers, he was spending the summer lying in bed and reading ten science fiction novels per week. He turned up for work in a denim jacket and jeans, looking fairly tidy and trim. His hair was feathery, freshly washed. In the bright morning sun, it glowed like filaments of fine copper wire.

Mr Crawford had taken him on on Rob's say so, but after a brief trial classified him as unsuitable for clerical work. He couldn't read his handwriting nor could he understand a word he uttered. Stuart was to go into the packing room with Hadas, the lucky bastard, while he struggled through another few days of copying last year's sales figures onto ruled graph sheets. The taxman was coming next week, Crawford explained to him. That's what he was there for, and Rob just had to buckle down to it. Hadas was drafted in to speed things up sometimes. He had worked on steadily and efficiently, which certainly wasn't the case with Hadas in the same room, nor when he left to check up on them in the packing room. Eventually Rob made it back there for the afternoon shift on carding and radio listening to find they'd already bonded over a fierce argument about Middle Eastern politics and were getting on together like a burning building. They looked up at him with half-amused, vaguely tolerant pity.

"Is it true that you're on 15p an hour more than us?" Hadas asked immediately.

"He's the senior man," Stuart said treacherously. "Crawford thinks he's more intelligent than us."

"Just because you're from the third world," Rob said sarcastically.

Hadas flung down her key ring in fury and stood up. "I'm not having that," she said. "Crawford can fuck off if he thinks he's going to discriminate against me as a woman – it's just wrong. I'm going to talk to him." She banged impressively out of the room to confront Crawford with her demand for equal pay and equal rights.

"Why did you tell her about the money?"

"You don't mind, do you?"

"No," he said. "Except he told me to keep it quiet. What do you think of her?"

Stuart looked blissfully happy. "Great," he said. "She's brilliant, isn't she?"

Brilliant or not, she easily got her way. She soon intimidated old Crawford and from that moment on she and Stuart were on the same hourly rate as him – and Rob's senior man status came to an abrupt end. The old man thought considerably less of him after that. He realised he should have kept his mouth shut. Crawford told Rob as much. He'd given away his small advantage to people who weren't going to be particularly grateful. Stupidly, he'd worsened his own position – and the worst thing about it was that he had done it himself, almost willingly, even persuading himself to think it was a right and just and fair settlement. Rob could tell Crawford wanted to sack him with immediate effect, but he didn't.

Hadas and Stuart began spending time together out of working hours, drinking and talking, about the Middle-East, and he learnt things about her she never directly told Rob. She took a lot of pleasure in preferring Stuart to Rob: she told him that much, and he could see how much she enjoyed his disappointment. But although an air of mystery and exclusive intimacy surrounded the things she told him, Stuart nevertheless doled them out to him in dribs and drabs when they were alone together.

Her real name was Daphne, and she was living with her parents for a while after having got into trouble in London. She'd been living with a man, a heroin addict, who'd got her hooked on the stuff, and … anyway, now she was recovering, trying to get her life back together. And that was why she wanted to go to off to Israel and start afresh.

"The culture's in the religion," she explained. "You've got to learn Hebrew properly to understand it."

"Ancient Hebrew?"

"Well, yeah, obviously. Modern Hebrew too."

Rob's father used to pick him up every night in the car, although he could easily have suggested he leave me to it. I could get the bus, the 215, later. But he wasn't going anywhere with Hadas, that much was obvious. She'd amble across the road after work, with her slow, masculine gait, onto the path through the woods leading to the deep mysteries of Claygate. His father had told him it was called after a brickworks that used to be there, but now it was very much a middle-class enclave. He had a school friend who lived in Dalmore Avenue. They used to play music together, smoke dope in his mother's attic, and even did a couple of gigs in the pub there – Rob's songs, his slide blues playing – in The Swan, next to the cricket pavilion which faced onto the manicured green. Hadas would doubtless be ambling across it on her way back to whatever gabled mansion she lived in.

Stuart liked getting blind drunk, which sometimes reacted badly with the valium he was taking for his driving lessons, so when she gave him her address and told him to come around sometime he thought this would be a good way of getting up the courage to go. He'd turned up drunk in the front garden of a large detached house and began throwing stones up at what he thought looked like her window. No response. Eventually he knocked on the front door and a nice middle-class lady answered and politely asked if he was a friend of Daphne's. And called up the stairs after her: "Daphne! Daphne! Somebody to see you!"

That's how he learned her real name. She was out, but her mother told her of his call and she returned the visit a bit later. Stuart's mother woke him up and they went out on a pub-crawl. Hadas, or Daphne, drank him under the table.

"So, it's Daphne is it?" he'd smiled at her.

"If you tell anyone my name," she said. "I'll fucking kill you, alright? Especially that idiot little friend of yours."

He told Rob about all this on another pub-crawl, a week or so later, but there wasn't much to tell. "I didn't even like her," he muttered vaguely, despairingly, deep in his cups. His friend knew nothing had really happened between them, but now that he had nothing to be jealous about he wished they'd become lovers, boyfriend and girlfriend, for the whole thing to have been a spectacular turn up for the books, a reversal. But it was impossible. They were kids after all, getting pissed up and spouting crap, and she was a real woman. Things like that just didn't happen. At closing time Rob had delivered him back to his mother, a trim, competent woman with a wry smile, a large family to look after, an ironic tinkling laugh. She found him a couple of blankets.

Rob prepared to sleep on the couch. "I expect you've been hearing all about dear Daphne," Mrs Mcleod laughed ruefully. "She thinks a lot of herself." She laughed again, her light laugh.

Mcleod was off sick for the day and Hadas and Rob were carding together in the back room. He didn't call her Hadas, or anything else. He'd been too shy of her to use her name, especially such an important sounding one. Somehow or other, a real woman, she had refused even to be named by him, let alone as the ludicrous Daphne, and anyway he preferred her adopted name. But, in truth, he couldn't believe she didn't like him in any way at all, that his interest in her wasn't somehow reciprocated.

"You like Stuart, don't you?" Rob asked. "You seem to get on well."

"Yeah," she shrugged. "He's quite an interesting young man."

"You can get out of whatever trouble you've been in," he said later.

"I know I can." She looked at me more directly. "Look. It's none of your fucking business."

"Just do something else. You can do whatever you want."

"Well. I hope so."

"I really admire you." Rob said this in a brotherly way.

"I know you do."

"How do you know?"

"Because you make it so fucking obvious," Hadas said. "Look, you know fuck all about women – these girls you hang around with, they aren't real women." She looked down at her pile of crappy golden key rings, many of them destined to personalise some idiot's car keys. "They probably never will be either."

"What do you mean?"

"Oh, you know – just shop girls."

Rob was revolted by this attitude. "I was only trying to be friendly."

"I'm telling you the truth. I don't like the way you talk to me, Rob. I don't like it at all. You obviously think you're intelligent – and you aren't."

"I don't know how intelligent I am, not really." Rob shrugged. "Nor do you."

"But I do," she said. "Stuart's not really clever either, you know." She winced in sympathy for his friend. "He's got problems."

"Stuart's got a lot going for him."

"Keep telling him he's brilliant," she said. "It might work."

The summer wore on in a luminous, repetitive false-eternity, and not many weeks later the job came to an abrupt end. Crawford suddenly sacked everybody, but he got rid of Rob first because he had divulged his higher wages to the others and so broken his employer's trust. Hadas finally got her way and met Malcolm, his friend with the Dracula cape and the Austin Cambridge. Apart from anything else, this had been the only way to get her to show up for a drink in the pub on the corner – the Orleans Arms, or perhaps the Marquis of Granby, just before the Scilly Isles. This was the name of the large roundabout which Stuart had driven across recently in a valium-induced stupor.

It had been an idle game of hers to find out who was the cleverest, and she'd already decided that it must be Malcolm. Malcolm duly swept in, primed for the encounter, and they plunged immediately into congenial conversation. Rob couldn't remember what it was all about, only that Dracula had been charming and articulate and she had warmed to him, both of them effortlessly outclassing Rob and Stuart for half an hour or so in a spontaneously ostentatious enactment of superior cleverness and instant mutual admiration.

Rob used to find this sort of thing nauseating – but to him it was still funny. To Hadas it was clear that Malcolm was a real person in a way they were not, could never be, and to Malcolm, as to them, she was indeed an extraordinary woman whom he was delighted to try and impress. Stuart and Malcolm – a febrile, skinny, neurotic red-headed Scot and an imposingly confident product of the English middle classes – were a paired set of contrasting male types in an English novel, and they had been Rob's best friends at the time, dumped randomly and indelibly onto the blank white paper of his life.

That's exactly how it was and they served themselves up to her, giving her whatever they had, for her momentary interest and judgement. She really thought she was God, or that's how he would have put it at the time. That which you would like to show me, verily I would like to be shown it. And he imagined her raising her dark, partly-seeing eyes as if to some all-seeing rabbi, uttering some prayer of supplication: His judgement is upon all of us, and we in turn are always called upon to judge others: a task everybody seemed to assume more or less eagerly, young and old.

There had been nothing very much to steal amongst the stock of key rings and other petrol station trinkets, apart perhaps from some onyx eggs and some cigarette boxes made of the same brightly marbled stone. They came in a sickly duck egg blue and a sort of orangey brown, same as the eggs, and were held together by a frail golden hinge. Many of these were broken, and they were under strict instructions not to break any more of them. It didn't matter all that much as they were seldom ordered, whereas orders for more key rings seemed to come in every day. All of them were artefacts that had somehow fallen off the edge of culture, although they imitated valuable things. They were made for sale rather than for use. Essentially, Hadas thought, they were made for people who didn't know what they were buying. They were nothing but a cheap trick being played on the incontrovertibly gullible working-classes.

Rob hated all of the stock himself, but since he was one of those unfortunate folk, he managed sufficiently to persuade himself of the virtues of onyx eggs and cigarette boxes to secrete one of each in his shoulder bag and to take them home for his mother. She had been quite disgusted by his stealing from the job, and, anyway, although a heavy smoker, didn't think all that much of the onyx cigarette box. He'd managed to return it, smuggle it back into stock, although the pale blue egg, chipped but still sparkly, seeming to have been stolen from another, far distant planet, remained a fixture for years, balanced in the middle of a mid-tan onyx ashtray she had acquired somewhere or other.

There was nothing left now of those days, except perhaps the onyx egg was still hanging around somewhere, unrecyclable. Rob used to pick it up and look at it sometimes – tarnished, a hideous object – it reminded him of those moments of false promise and of his own foolishness. He could never really see why his mother hung on to it, unless it was because he'd given it to her. For all of them it had been a more or less hated place, one they were hoping to spring free from soon, but there was always something spongy about it and you hoped your feet hadn't sunk in too far.

Judge not lest ye be judged. He believed in that cautious maxim himself, although he still picked the odd mote out of his neighbour's eye. Rob wondered what became of Daphne, or Hadas. Rob wondered if she ever went to Israel; if she ever actually studied the Torah in Hebrew, did her national service on the West Bank, and became an academic in Tel Aviv. Somehow he didn't think she seemed clever enough: maybe it was just a fantasy of escape, a scheme, a counter to her mother's idea of what her life should be. He looked up her name on his phone, discovered it was the name of an ancient water-nymph: a fleeing girl, whose river god turned her into a tree to evade her unwanted suitor, Apollo. Fuck that, anyway.

Probably, eventually, he thought, she would have met a man, a man she'd considered good enough for her, and finally buckled down to being a middle-class housewife, Daphne, a woman from who knows where with that sweet old English name. Rob found himself cruelly hoping this for her: it was the best he could manage. He thought of her on her wedding day, spectacularly happy in a frothy white silk creation, then as she was, blunt, forceful, turbulent and beautiful.

"Never, alright?! Never!"

He thought of her stomping around wildly in her combat fatigues, refusing to put on the hated bridal garment. He played himself this scene, stood back and laughed at her. He wondered if she'd started her own business – perhaps something like Crawford's steady, lucrative key-ring operation. But how would he know? What business was it of his anyway how her life had turned out? Hadas had been a serious person and, of course, that meant something. Just curious, he supposed. After all, he knew what happened to the rest of them.

www.ingramcontent.com/pod-product-compliance
Lightning Source LLC
Chambersburg PA
CBHW030543030726
47495CB00004B/1115